FLIGHT 316

BOOK ONE OF THE SHeSHeD SERIES

MAURITA CHALICE BURGETT

Published in the United States by SheShed Press

Printed in the United States of America
ISBN 979-8-9900064-0-9
Library of Congress Registration Number TXu002432774

Cover Art: Karen Ducker
Writing Sherpa: David Moore
Theological Consultant: Dr. Dan Morris
Line Editor and Proofreader: Juli Burgett
Cover/Interior Design and Formatting: Champagne Book Design

Book One of the SheShed Series

For more information visit www.SheShedwriter.com or
email info@sheshedwriter.com

**SheShed
PRESS**

For God
You are the greatest love of my life.

For Reverend David Ebaugh
When I was a child you told me that finding heaven on Earth was God's purpose for me. And I believed you.

And for Don Burgett
When I was afraid you might not want to marry a zealot, you promised that if God's only purpose for you was to carry my bags you would stay with me all of your days—you deserve the title of The Rock.
You are the second greatest love of my life

FLIGHT 316

CHAPTER 1

S HE KNEW HE WAS AFRAID TO FLY EVEN BEFORE SHE REACHED her seat. Just minutes before she'd been rushing to the terminal, relieved to see the plane for flight 316 from Dallas to Honolulu was still parked at the gate but grew panicky as she witnessed the agent start to close the door. "Wait!" she cried out loudly. The agent paused, looked in her direction, and then surprisingly reopened the door. Grace stopped long enough to catch her breath and to have her boarding pass scanned. "Thank you!" she called over her shoulder as she raced through the open door, down the jetway, and onto the plane.

Once inside, Grace Jackson exhaled a quiet "Thank God!" as the flight attendant secured the latch and closed the airplane door behind her. She checked her phone to confirm her assigned seat number and moved quickly to aisle seat 4D not unaware of the annoyed glances of her fellow passengers. *Get over it*, she told them silently as she searched in vain for an overhead compartment with space to hold her carry-on bag. Sleet in Dallas had caused almost all the connecting flights to be late. *We're lucky to be leaving at all*, she thought.

To her delighted surprise while landing on the runway from Austin, she received a notification on her phone of an unexpected upgrade for her next flight. *How did that happen?* she thought as she stared at her phone. A vacant seat in first class to Hawaii? The plane she would be traveling on was actually a smaller, narrow body jet, not one of the larger ones usually scheduled. There wouldn't even be that many seats in first class. Thinking a free upgrade would be impossible she hadn't even submitted a request on the airline's website.

An attractive flight attendant appearing to be in her early thirties took Grace's coat and hung it in the closet by the door. She then moved swiftly and definitively towards her, opened the overhead compartment door directly opposite Grace's seat, rearranged a few bags, grabbed Grace's overnight case out of her hand and jammed it into the remaining space. She gave the compartment door a decisive slam indicating it was time to go.

As Grace approached her seat, the man assigned to the seat next to hers jumped up immediately and asked if she would mind changing places with him, giving away his fear of flying. He'd been assigned the window seat but preferred an aisle. Dark, handsome, either oilman or cattle baron, his request and anxious face said it all. Given the weather, the likelihood of turbulence, and that possibly the airline industry's choice of the word *terminal* might not be a coincidence, he wanted a seat as close to the exit as possible.

Grace's eyes locked with his as they both momentarily but thoroughly studied and sized up their evening and overseas travel partner. Raven black hair, blue eyes, dark eyebrows that slightly fanned, arched, and then took a sharp dive, Grace wondered briefly if she recognized him. Had he once been a patient? Lived in her neighborhood? Had she seen him on the internet? In the movies? She was the first to break eye contact.

She considered his request and was briefly tempted to decline. She didn't like window seats either but not for the same apparent reason. This was going to be a long flight and she hated climbing over people when she needed to get out to use the restroom. But that night, tired and just grateful to have been upgraded, she looked up at him once again, shrugged briefly, and murmured, "Sure." He thanked her politely and moved further out into the aisle, giving her plenty of space to slide past him.

Getting situated, she tucked her oversized purse under the seat in front of her and as she buckled her seatbelt she told herself it really didn't matter. She was probably going to sleep anyway. All she wanted was a smooth ride, a few free drinks, maybe a decent movie, and dinner that didn't come in a bag. Why not?

She'd originally flown in from Austin and sat on the runway in Dallas for nearly an hour because there'd been no gate available. Her last seatmate with nothing else to do decided to fill the time by giving Grace an unrequested thumbnail sketch of her life, covering all the emotional high and low lights. The woman had been married, divorced, and was currently in the middle of a court battle trying to evict her ex-husband, his girlfriend, and the girlfriend's three children (one of whom she suspected was probably fathered by her own cheating ex) who were squatting illegally in a home the judge and divorce decree had clearly granted to her. But because there were small children involved, the husband had filed an extension and the courts were bound to review it.

Only partially paying attention as her seatmate sat down and fiddled with his seatbelt, Grace reached up and tried to adjust the air vent blowing cold air on top of her. Finally able to close the vent, she gave a sideways glance to her seatmate and quickly determined that the man about to be her travel companion for the next several hours wasn't going to be much of a talker. Airplane passengers who choose not to socialize with strangers make no attempt to hide that given the choice the seat next to them would have remained empty. Once settled they don't even look up from their phone or computer when approached. They leave absolutely no doubt of their desire to be left alone. The man sitting next to her seemed no exception. After he thanked her again for exchanging seats, he pulled out his tablet and as far as Grace could tell was checking his email.

Settled and feeling done for the day, Grace leaned back and tried to let the ever-present stress fade away. She tuned out the familiar sounds of the flight attendant's take-off instructions and closed her eyes. She let her mind shift to autopilot but not before having a sudden and strange premonition sweep over her that the events of the night would be anything but ordinary.

CHAPTER 2

DESPITE THE CONTINUED RAIN, TAKEOFF WAS FAIRLY SMOOTH. Once in the air the flight attendant was back for their drink orders. Grace ordered the red wine and hoped the attendant brought it quickly. It had been a long day.

Her seatmate, however, was more discerning. He asked what kind of scotch they had and if she knew if the wine was a cabernet, a merlot, or a pinot noir. The flight attendant was only too happy to provide a detailed account of every choice available. He settled on the scotch and she laughed prettily, as if his final choice was the most charming and interesting request she'd had all day.

Bypassing the passengers in the first three rows and before Grace could even pull out the additional small tray table between her and her seatmate, the flight attendant quickly returned with both their beverages and waited patiently for them to get situated. She smiled at Grace's seatmate, waiting as he pulled out his tray table, and then leaned over him, unnecessarily close, Grace thought, as she placed small cocktail napkins imprinted with the colorful red, white, and blue airline logo on the small surfaces before setting their drinks down. She then placed a small white ceramic container of warm mixed nuts next to each drink.

She returned to the galley and served the other passengers their drinks and nuts before enthusiastically returning and announcing the evening's dinner selections to Grace and her travel companion. When she was finished she asked politely, "Ms. Jackson?" without showing any particular interest in Grace's choice. However, her voice turned silky when asking the gentleman traveler if he preferred the chicken dish or the vegetable pasta.

Grace had unsuspectingly ordered the pasta. When it was her companion's turn to choose the flight attendant smiled at him, lowered her voice, and said as if revealing a confidence, "I'd get the chicken," and winked at him. He did and the flight attendant nodded her head at him meaningfully in obvious approval and then scurried up the aisle taking orders from the remaining diners. Grace looked directly at her seatmate as he smiled to himself and looked down at his tablet. She turned her head, rolled her eyes, and looked out the window.

A loud Texan in row two on the opposite side of the aisle let out a war whoop laugh and shouted, "Well, lookie here!" causing Grace to look away from the window. When she entered the plane she had briefly noticed a man wearing a large Stetson cowboy hat. Someone had obviously given him a paper lei made of purple and yellow flowers that his wife had pinned to the back of his cowboy hat. He had on a purple button-down short sleeve shirt with two parrots in brightly colored flowered shirts holding tropical drinks playing at a craps table. In large print the shirt said, "Living it up in Pair-a-dice." He stood up and was swinging his head back and forth displaying his wife's handiwork. The flight attendant passed laughing and told him he was cut off. No more drinks for him, she teased.

Grace took the distraction as an opportunity to further study her seatmate. He was very nice looking, she concluded, in an understated, wholesome, good guy way. About forty, probably about six foot two, broad shouldered, nicely dressed in a pair of black jeans and a starched button-down lavender shirt and black lambskin leather jacket. Even though it was the dead of winter he had a tan that made her think he spent quite a bit of time outdoors. She decided on rancher as a profession, probably with a bunch of horses somewhere. *He probably has a nice wife, a couple of kids, and a big dog too*, she thought. She checked and noted he wasn't wearing a wedding ring but that didn't really mean anything, she reminded herself wryly.

Grace leaned down and pulled out a *People* magazine from her purse. Sipping her wine she perused the articles, picking through the nuts in the container for only the almonds, until the flight attendant returned with dinner. As she served their orders she introduced herself as Katie and announced she was from Dallas.

Katie looked like she was from Dallas. She was tall, statuesque, and voluptuous with a slender but curvy hourglass figure with a narrow waist and large broad hips. She had a full mouth that had been recently swathed with bright pink lipstick and topped off with a shiny gloss and the two mixed together mimicked the exact same shade and shine as her long square-shaped fingernails. She had long dark eyelash extensions, and although tasteful would have resembled spiders if any longer, Grace thought. Her perfume smelled like orange blossoms and jasmine, and she wore a pair of medium-sized square cut diamond stud earrings. She had tan skin with high, bronze and rose-colored cheekbones and a small mole topped off the corner of her right upper lip.

Her honey-colored side bangs dropped down and covered her right eye while her ponytail pulled high, also shiny, swished from shoulder to shoulder when she walked.

Soon Katie was joined by another pretty young flight attendant who came to the front, recruited to help with first class service. While Katie wore a tight, and somewhat revealing, navy blue dress, navy tights and heels, her co-worker appeared in a crisp white shirt, modestly covered by a thin navy blue sweater. She also wore navy tights, but her shoes were flat and although stylish were more sensible and obviously chosen for comfort. Below her meticulously placed airline pin was a nametag that read, "Anna."

Soon Katie returned with a basket of bread. "Whole wheat, white, or sourdough?" she asked efficiently yet prettily, with tongs hovering expectantly. Watching her weight Grace refused while her seatmate chose the sourdough. Katie gave him two extra pads of butter and told him she had softened them specifically for him, so he didn't have to struggle with the frozen packets. She had discovered over the years that frozen butter is just so many men's pet peeve, she sighed knowingly. He smiled appreciatively and thanked her.

Katie and Anna delivered the remainder of the meals and drinks and bread to the other passengers. Once finished they hurried about, alternating between the galley and aisle, offering drink refills. Katie reminded them both to check out the airline's music and movie selections, brought water, and then, unasked, returned with an overflowing cup of lemon wedges for her seatmate only. "You might like these," she drawled charmingly, setting them on the man's tray table.

Not bothering to hide it, Grace rolled her eyes once again at the excessive attention. He smiled, thanked Katie for the lemons, and returned to his meal.

Dinner on an airplane is usually the time even non-talkers might share a few pleasantries. "Where are you headed, how long have you been away?" sort of chitchat. Sometimes people graduate to a slightly more intimate level of conversation such as marital status, number of children, occupation, and what event took them away from home.

Even though she was tired, courtesy and habit won out. Eight and a half hours on a plane is a long time and it would only be polite to initiate some conversation during such a long flight. In between bites she asked, "Are you staying in Honolulu, or do you have a connection once we land?"

He didn't look up from his salad, intent on picking out the tomatoes. "Just Honolulu," he responded without asking her plans.

"Me too." Wishing she could have his tomatoes she continued, "How long have you been traveling?"

He turned and looked her once again full in the eyes, seemed to search for something, and upon not finding it turned back to his meal and said, "All my life."

She gave an easy laugh. "Yeah, me too. I heard a guy say once he was born married and went to work the next day. Sometimes I feel the same way."

He gave a half-smile but didn't say anything. Feeling a little shut down she shook it off, decided to finish her meal in silence and allow him to do the same. Still, she looked at him again sideways. She was almost certain she recognized him.

Once they were both finished Katie came by, removed their trays, refilled their drinks, and eventually brought out a tray of recently microwaved cookies. It was an overnight flight to Honolulu and there would be additional snacks available. Grace declined but he took a cookie and stuck it into his mouth as he leaned down and reached into his briefcase and pulled out a laptop.

Grace resumed her magazine but out of the corner of her eye

couldn't help noticing how his fingers moved rapidly and efficiently across the screen. As she continued to peruse the articles she watched as he appeared to be making changes to 3D images that looked like some form of building structure. *Okay, maybe an architect not a rancher,* she concluded.

She quickly surveyed the other passengers in the cabin. She and her seatmate were in the fourth row on the right side of the airplane facing the front. Directly in the row behind them was a young couple traveling with a small baby who was thankfully sleeping in her mother's arms. Grace noticed the mother had declined dinner not wanting to wake the baby. Anna had promised to keep her meal warm until her husband was finished and could take his turn with the baby.

Across the aisle to Grace's left, catty-corner in the last row, were two men, both appearing to be in their mid- to early forties, animatedly talking. It seemed they were probably traveling together and looked more like business associates than Hawaiian vacationers. In the row in front of them, directly across the aisle from Grace and her seatmate, was an elderly couple probably in their mid-seventies, definitely tourists, with brightly colored Hawaiian clothing. The woman sat by the window with her husband in the seat closest to the aisle. They had recently been blessed with their eighth grandchild, who, based on the pictures they whipped out, Anna had already deemed the cutest baby she'd ever seen.

In front of them was the boisterous cowboy Grace estimated to be about seventy, who was accompanied by his wife. She was a matronly but well-groomed stout woman with shoulder-length white bobbed hair. She wore a bright kelly green and lemon-colored three-quarter sleeve tunic top with large white flowers and a pair of Eileen Fisher wide-legged white linen pants. Her gold strappy sandals with large colored jewels cut into her skin and appeared to somewhat interrupt the circulation to her large swollen ankles. Around her neck were at least three paper leis, all of varying shades of purple, green, yellow, red, and orange. Under her seat she had stuffed an oversized woven beach bag with 3D pink flamingos on the front.

Through the crack in the seat Grace could see the back of the head of one of a set of identical twins in row two seated by the window. Grace had noticed the sisters when she'd boarded. They appeared to be in their early eighties and were dressed completely alike in blue jean jackets and pants adorned with colorful floral appliqués.

In the bulkhead was a woman and a young boy Grace assumed was her son, about ten. In the bulkhead to the right was a teenager and a man Grace thought might be his dad or an uncle. Behind them in row two sat a large woman who appeared to be in her sixties with teased red hair and a bright colorful top who, from what Grace could tell, was also traveling with her husband. He sat next to the aisle and wore a straw fedora with a red band and multi-colored feather attached to it.

Directly in front of Grace was a couple of young newlyweds on their honeymoon. They huddled and kissed and shared their food, each preferring the other's meal choice to their own. Katie had grabbed the girl's hand and exclaimed loudly over the size of the diamond in her ring. The girl waved it excitedly in the air and told Katie they hadn't even been married for twenty-four hours. Although Grace couldn't see much of the young woman since she was seated by the window, she could see her husband's young face beaming with pride and excitement. They were headed directly to Maui after they landed and would be in Hawaii staying in his parents' time share for an entire ten days! She had brought four new swimming suits. He told Katie he couldn't understand how four bikinis and a couple of pairs of shorts and some T-shirts could take up the two large suitcases his wife insisted on bringing. He lingered on the word "wife," obviously enjoying the new privilege of saying it.

Grace sat smiling for a moment, listening to the young couple's chatter until they finally started watching the same movie on different laptops. Each started the movie at exactly the same time so they would be perfectly in sync. Katie brought them each a small bottle of prosecco with two glasses and apologized it wasn't better champagne, but she hoped they would enjoy it.

Grace opted not to start a movie and replaced the *People* magazine with a book she pulled out of her purse. She was reading a current release by an author famous for self-help books that leaned towards self-actualization, self-empowerment, and self-love. A prominent and respected psychologist, well-known beyond Texas, Dr. Grace, as she was known, was always searching for new tools and techniques to help her patients successfully negotiate the highs and lows of their lives.

"Each person's life and individual circumstances are simply the by-product of his or her belief system," the author claimed. "Each person's thinking creates his world, garbage in—garbage out. Control your thoughts, control your world, control your happiness," he promised.

She laid the book down for a moment and closed her eyes. She'd read several along the same vein recently and gave a small sigh. She admitted to herself, like many others in her field openly confessed, she had sought out a career in the mental health field looking for solutions to her own problems as well as those of her patients. Recently divorced and squabbling with her mother and her sister, she was starting to wonder if intimate relationships were really her strong suit and if she had chosen the right profession. After all, if she couldn't even manage her own relationships successfully what business did she have giving advice to others on the same subject, she wondered.

Happiness? she asked herself wryly. *Good luck on that yellow brick road.* She then chided herself for her pessimism, picked up the book, and absently thumbed through it while wondering if there was any value in continuing. She took another long sip of her wine, swirled the contents, and stared into the glass.

Recently, in an act of unusual courage, she'd taken a deep dive into brutal self-examination and in the process Grace came to the realization that she was unhappy. The full and sudden revelation of what had previously only been a nagging suspicion had shaken Grace to her core.

But why? she asked herself silently as she stared out the window into the black and gray cumulus clouds that seemed to encompass and guide the aircraft through the turbulent sky. Grace closed the window shade and turned off her overhead light, leaned her seat back, closed her eyes, and reflected back to her recent journey through self-analysis.

It wasn't just the divorce, she told herself. Grace realized that losing her sense of purpose, her joy, and if she was totally honest, any real enthusiasm for getting out of bed in the mornings, had been like air slowly seeping out of what had once been a shiny, bouncy, helium-filled and celebratory balloon now sinking slowly, barely hanging on at half-mast. She knew she was hovering dangerously just this side of depression and unless something significantly changed, she had no reason to think that all her tomorrows were going to end up looking any different than her boring, lifeless, unfulfilling todays.

She shook her head again and felt tears spring to her eyes. *Where the hell's my happy? I don't have any reason to feel this way*, she chided herself. The observation almost caused her to panic. She felt her heart beat fast and she took another drink. She opened the shade and looked out the window again and thought, if all the boxes were already checked, how could she ever buy, drive, wear, seduce, decorate, or stumble across anything or anyone to possibly help change things? She already had everything she wanted, she told herself, and then corrected, well almost. Someday she'd like to be married again. But not yet. Not until she could be assured that she wasn't going to attract another man just like the jerk who'd just left her.

But even a new man wasn't going to make her happy, she assured herself practically. She knew that. She was a therapist, for heaven's sake. Even if Prince Charming rode right up to her door on a big white horse, sweeping her away to his castle, making her his nation's first and most adored therapist queen, capable of setting all men, women, and children free from their emotional prisons, even that wouldn't make her happy. No. Something else was wrong. Something inside. Something important was missing. Grace knew the problem was that she had no idea what that something could be.

By all traditional measuring sticks, she was the picture of success. She knew that. She was high-functioning and self-reliant. Grace was well-educated, professionally respected, published, sought after as a speaker, articulate, funny, attractive, and caring. She had a strong moral compass and was all around physically, mentally, and financially healthy. Mentally healthy? Grace assessed herself again scrupulously. Yes, she was mentally healthy. She wasn't happy, but she wasn't dysfunctional. There's a difference, she reminded herself. What she was, Grace realized suddenly, was empty.

But what do I do if there's nothing else I want? she asked herself almost desperately. *Isn't there something or someone else I can make myself want? Something I can get to at least fill the hole and bide some time until this passes?* She reached into her purse and grabbed a mint. Time with her own therapist hadn't helped her get rid of anything but hope and money. She drained the last of her wine and looked at the book again. *I can't believe I don't know how to fix this,* she thought silently. She considered medication. *Really?* She wrinkled her brow at herself critically. Grace wasn't against taking an anti-depressant. She had recommended either anti-depressants or anti-anxiety medication or both to the majority of her patients. But always just to get them over the hump. Never as a permanent solution.

She cringed when she remembered that earlier in the day she had googled Hawaii to see if they had lifted the ban on recreational marijuana and toyed with the idea of getting some while she was there. Grace shook her head in confusion and dismay. No. Pot and/or medicine was not going to be a long-term solution for her, regardless of how legal or socially acceptable they'd become. Maybe she could accept both as a temporary bandage, a bridge, but nothing she was willing to take on as a permanent part of her routine. Not yet anyway.

Grace opened her eyes, reached up and turned her light back on. She closed her book and stuffed it in between her seat and the window and pulled out a *Good Housekeeping* magazine that someone had left in the seat pocket in front of her. She perused the magazine cover checking out their feature stories. "Shed Five Pounds in Five Days Eating Pasta," one article promised. "Time Management Tips from a Mother of Five." "Super Savings without Cutting Coupons." "How God Saved My Marriage."

"Hmph," she grumbled, sullenly flipping through the pages. "Well, he sure as hell didn't save mine." The bitterness of the accusation surprised Grace. She hadn't given God more than a passing thought in years. *Why now?* she wondered. Grace briefly pondered the question while taking a sip of her remaining water. She gave a silent half laugh derisively. *Certainly I don't think God is the answer,* she chided herself. *I'd rather have to smoke a joint every day of my life than go down that road,* she thought wryly.

Grace thought back on her youth, which was the last time she remembered thinking much at all about God. She'd been raised in a traditional Christian household. Her parents began attending church shortly after they'd survived a potentially fatal car crash, walking away virtually unscathed. Deemed a wake-up call from God, they marched their family off to their new church home whenever the doors were opened.

She turned and studied the various passing shades of darkness outside, surprised to remember that as a child she had actually once loved God. In fact, she remembered, she had *really* loved him. She'd gone to church camp, Bible school, and other youth activities and participated with great enthusiasm. No one had to force her. From the first time she'd first heard about Jesus, Grace was hooked. Where other girls dreamed about pop stars, Grace was starstruck by Jesus.

Watching the gray clouds pass she remembered often dreaming about him at night as she floated off to sleep. In her dreams Jesus would come and offer his hand and they'd dance on a balcony while love songs played somewhere inside.

Actually, the music came from her older sister's record player and to Grace Jesus bore a striking resemblance to Mel Gibson's character in the movie *Braveheart*. But to her he was Jesus, and he was her hero. She loved him with all her heart because she knew one day she and Jesus were getting married.

Her favorite Sunday school teacher had told her so. Mrs. Paulus knew everything about Jesus and heaven. One Sunday morning she read out of the children's Bible to the entire class that Jesus would be coming back to Earth and would choose a bride. She read Jesus was in heaven preparing a place for everyone to live. When it was finished, he planned to come back and anybody who didn't deny they knew him would be invited to his wedding. There would be a big celebration and then everyone would move to heaven and live in the same neighborhood as Jesus.

When Grace heard the story she knew immediately she would be the bride. She was sure of it. She loved Jesus. In fact, she didn't just love him, she was obsessed with him. She had his picture in her room.

Jesus loved her! He was already dancing with her in her dreams, wasn't he? Of course it was her!

Grace remembered one Sunday she made the decision to totally devote her life to Jesus. She had shyly suggested to Mrs. Paulus after class that she thought she might be the bride. Her teacher enthusiastically agreed, beamed with delight, and told Grace she was very proud of her. Mrs. Paulus even suggested they pray together right there so Grace could tell Jesus of her commitment to him and invite him into her heart.

They knelt down and Grace prayed. Afterward Mrs. Paulus cried and hugged Grace, assuring her she would live in heaven forever with Jesus. Grace proudly told her parents after church she had prayed with Mrs. Paulus and accepted Jesus into her heart and one day he was going to marry her! Nobody questioned the story. Her parents, too, were thrilled. Like Mrs. Paulus, her mother cried. They all went for ice cream.

Grace went for years believing in Jesus' love for her and living her young life preparing herself for him. But then one day Grace graduated and moved from Sunday school to the church's large and flourishing youth group. However, Mrs. Paulus and her stories of love and marriage to Jesus stayed in children's church.

As she progressed through the religious system Grace learned the best way to love Jesus was to serve him. Dancing on the balcony *with* him was replaced by handing out tracts *about* him. Jesus had high standards. Many people were going to hell. The stakes were getting higher. Jesus stopped visiting her in her dreams and in her mind he stopped looking like Mel Gibson and more like the school principal.

It didn't take too many more years before Grace came to the conclusion she thought more highly of Jesus than he thought of her. She was a sinner. He was perfect. She wanted a boyfriend who told her she was beautiful. She was told her Jesus thought she was a filthy rag. Not a good foundation for a marriage. The relationship cooled.

As her image of Jesus and what he wanted from her and for her continued to change, Grace eventually left God and the church. Initially, she didn't want to abandon her Jesus but obviously his will and hers had grown incompatible.

When she announced to her parents she was leaving the church her mother commissioned the preacher to pay Grace a visit. He came to her apartment and warned her sternly, "Do not forsake fellowship with other believers. What about worship? What about communion?" Grace lit a cigarette, opened a wine cooler, placed two Ritz crackers she pulled from a bag onto a small plate and offered them to the preacher. He stared, declined, and she shrugged her shoulders, taking a long drag on her cigarette.

The preacher, undaunted and determined, cautioned and told her obedience was required to please God. The world is a dangerous place. How could she expect protection or provision from a God she wouldn't obey?

She politely listened and considered all the preacher had to say. When he was finished Grace stubbed out her cigarette, stood up, smiled, thanked him for coming, and with the finality that left no room for discussion informed the reverend as far as she was concerned if God wanted obedience he should get a dog and showed him to the door.

Grace sipped her water and asked herself how Jesus went from sweetheart to principal to mafia boss. Deeply wounded by the extreme guilt and shame her parents, friends, and other church and family members employed to coerce her back into the fold, Grace had become if not completely atheist, at least agnostic.

Suddenly tired, she looked down at her hands and wondered again if there was a God, if he had ever really loved her, and if so why did he let her leave without even putting up a fight? Let alone end up with a loser husband who after ten years of marriage cheated on her, drained their bank account, stole her dog, and then left her for his hairdresser. How could she, even as a child, feel such love from and for God and been so wrong? Her mother and her sister told her the problems of her life was God's punishment on her for leaving the church. Her sister told her she was too self-centered to ever find love. She couldn't even keep a dog let alone a husband. Grace's jaw clenched at the memory.

She shook her head and wondered how God, once so important to her, was now nothing more than a subconscious disappointment. She didn't know but questioned if it all hadn't just been merely a child-hood fantasy. Certain that no answer existed for her, certainly not that night, she took a drink of water and flipped through the magazine, de-termined to discover how to lose five pounds and still eat pasta.

CHAPTER 3

SOON THE FLIGHT ATTENDANT PASSED BY WITH MORE COOKIES and this time Grace couldn't resist. She took one as did her travel mate. They both ordered coffee. Katie took their empty drink glasses and soon returned, placing the first cup of coffee on Grace's partially opened tray table. As she sat it down they hit turbulence and before the flight attendant could steady it, the cup tipped, dumping the coffee onto the table which then made its way into Grace's lap. Immediately she felt the liquid reach the back of her seat. Trying to keep it from soaking her pants she instinctively lifted her bottom and in the process accidentally hit her leg on her tray table scattering the contents.

At once, as the remaining coffee tipped into Grace's lap, she and Katie both simultaneously and involuntarily swore out loud. As if connected, every head in the cabin simultaneously turned to witness the catastrophe. As Grace scrambled, trying to reduce as much damage as possible, she realized later the man sitting next to her did something out of character for someone who hadn't said a dozen words. As he and Katie quickly moved to let her out and into the aisle, he laughed.

Before any more injury could be done to her suit or her ego, Grace made her way to the lavatory to see if she couldn't control the damage. She tried unsuccessfully to blot out the coffee stains. Realizing the water was making it worse she gave up, left the bathroom, and, trying to avoid looks of amusement from the men and sympathy from the women, she slid past the stranger who had stood up to let her back into her seat. Katie had been there in her absence and the only remaining evidence was Grace's magazine and book, both wet and coffee-stained, newly tucked into the seat pocket in front of her. She glanced over and found the man openly studying her.

"What?" she asked a little irritated.

"I'd give ten bucks to see the replay."

She muttered another oath taken aback by his response. Katie came to check on her and asked if she wanted coffee or another glass of wine. Somewhat curtly she answered wine, and Katie was right back with a fresh glass filled to the top. She sat it down on Grace's tray table along with several napkins and a weak smile as if to say, "Just in case . . ." Instead, she said, "Ma'am, I am so sorry."

Grace gave a weak smile and said graciously, "It wasn't your fault. Let's just blame Mother Nature." Katie apologized again, brought Grace another cookie unrequested, and made her way back to the galley.

Grace took a few minutes to compose herself. She took a small bite of the cookie and noticed her seatmate had not pulled out his computer and was still looking at her and then heard him slightly chuckle. She turned and looked at him squarely. "Hasn't your wife ever taught you to laugh at a woman who doesn't intend to be funny is rude and, depending on the woman, possibly dangerous?"

"Sorry."

It was obvious he wasn't. "Well?" she waited, smoothing her suit the best she could.

Aware she expected an answer he asked, "Do you want to know if I'm married?" He was surprised but amused.

"I do," she agreed. "I've been watching the flight attendant flit around you for the past hour. You aren't taking the hint she's interested. If you're married do us both a favor and tell her so she'll quit drooling over you and watch what she's doing."

He openly studied her face. It was as if he were looking for some clue that would tell him something he wanted to know. He turned away. "No, I'm not married. I'm also not interested but I like the attention. She's cute."

"Cad," she accused a little less ruffled.

"I'm not a cad. Just a man," he smiled unapologetically.

"She is pretty cute," Grace pursued. "Why aren't you interested?" Her brazenness surprised them both. He opened the door, she reminded herself.

"Rejection issues," he said with a smile. "I'm afraid no self-respecting woman would have me," he said with mock self-depreciation. He finished his cookie in two bites.

"That's not the only thing you're afraid of," she observed equally candidly. "You're also afraid to fly. I saw you when I got on this plane. You were nervous as a cat." She liked men who were good at bantering. She especially liked men who were so good-looking while doing it. Upon closer examination she noticed his dark blue eyes were accompanied by long, dark eyelashes that curled slightly at the ends. She studied him intently. *Where had she seen him before?*

"Guilty as charged," he conceded, showing a lopsided grin indicating a good orthodontist at some point. "What can I say?" he shrugged. "I'm afraid of falling. I only fly when I can't avoid it. I also stay off bridges, skyscrapers, stilts, tall peoples' shoulders . . ."

So, the non-talker switched over into talker mode and revealed a secret fear. Spilled coffee and personal troubles temporarily forgotten, eight looming hours of boredom and years of training kicked in and she mentally rubbed her hands together and prepared to put him on the couch.

She looked at him intently and asked, "Why are you afraid of falling?"

Again, the penetrating look. "Well, I took a fall once and it had a disastrous effect. It happened a long time ago. I never really got over it." Katie brought him a coffee refill with some additional sugar packets and creamer. He added them and took a small exploratory sip of his drink.

She pursed her lips. Freud, move over. Aloud she said, "Well, we have several hours left just the two of us, plus a third ear in case we need Katie, and I have a few fears of my own. You tell me yours and I'll let you in on a few of mine." She leaned in and smiled at him encouragingly. "Since you're on a roll why don't you go first?"

He stared at her for just a moment before he asked a question that she debated every day of her life afterward. "Do you think God sent you to me?"

She wondered if she'd heard him correctly. She cocked her head slightly. "I'm sorry?"

"Do you think God put you on this plane for me?"

This was getting more interesting by the minute. "If I had that kind of relationship with God do you think I'd be sitting here with coffee stains on my pants?"

He laughed out loud but seeing his disappointment she quickly followed up, surprised, "You don't seriously think God hand picks your travel companions, do you?"

"Not normally, but I have a problem and I'm stuck," he answered defensively. "I asked God for help. I need someone to talk to. You're so anxious to analyze me I thought maybe you're the help he's sending. I thought maybe the coffee incident was just what we needed to break the ice and get the ball rolling."

"I am a trained psychologist but I'm not anxious to analyze you," she retorted, embarrassed at being so obvious. Feeling more than a little curious though, she pursued. "You're religious? You think God spilled coffee on me to get us to talk?"

He smiled and said, "No, I'm not religious. No, I don't think God dumped coffee on you, even though he does have a good sense of humor. It's just that when I ask him for something I give him the courtesy of believing he'll answer. I thought maybe you were it." He looked at her, shrugged his shoulders and smiled. "Guess I was wrong."

"Hmm, I see." This guy was nuts. She finished her cookie, wiped her hands, and took a sip of wine.

"Now, Dr. Laura, don't flip your tone like that telling me my credibility just went down a couple of notches. Don't you believe God cares about people and helps us out when we ask?"

Maybe not nuts she decided, just delusional. "It's rude to make up names for a person just because you don't know her real one. If we are going to continue this conversation any reprimands should be addressed to my real name, which is Grace. And you are?"

"Adam." He extended his hand and they shook. Nice hands. Katie really did miss out.

"So you have a problem and you're stuck. You wonder if maybe this is a divine appointment. Hmmm . . ." She decided she needed to be honest, with at least herself, about her true motives in pursuing a conversation. She wanted to analyze Adam because she was bored, she wasn't in the mood for a movie, and she was tired of thinking about her own issues. He was good-looking. Smart. A little weird. An unofficial, off-the-books nighttime counseling session over drinks, sitting in the dark, whispering secrets with a good-looking mysterious stranger could be the perfect solution. She felt a small rush of adrenaline and inwardly celebrated.

However, she paused, she didn't believe in God anymore. How much help could she really offer? Still, unwilling to let that be a deterrent, she decided *how hard can it be?* Instead she quipped out loud, "Maybe God did send me. I haven't talked to him for some time, and it scares me a little to think he still has my number, but I used to dabble a little in the God business." She leaned in and smiled deviously. "In fact, now that I think about it, maybe a higher power did put us together. I have a little history with religious fanatics. Maybe I *am* just the person to help you!" she snickered. *This is going to be so fun!* she thought excitedly.

His smile disappeared and his blue eyes turned to icy steel. He turned away, finished his coffee, stuffed the empty sugar packet and creamer container into the empty cup, and said coolly, "If you want to be taken seriously in the medical field you might consider not referring to your patients as fanatics." He reached over and started to pull out his computer.

Warning bells indicated she had clearly misread the moment. She was instantly and genuinely contrite. Not to mention embarrassed. She could usually be counted on for her empathy and professionalism, both of which obviously got lost in the last glass of wine. "I apologize," she said quickly. He glanced to see if she was mocking him. "No, I really am." She touched his arm gently. "I'm sure I'm overly glib because I guess if I'm honest I've got some major unresolved religious issues," she confessed. He didn't respond but made no further move towards the laptop so she said hurriedly, "Like I said, God and I aren't exactly on speaking terms these days."

Adam gave a slight smile and she continued, "Please forgive me. I really am sorry." She smiled at him again kindly and he saw genuine sincerity in her eyes. At least he hoped it was.

He scrutinized her intently without hiding the fact he was doing so. She was a little taken aback by his inspection but allowed it as an act of contrition. He studied her more closely.

Adam also was a good judge of people. After a few moments he deduced that the woman seated next to him was open, intelligent, and certainly beautiful. He loved old movies. In fact he thought he'd seen just about every old film ever made. When Grace first stepped onto the plane he had gasped under his breath. The woman about to be his travel companion for the next eight and a half hours looked like she'd just stepped out of a vintage Hollywood magazine. Tall, blonde, sleek, and chic in an off-white linen suit. He couldn't believe his luck when she approached his row and agreed to switch seats with him. Standing with her in the aisle when she first got on the plane, all he could do was stare. Then he'd been so taken aback when she'd first spoken to him during dinner he couldn't think of one intelligent thing to say.

Adam had been praying for a sharp, open-minded, empathetic sounding board. Grace looked like a combination of Michelle Pfeiffer and Grace Kelly. A wee snarky, he thought, but a trained psychologist and a willing and captive audience for the next several hours. Plus, she was encouraging him to spill his guts. *Thank you, Jesus*, he thought.

He paused and reflected. There was a good chance this conversation would not end well. He momentarily hesitated. He looked at Grace's kind, expectant face, threw caution to the wind, and decided to risk it. If she thought he was crazy he'd change seats with someone and she'd never have to see him again. "Well, God and I are definitely on speaking terms. That's not the problem," he offered. "You said you have a history with God? Do you know anything about the Bible?" he interviewed.

"Oh yes, never missed a Sunday service when I was a kid," she responded promptly. "Include summer Bible school and church camp until I was fourteen. I once won a trip to the Illinois State Fair for memorizing more Bible verses than any other camper." Her smile was dazzling. "Also, under duress I will admit, I listen to a weekly recap of my mother's preacher's sermon every Sunday night along with commentary as to how it applies to my life."

"Impressive qualifications, doctor. You'll do." He said drolly and she was relieved he'd forgiven her. There was something interesting about him, she thought. The look behind his eyes along with his easy and confident demeanor indicated he was someone extraordinary. He seemed intelligent and fun-loving, yet intense with an above average self-awareness. Comfortable in his own skin. He talked about God as though they were golfing buddies. She did a quick physical re-appraisal. Expensive shoes, nice briefcase, it was obvious he wasn't going to hit her up for hotel fare when they landed. His self-confidence was evident but so far not a hint of ego. Yet not married. Go figure.

The pilot's voice came over the intercom informing them of their current weather conditions. He was sorry for the earlier turbulence and had adjusted the plane to an altitude that would hopefully avoid any further roughness. The newly married couple in front of them had put their movies on hold, had their heads together, and were whispering and giggling.

Grace started afresh. "Why are you stuck? Are you a minister or philosophy teacher and have a problem with some sort of biblical doctrine?"

"Neither," he answered. "I'm just a not so normal guy in need of an intelligent yet open minded," he paused and looked at her meaningfully and repeated, "*very* open-minded sounding board. I have a problem—a unique problem—I can't resolve myself and honestly can't discuss it with," he hesitated for a moment, "well, really anyone. And since you volunteered . . ." he trailed off.

"Are you gay?" she asked practically. "And wonder if God has a problem with it?"

He laughed. "No. But I'm glad you're ready to consider all possibilities."

"Hmm. And since we're sitting here together in the dark and you'll probably never see me again . . ." she continued. "Full disclaimer, I'm pretty sure God's got nothing to do with it. Like I said, we aren't exactly speaking . . ." She looked at him again and he seemed unbothered. Satisfied, she nodded her head and continued in her best professional voice, indicating she was ready to get started, "Okay then. Why don't you tell me what's bothering you and let's just see where this night takes us!" she smiled encouragingly.

He reached up to adjust the air vent above him. "Let's see how good of a sounding board you really are," he started. "Summarized, here's my dilemma." He grew serious. "My relationship with God is the most important thing to me. However, all of a sudden I'm having trouble hearing from him. He's gone quiet. I can still feel him but he won't engage with me in conversation. It's either that, or more likely, I've got something blocking me."

Grace wrinkled her brow but was careful not to let any skepticism or concern show on her face. He was hearing voices. She asked cautiously, "But you could hear from him before?"

"Yes."

Establish rapport. Establish rapport. "How long's he been gone?"

"Maybe a month."

She paused. "Did anything happen of significance during the time around his, um, departure?"

"No," he said a little miserably.

Grace grew matter of fact. "If you had to guess, why would you say he left?" In her practice she'd discovered that most people know the answers to their own questions but aren't confident enough to verbalize their hunches. Getting them to guess often times allows the answer to surface without causing the patient to feel as though they're committing to an answer.

"I don't know. Maybe because I took something from him," he answered unhappily.

The newlyweds in front of them stopped giggling and the bride lightly but definitively smacked her new husband on the head and said, "Absolutely not. Forget it!" Her husband protested as if in physical pain. Grace smiled and studied the pattern a drop of wine had made on her napkin and posed her next question. "What did you take from him?" she asked.

"Just his whole world," Adam answered sadly.

Grace reached into her briefcase, pulled out a leather portfolio, and inserted a fresh pad of paper. Solving relationship issues with God was not exactly her strong suit. *This is going to be a long night,* she told herself, *I'd better take notes.* She narrowed her eyes and studied her seatmate thoughtfully.

CHAPTER 4

KATIE WAS BACK. THIS TIME TO ANNOUNCE THEY SHOULD expect additional turbulence. When she spoke she primarily addressed Grace. Mild apprehension showed on her face. She was still remembering her part in the spilled coffee escapade. Grace nodded her head indicating they had her permission for the flight to continue. Katie walked away but stopped to let the Texan with the cowboy hat, struggling to slide past his seated wife so as not to disturb her, into the aisle.

Grace watched her walk away and commented encouragingly to her new friend, "She is so cute." She wondered if Adam would allow her to delve at least a little into his love life. Maybe God wasn't his only problem, she speculated shamelessly, yet somewhat hopefully.

Slightly aggravated but needing her help he said, "Grace, quit worrying about my love life. I have more to tell you that I'm afraid, yet grateful at the same time, is going to push all thoughts of romance out of your mind. Even though I'm worried you may have trouble believing—" he was interrupted by the pilot making an announcement that the beverage service in both cabins would be temporarily discontinued and he was turning on the seatbelt sign until the flight smoothed out and it was safe to continue.

"I pride myself on having an open mind," she encouraged and put her hand over her wine glass to avoid future spills as the plane took a slight lurch.

Adam glanced tentatively past her out the window and his tan face paled slightly as the plane jerked back and forth as if it was having trouble shifting gears. "I was married before," he admitted finally. "In fact, several times. However, the reason I'm not married any more is because the circumstances of my life are so extremely unusual, bizarre really, I have found it impossible to find a woman who is realistically able to share that life. Therefore, I keep my relationships light, on the surface, and have learned to live with being alone." He shrugged and gave a slightly sick glance out the window again.

She watched the Texan come out of the restroom, stop and ask Katie for another drink, and then insist his wife stand up to let him back into his seat instead of crawling over her again. She was knitting something and it took her a minute to gather her yarn, needles, and project, struggle out of her seat, and into the aisle. Grace didn't know why but she was surprised by the confession of multiple marriages. First appearances indicated he was the settling down type. "Do these unique circumstances relate to the problem you're having with God?"

"Maybe." He took a deep breath. "Grace, I'm about to tell a story that will be very difficult for you to believe. It will sound crazy. You'll have to suspend your belief in what's possible. Can you do that? If not,

I need you to tell me now before I say something I can't take back. If you have any doubt then we should stop, have another drink, and talk about something a little more uh . . . safe."

Now beyond professionally curious, she leaned in and encouraged, "You can trust me, Adam. Tell me what's going on."

"This will be a difficult conversation," he warned again. "*Very difficult*," he emphasized.

She nodded her acceptance. He had her total and undivided attention. This plane could be struck by lightning, and on the way down she'd still say, *We'll be fine, Adam, really. Just tell me what's going on*, she thought, completely intrigued.

He carefully pondered his next sentence. He closed his eyes and she had the distinct impression he might be praying. He took a deep breath and without opening his eyes said, "Grace, I'm not just any Adam. I am 'the' Adam. The Adam from the Bible. I am God's first created being." He was silenced by a sudden lurch of the plane.

CHAPTER 5

AFTER A MOMENT OF LETTING HIS STOMACH SETTLE AND HIS words sink in he opened his eyes, looked at her, and waited for her reaction. When none came he quickly asked, "Did you hear me?" She simply stared at him as if waiting for the punchline. He continued, "I'm serious. I am 'the' Adam," he reiterated. "I messed up God's world. I've tried for centuries to fix it but eventually I realized there's only so much I can do. At one point I completely lost my relationship with God but over the years it's been repaired. But like I said, something's happened and now there's this void. I've lost contact with him. I need someone to talk to who can help me figure it out. I'm lost." He exhaled and sat silently, anxiously awaiting her response.

She was momentarily taken aback but quickly remembered their earlier bantering. He was retaliating against Grace for calling him a religious fanatic. When she was certain he'd concluded his prank she gave a half laugh and rebutted sarcastically, "Oh *that* Adam! Why didn't you say so?" she mockingly looked around. "So where's Eve? Flying coach?"

They hit another small pocket of turbulence, the plane swerved, but Adam barely flinched. "Grace, this isn't a joke."

She laughed out loud. "Then I just *have* to have the name of your plastic surgeon," she drawled.

No smile. "I'm telling you the truth," he said quietly. "I've had many wives since Eve, many careers, which have spanned multiple lifetimes. My life's purpose is to partner with God, help others find their way into the Garden, and be here to help usher in the New Jerusalem but for some reason suddenly I can barely even hear him now!"

She paused and looked at him completely bewildered. His face held no hint of a smirk. No smile in his eyes. No further elaboration to keep the joke going.

She stared at him quizzically and did a quick reassessment. A fellow traveler turned patient, straight-faced, telling a fantastic tale, and asking her to temporarily suspend reality and contemplate the possibility and tragedy of it. "You don't actually expect me to believe you, do you?" she asked without smiling this time. He said nothing awaiting her next reaction.

The plane hit another bump and Grace again placed her napkin and her palm over the top of her wineglass to keep the contents from sloshing outside. She stared at her hand without seeing it. She'd analyzed hundreds of patients in her practice. Her specific gift was quick and accurate patient evaluation. During their short encounter she'd assessed Adam to be of sound mind. Regardless of these current and ludicrous assertions she found herself unwilling to immediately discard her original assessment. She narrowed her eyes and studied his face intently.

She scanned her internal database for possible explanations. Suddenly she remembered a patient she'd had several years ago who'd engaged the services of a charlatan therapist, one who specialized in past life regression therapy. Adam said he'd suffered a fall. Possibly the fall had been severe and there'd been some head trauma. Maybe during the recovery process he'd fallen prey to a past life regression therapist who'd seeded the Adam theory.

The planted memory could've led Adam to assume a false sense of responsibility for the world's troubles. She turned to look out the window as the plane took another lurch. Head injury notwithstanding, Adam seemed too practical to have ventured down such an unconventional path. She looked at his face, which was white. She wasn't sure whether it was the weather and the unsteadiness of the plane or the topic of conversation.

"Are your memories based on something you think happened to you in a previous lifetime?"

"*What?* Of course not!" He shook his head and looked at her in disbelief. He decided to abort any further discussion, considering it emotional suicide. *What was I thinking?* he chastised himself. He was searching for a way to change the subject when he looked into Grace's eyes. The teasing sarcasm had been replaced with concern, compassion, and a desire to help.

He wavered. He hadn't had a conversation with God in over a month. They were partners. They talked constantly before that. Adam felt desperate. He studied Grace again. It had been years since there'd been anyone in whom he could truly confide. Even cautious and calculated attempts to share his story almost always resulted in a tsunami of rejection, derision, and eventual misdiagnoses of mental illness. Eventually, he abandoned all attempts at meaningful conversation with others which left him alone and tortured.

But the longing to share his heart, his *story*, with another human being had been rising within him for some time even before he lost contact with God. Was God's absence intended to force Adam's hand? Was he telling Adam to try again? He looked at her profile against the filtered light coming in through the window. Could he trust her? Adam turned to look out the window across the other side of the aisle. He prayed again, *Jesus, if she can't handle this show me now. Please!*

After a few moments of further internal debate, he opted to continue, deciding he'd already exposed too much to make a clean exit out of the conversation anyway. The teenager in the front row with short, cropped hair wearing a T-shirt with a guitar, a cross, and a dove on it that said "Rock in Peace" got up to use the restroom. Anna, sitting in the jump seat next to Katie, reminded him the seat belt sign was still on. He looked at her blankly but returned to his seat.

Adam turned back to Grace and continued soberly, "I'm not sparring with you, and I don't think I've been reincarnated if that's what you're suggesting. I told you early on this was going to be a difficult conversation. You said you could handle it," he reminded her.

She stared at him.

"I'm asking you to consider," he continued calmly and slowly enunciating each word, "the possibility that I am God's original human creation. I am not any Adam; I am *the* Adam," he reiterated. "God created me, put me on Earth, and I have never died. For purposes of a one-time discussion, I'm asking you to at least pretend to believe me and let me tell my story." He almost pleaded, "I need somebody to talk to." And then added almost in reproach, "You said you could handle it."

Warning bells screamed loudly from within. Grace managed to choke out, "How did you not die?"

Adam shook his head miserably. "I ate from the Tree of Life before God could ban it."

She suddenly remembered her Bible and said, "No. The Bible clearly states that Adam died when he was about eight hundred years old." *How did she remember that?* She shook off the question as her head started to spin.

He was silent and then said, "It was then that I disappeared from my family and society and became a complete recluse. My family and everyone thought I died and in a manner of speaking I guess I did. I took another name, moved to a different land, took a different identity." He looked at her miserably and shrugged. "I wasn't aging like the others, and I couldn't fake it any longer. It got complicated, Grace."

She was silent, too stunned to continue. The captain came on the intercom to announce he had temporarily risen above the turbulence but thought more was coming. He was turning off the seat belt sign but people who needed to get up should do so as the likelihood of it soon being turned back on was probable. The teenager jumped up, used the restroom, and returned to his seat.

Grace downed the last of her wine. When she could finally speak she angrily stowed her tray table, threw her notepad and pen into her purse, grabbed her empty glass, jumped out of her seat, and commanded angrily, "That's it! Let me out!" Sparring with a stranger was one thing but participating as the butt of a juvenile and cruel joke was quite another.

He stood, let her pass, and she made her escape. She thrust her empty glass into Katie's surprised hand, entered the lavatory and slammed the door, noisily locking it behind her and leaving him to face the probability of a future storm alone.

CHAPTER 6

S HE DIDN'T COME BACK FOR A LONG TIME. ADAM LOOKED UP and saw the lavatory occupied light was still illuminated. She was in there thinking only God knew what. Probably wondering how she could exchange seats with someone else. *At least she didn't call security,* he reassured himself.

The elderly couple across the aisle had taken out a deck of playing cards and the woman shuffled them loudly. "What are we playing?" her husband asked.

Adam glanced briefly out the window and gave a heavy sigh as his mind reverted to an age and place no longer in existence. He felt his throat tighten. *At least I didn't lose the memories of Eden,* he thought dejectedly.

Adam thought of another tree, the tree that had been the source of his problems, the Tree of the Knowledge of Good and Evil. It had been positioned at the far edge of the Garden. Of all the trees it was the least unique. Its leaves were small and dull, its fruit unremarkable in color. Adam remembered the warning his father gave him about the Tree and the devastating effects it would have if Adam consumed its fruit. He recalled with great sadness the Lord's explanation of why he'd given Adam access to it in the first place.

‿჻

Every evening during Adam's life in the Garden was the time the Almighty normally came to visit with him, and they walked and talked together enjoying the coolness of the early nighttime breeze. Adam loved his dad, and their walks were the highlight of his day. On their evening excursions Adam took every opportunity to emulate his Creator. If God took long strides, Adam took long strides. If God stopped and pondered an animal, Adam would tilt his head and adopt the same contemplative pose. When his father scooped up handfuls of water from the river, Adam cupped his hand and learned to drink the same way.

Adam loved the sound of his father's laugh and went to great lengths to tell his dad all the things he'd seen and done during the day, especially the stories Adam knew would humor him. When God laughed, Adam would retell the same antic, often repeatedly, in a slightly different way. God laughed just as hard each time. Adam lived to hear his dad laugh. God laughed freely because there was nothing on Earth he'd created that he loved as much as hearing his son tell him a story.

God deeply loved Adam and with joyful anticipation also looked forward to their evening visits together. The Creator had spared no time or resource as he carefully planned, designed, formed, and adorned the most perfect dwelling place his mind and heart could conceive, the Garden of Eden. He'd then placed his human son, the first of many to come, into his new home. Eden was the perfect setting for the greatest love the Almighty would ever have, his family.

Together God and Adam explored the Garden, sampling the fruits from the different trees and discussing their differences. Only one tree had been off limits. God never ate from the Tree of Knowledge and instructed Adam to also avoid the Tree. Adam only did what he saw his father doing. If God stayed away from the Tree, then so would his son.

After a time, Adam thought to ask, "Why do we avoid the Tree at the Garden's edge?" Not only had they not eaten the fruit, but they had also never touched the Tree, examined its bark, or rested in its shade.

He posed the question one late afternoon as they stood shoulder to shoulder watching a pride of lions playfully attack one another near a bluff. Adam felt his father sharply inhale and it was a moment or two before the Lord responded. Suddenly losing interest in the cat games he turned and motioned for his son to walk with him.

The pair traveled amiably along a path until they came to the center of the Garden where the four rivers divided. Adam could feel the additional coolness the waters added to the evening breeze. God sat down on the blue green grass sprinkled with springtime wildflowers in colors of lavender, green, and yellow, and indicated his son should sit beside him.

Adam flopped down happily. He loved the rivers that flowed through the Garden and this place where all four major tributaries originated was magical for him. The stories his father told him when they were next to the rivers were always the most meaningful ones and Adam cherished the endless wisdom as well as the waters that flowed from there.

The Almighty looked his son squarely in the face and when he knew he had his full attention he said, "I love you, you love me . . ."

Adam looked at his dad, smiled, and as if on cue, finished the sentence. He'd heard it so many times in his young life he could recite it in his sleep. "Nothing else matters . . ." and they both finished together, "much!"

Both smiled and the Lord continued. "You and your heirs are my children. Not my servants. Not my counselors. You're blood of my blood, bones of my bones. Because you are my family you are special and set apart from all other living beings." He paused, giving Adam a moment for the concept to sink in. "You share my highest attributes. I have patterned you, and your sons and daughters, after myself. God Most High. No other creation will ever be offered such a design or inheritance as yours and that of your children."

"You patterned me after *yourself*?" The Lord looked kindly upon his son and gently nodded. Adam lifted his hands to the air and exclaimed emphatically, "Then all I have to say is thank God for God!"

God laughed good-naturedly with his son before he added excitedly, "Oh, the places we will go! The things we'll see. The life we'll build. The two of us, the enchanting spouse you have yet to meet, plus all your beautiful, precious heirs! Your young eyes have not seen nor your mind able to conceive of all the plans I have for you."

Adam's eyes gleamed and he said, "I can't imagine how my life could get any better. But I know you're right because every day I find new and amazing thoughts and abilities inside me I didn't even know existed! Some aptitude I didn't see the day before and new ways to apply it."

The Lord smiled and said, "Son, not all that newness you're seeing is in you. Many new possibilities you're seeing are available in me being made visible and accessible to you."

Adam contemplated his father's words and said, "Maybe you'd better explain that."

His father leaned back on his elbows, ran his fingers back and forth over the clean, warm grass as if petting it and said, "All things are possible through me, Son. In unity and partnership with me you're able to do and have anything you'll ever need and mostly whatever you want."

"Anything? Forever?" Adam asked incredulously.

"As long as you stay connected to me, then yes, forever." He looked at him proudly and reiterated, "Like I said, you're my family and I'm yours. There are many trees inside the Garden of my body. You can eat from the fruits of them all with the exception of the Tree of the Knowledge of Good and Evil. You can see the best way to do things, but you can't see every way. Not until I say you're mature enough to handle it. Not until I tell you you're ready."

Adam was confused, "How can I see what's inside you?"

The Lord answered, "My Holy Spirit lives inside your spirit and acts something like a spiritual umbilical cord and a bridge between us. It's a conduit that transfers thoughts, emotions, communication, and substance between us. Whether you need a new idea, a different perspective, peace, strength, literally anything, Son. When you want or need something and look to me, then through my Spirit I send you what you need."

"Anything?"

His father nodded, "Anything. You're a pure conduit, Adam. You are without sin, lies, or any form of unhealthiness. These could all be obstructions but as you are free from these incumbrances and our wills are the same there's nothing blocking the bridge between us. Because of your wholeness, your complete emotional, mental, physical, and spiritual health in addition to your faith in me both the *transfer and the receipt* of whatever you ask me for is almost always immediate."

Adam said practically, "I get it. Just like the other day when I needed an element to help finish the bridge we were working on. I had options and didn't know the best one. I asked you about it and in an instant my mind knew exactly which one would work the best."

The Lord nodded and said, "Yes. As soon as you asked me, I transferred what you needed through my Holy Spirit. It works so quickly because there are no barriers between us. You see what's possible, ask me for it, I confirm I'll do it, you believe me, it's done!"

"It's because I'm your son, isn't it? You love me because you made me, I love you because you gave me life. You're my dad. You wouldn't have made me if you didn't want me."

"That's right," he looked at his son with misty eyes. "I want children to call my own. To love and to love me back. My goal from the day I conceived of you was to make your life and your future an eternal Paradise. You're my first created son and there's nothing I love more than I love you."

Adam cocked his head, pursed his lips thoughtfully, and then slowly nodded. "That's right. That makes me God, too, then. So I guess what you're really telling me is that once I've fully matured I can have whatever God can have and I'll be able to do whatever God can do."

God's firstborn suddenly threw his head back majestically with his dark hair shining brightly in the sun and the Lord witnessing the toss of his head, the proud line of his face, nose, and jaw, the elegance and simplicity of the remaining lines of his body could not find much to dispute. However, he smiled and said, "Not exactly."

Adam said innocently enough, "Why not? You said I'm a son of God. That makes me God then, too, does it not?"

"Well, Son, it's complicated but let's just say this. You have all the necessary components to look and function at a supernaturally high level. When connected to me, *touching me* through my Spirit," he emphasized clearly, "you have access to everything you need. But I'm God all by myself. I have a holiness, a glory, a spiritual presence as well as other attributes that simply could never be replicated. I don't have an attachment to a source; I *am* the Source. The head of the line, so to speak."

Adam shrugged and said, "Okay. But I still have access to all your resources, right? I can do whatever I want with them."

His dad smiled. "Well, let's just say for now you've got all you need. And as long as you stay connected to me, and the bridge between us stays unclogged, you'll never want for anything. It's a covenant I make with you and all your heirs, Son. Forever."

Adam looked to the sky and then asked, "What would happen if we disconnected?"

His father turned to make sure his son could see his face clearly before he said, "Your humanity would eventually self-destruct."

"I would die?" Adam asked surprised.

His father nodded, "I'm the power source, Adam, for all things. Your connection to me is what keeps you alive. I'm not just your dad, I'm the source of life. *Eternal* life. You have to stay attached in order to live." The Lord looked directly at Adam to ensure he understood the gravity of his remarks.

"I would die if we weren't attached?" he repeated with more than a little surprise. The thought had never occurred to him before.

His father nodded. "I don't have power, Adam. I am Power. Without my Spirit, alive and active within you, your life, your mind, your heart, all would eventually . . . power off."

Somewhat concerned, Adam asked, "What keeps that from happening? What keeps us attached?"

His father answered, "Just an agreement to stay together. If we want to be together, we each have to agree not to leave."

Adam looked towards the sky. After a moment he turned back to his father and said, "Well, I agree if you do."

His dad laughed, somewhat relieved, and said, "Well, then I guess it's settled." But soon added, "Son, I vow to you I'll never leave you. Ever. But if you ever change your mind about me . . ." he glanced quickly at his son and left the unsaid words hanging in the air between them.

Adam quickly interjected, "But if I promise never to disconnect we don't need to worry about that, do we?"

His father ruffled his son's hair fondly and said, "No, we don't," then added truthfully, "You're the apple of my eye, Son. There's nothing I love more than you and nothing I would ever withhold."

"I thought you said I can't eat from the Tree of Knowledge? That's something you're withholding though, right?"

"I'm telling you not to eat from it because it would be very bad for you, for me, for your heirs, and your entire world."

His son raised his eyebrows and asked, "If it's bad for me why would you let me see it?"

"I'm telling you not to eat from the Tree. That should be enough. You're a son of God. The title deserves respect. I told you eating from the Tree would destroy you. I believe you can be trusted to know what that could mean and respond accordingly."

Adam nodded his head in understanding. "Of course. In fact, thank you for giving me the respect of making the choice for myself. I would absolutely *hate* to be controlled. Or treated like a child. It would seem, I don't know, foreign. Embarrassing almost, like I couldn't be trusted to do the right thing by you simply telling me."

"That's right, Son. Freedom is a primary food group to the sons and daughters of God. You can't thrive without it, and I would never disrespect you enough to take control of your life away from you," he spoke candidly. "Not as long as my Spirit remains within you or there's any chance that I could possibly return if you ever rejected me."

Adam looked squarely into his father's eyes as if receiving a new revelation. "Even if I was hurting myself? Or others?"

The Lord sighed. "Let's not go there."

Adam nodded and said, "There's a lot of responsibility in this then, isn't there?"

His father nodded slowly and meaningfully. "There is. You aren't like the animals. You're above everything else I've created. Your position carries great authority, power, and privilege. But that also means the weight and responsibility of it can be heavy at times. Consequences for abuse are much more severe even than for the angelic beings."

Adam wasn't quite sure why he suddenly felt so overcome by the revelation of a gift he already possessed, he just knew he had a greater understanding of its value and that the attachment to his father, to his Holy Spirit, the conduit to everything Adam would ever want or need, was not necessarily his birthright but an honor. Adam was a son of *God*. All future generations would make the same claim. Everything in God, all his love, his favor, his resources, were Adam's just for the asking. And all he had to do to receive them was to acknowledge his father, the bridge that held them together, and not mess it up.

Two sets of eyes appearing almost identical in shape and color gazed upon each other. The primary difference was one set was filled with a deep and endless well of love and wisdom, the younger, full of love, innocence, and hope.

Adam studied his father's face slowly and intently absorbed the truth of his words, "Nothing I love more than you." As the declaration of the Father's deep and abiding love penetrated into a hidden layer of Adam's heart, unexpected tears pooled and hovered in his eyes.

He bowed his head and held his hand up, indicating his father should give him a minute. A grasshopper jumped and landed on Adam's arm. They studied each other momentarily before the insect sprung away quietly making his escape.

Adam looked up at his father and shook his head almost disbelievingly. *Who am I that God considers me the apple of his eye? Would grant me a seat at his dinner table? Crave my company? My conversation? Give me a humanity designed to enable me to soar into the Great Beyond forever loved and protected by his side?* Adam wondered for the hundredth time what it was about him and his future species the Lord considers so exceptional to have earned the place in the universe and God's heart as "favorite creation." The only living creation God has personally chosen to live with *in tandem*. Unable to speak he simply looked up at his father and nodded.

The Lord continued, "Son, I'm the same today and tomorrow as I was yesterday. My nature will always stay constant. However, everything alive including me changes and grows."

"So, you stay the same, but you're always changing?"

The Almighty nodded. "The important parts stay the same. In my nature and ways," he pointed to a large and sturdy rock by the side of the river, "I'm that rock. You can't move me." He motioned towards the river. "However, I'm also the living waters that flow from here, I'm not stagnant either. Everything alive stays the same in some respects yet evolves and changes in others. This garden in which I have placed you, and all its splendor, looks very little like what it will eventually evolve into under your leadership and partnership with me."

Adam nodded in agreement. "It's already changed. I can see that. Before we built this bridge between my house and these rivers, I kept thinking about how helpful a new bridge would be. I couldn't get it off my mind. Finally, I talked to you about it, and we agreed that a bridge was a good idea. So, we built it."

The Lord nodded. "That's right. In your mind you could see it, you thought about it, wanted it, talked to me about it, and then I transferred all the missing pieces. That's how it works. If you ever want something to change, follow that process. See it, decide if you want it, talk to me about it, once we're in unity about the details, the resources will automatically transfer. Done!"

"Why do we have to be in unity? I thought you weren't going to control me?"

His dad moved to let a paddling of ducks pass between them. He simply said, "I'm responsible for the entire universe, Son. Not just you. I have a plan for everyone that stretches into eternity. That takes a lot of coordination. This garden is yours. I've given it to you. No one can take it from you. But I have other gardens planned for your children, and their children, and for endless generations to come. I have a perfect plan for each one, completely individualized, designed to thrill and delight you all. All choreographed by the master conductor but not master controller. You have to trust that although I promise not to control you, I also won't give you the keys to anyone else's garden. If you try to access their gardens, or mess up your own, my well will automatically shut itself down. I won't stop you, but I also won't enable you."

Adam pulled at a burr in the mane of the lion that had strolled up and laid down behind him, silently requesting to be used as a pillow as his young human friend had done dozens of times before. The Lord took a mental picture of his son and the lion laying comfortably in the rays of the setting sun and stored it in his memory box of favorite images.

Two bluebirds flew past them chattering happily. Adam watched them fly into a nest in a nearby tree. He could hear baby birds crying excitedly, anticipating their evening meal. A strong breeze swept across them. Adam lifted his face and breathed in new smells introduced by the wind. The evening sky had turned from shades of orange and blue to pink and lavender as the sun began to set behind them. Relaxed and at peace in his father's presence he suddenly remembered to ask, "But what does any of this have to do with the Tree?"

CHAPTER 7

THE LORD PICKED UP A BLADE OF GRASS AND TWIRLED IT in between his fingers and seemed to study its design for several minutes before answering. Finally, he took a deep breath and replied, "The Tree of the Knowledge of Good and Evil is unique because the fruit it bears, if ingested, opens a secret door within you. Another door that until now you didn't even know exists."

"What's behind it?" Adam, who possibly loved adventure and mystery more than anything else in his father's well, asked excitedly.

His father sighed heavily and said, "It's the door of separation. The door to self-reliance, which ultimately leads to powerlessness, death, and possibly hell."

Adam was stunned. "What's hell?"

The Creator studied young, curious eyes and knew he owed his son, the universe, and the future of all mankind the best explanation he could possibly give.

"Hell, Son, is the sludge that comes from pulling up resources from other wells than mine."

"Well, we certainly would never want that," Adam brushed off the explanation. When his father didn't comment but simply looked at him he countered with surprise, "Would we?"

His dad said, "What's inside me, Adam, and all that you see, is holy. Holy means 'the best.' When you ask me to show you something or pray for what you need I only send my best. The highest and most pure. Things that have been designed and earmarked just for you. Not for your neighbor, not your sons and daughters, but for you. Gifts that enhance your life and keep you moving along the path of eternal growth and maturity as well as preparing you for your next awesome adventure. He elaborated, "I would never look outside my own wells to inferior options and say 'Hey, try this out.' Love wouldn't do that." Adam nodded in understanding.

He continued, "I'm telling you that opening the door and exploring options other than what I provide would lead to your destruction, devastation, and would be a tremendous mistake. Once you open the door you can never get it closed again. You would never be able to unsee what's you've seen, never cleanse your soul of the rot, never forgive yourself for letting it get on and in you."

"But yet I have access to it?" his son asked in disbelief.

His dad nodded. "The door to the outside is always open to the sons and daughters of God. Like I said, the title deserves respect. I have determined you are mature enough now to exhibit self-control. Therefore I won't demean you by limiting or controlling your choices. I'll tell you not to open that door, but the choice must ultimately be yours."

Adam arched his eyebrows. Until that moment he hadn't realized his perspective and his choices were being filtered.

"That's right, Son, all possibilities, good and evil, are both available to you. You are not your haven's prisoner. But I've seen the evil outside your Garden, I won't live there, and I don't want you to live there either. If you choose to explore all your options, you'll have to do it without me."

"But what's wrong with me seeing both sides if you do?" The wind picked up and Adam experienced an unexpected and unfamiliar chill.

"You do see everything I see. You just don't see what I have chosen not to see."

"Why not?" Adam insisted. "If it's possible then why can't I see it and decide for myself?"

His father answered him candidly, "You're too young. You have truth but not much wisdom yet. Outside the Garden there are too many hard choices. You don't have the necessary tools to sort through them yet."

Adam looked at his father, shrugged, and said with obvious disappointment, "Okay."

The Lord examined his son, not satisfied with the turn the conversation had taken. "Son, in the event you open the door to the knowledge of evil you will find yourself in nothing short of a nightmare. Captured and tortured by a force I won't even try to fully explain; alone, fearful, hating who you are, what you've done, and constantly on guard awaiting the next brutal attack on your heart, mind, body, and those of your family, which, trust me, would be worse for you to watch than an attack on your own."

"How could that happen?" Adam asked, stunned.

His father took a deep breath and said, "Because we have an enemy who would destroy us both if given the chance."

"You have an enemy?" he asked somewhat in disbelief.

His father nodded. "We both do. An adversary whose goal is to take control of everything and everyone that I love. One whose sole objective is to divide and conquer, turn you against me, render you powerless, and possess your inheritance."

"How could he do that?" Adam asked aghast.

"He couldn't unless you hand it over to him. The governance of your garden belongs to you, Adam. I've given it to you to manage. What happens to it is up to you. I'll always be here to help but I won't take control out of your hands. I'll never take back a gift I've given. No matter what you choose to do with it. Ever."

Adam was silent for a moment. He suddenly felt as if he'd aged considerably in the last few hours and knew after the evening's conversation, his thoughts, his perspective, his outlook on his life and role would never be the same. He looked at his father sideways and wondered what else he wasn't telling him and the question disturbed him. He asked cautiously, "What methods would this enemy use to destroy me?"

"His first goal is to take possession of your mind. If he could gain entry and dominate your thoughts, he could eventually take control of your entire world. His primary strategy, to blow up the bridge between us. Cut you off from me, my voice, my will. He would love to have access to my resources but knows I'd never allow that to happen. But you still have considerable resources within your own human strength, even without my Spirit living inside you. As a son of God you still have my DNA. Your body is strong, you have an excellent mind, and your spirit springs from my own. Like I said before, there's never been a creation with your design. The enemy knows that, and you would make the perfect host victim if he could ever possess you."

"How could he cut us off from each other?"

His father looked compassionately at his troubled son and although would have loved nothing more than to change the subject he forced himself to continue. "He'd start out by destroying your faith in me. It's your faith that pulls my will for you, and my resources into your world. Nothing transfers from my table to yours without faith. So if you ever lost it, you'd be on your own, and vulnerable, forced to engage in whatever methods your human imagination and strength could devise for your very survival. But without me to guide, protect, and support you, you'd be at the mercy of every cold wind that blows."

"So that would be his goal? To isolate me and make me think all my future, my survival, my burdens were my own? That would force me to do his will, not yours?"

His father nodded. "By convincing you your survival is completely up to you, telling you truthfully you aren't up to the task, making you fight and develop more human strength and power, he would fund and fuel his own agenda. He'd make you think all those burdens, which would exponentially multiply, are all on your own small shoulders. He'd convince you to develop and rely on your own limited human strength and that of other humans around you and forget about depending on my supernatural one to handle them all.

"The enemy is a leech," he spat out angrily. "He has literally *no strength* of his own. The only power he could ever get would be if he gained access to the watered-down fuel reserves that he could steal from my children's flesh. Knowing that if he could somehow convince my family to abandon me and rely on their own internal and limited reserves, he could potentially dominate and eventually destroy your entire kingdom. With all your heirs in it. He knows that even a little dependance upon me lessens his hold over his host victim. Therefore he would do anything to keep us apart."

Adam's eyes were wide. "What would he say to make me lose my faith in you?"

His father answered, "First of all he'd tell you because of your sin I'd abandoned you. He'd say your sin killed my love and respect for you. He'd lie and say that I withdrew my Spirit from you out of anger and disappointment when really it would be because I can't share space with a cockroach. But instead of telling you the truth he'd convince you I'd left because I don't love you anymore and had made you an orphan. If you doubted him, he'd remind you of the numerous troubles you'd already experienced and use them to illustrate why I can't be trusted enough for you to rely on me. He would say it's because there's something 'not enough' in both of us. He would say my love is conditional and you don't meet the requirements. It would be his number one strategy to destroy the world."

"But if the enemy trapped me, why wouldn't you drive him away? You're God. Can't you overpower him?"

The Lord shook his head. "You said you would *hate* to be controlled. You said you don't want to be told what to do. You don't want me to take away your choices. You said you understand the responsibility that comes with the sort of future only I can offer and accept the consequences of those choices. I have already told you what it takes to keep evil from your world. You can't have it both ways, Adam. I didn't design a contingency plan. The enemy can try to steal your faith, your power, but he can't force you to give it up. So you need to *trust me* and hang onto it. No matter what."

Adam shook his head not willing to believe his father's words. No place in his mind would allow him to believe his dad could allow such a fate to befall him. Even if the mistake was his own doing. "But you love me. I *know* you'd rescue me because your heart could never stand to watch me suffer," he challenged his dad.

His father stared at him and answered quietly, "Do you want me to limit your free will? Take away your choice? If so, tell me now. Like I said, you can't have it both ways."

His son was unwilling to yield. "But Dad," he insisted, "just tell me if I mess up you'll fix it."

His father was unmoved. "It's why we're having this conversation, Adam. Yes or no?"

Adam was overcome by his choice. Life in the shadows of temptation of what was sure to be the greatest and most daring adventure yet forced to exercise enough self-control to resist it or fall from grace and face the consequences. Both choices seemed overwhelming. He needed all the facts, he decided. He asked tentatively, "So what exactly would happen if I did happen to fall?"

"Son," his father said clearly, slowly, and distinctly, "if you intentionally give the enemy the keys to your garden, we would immediately separate. My Holy Spirit cannot live inside a vessel the enemy has infiltrated. I would never give him access to my Spirit through yours. Therefore, I would have no viable choice but to withdraw from you, then stand by and watch the destruction."

He elaborated sternly, "Even if I could implement a solution it would not be a quick fix. You and your heirs would suffer for a very long time. The damage would be indescribable. The cost to you and your children to pay for all that damage, unaffordable." He had a sudden foreshadowing and his face darkened considerably. "And your rescue would come at a price I cannot even fathom."

The wind picked up and blew gently across the field. The lion edged closer to the Lord, discomforted by the tone of the conversation. He nudged his hand to be petted as if for reassurance. His creator complied, stroking his fur back and forth until soon he and Adam could hear the sounds of light snoring. Two deer had wandered close to them and soon a baby fawn joined them. They grazed in the lush grass and eventually wandered into the river for a drink. After a while, the Lord said, "Look at me, Son." Adam obeyed and the Almighty, looking him squarely in the face and directly into his wide, astonished eyes, re-stated the same words with which he began the evening's conversation. "I love you. You love me . . ."

Adam said tightly, "Yeah, I know."

Ignoring the tone, his dad said, "You need to tell me, Son. Board up the door, take out the Tree, or leave it? It's up to you."

Adam calmed down, but only slightly. Finally, with hurt and con-fusion in his eyes he all but demanded, "Why would you tell me about the Tree in the first place? You could have kept it from me! Why put that burden on me? When you know how much I love an adventure, especially one with some risk? Knowing how bad it could hurt me?" Father and son stared silently at one another, and both were aware it was the first time Adam had ever questioned his father's judgement, not to mention posed a question that bordered on accusation.

The Lord took a moment and then answered calmly, patiently yet firmly, "I'm not a jailer or a dictator. You are my son. My long-term goal for you is complete freedom, power, and the full authority to use it. You are higher than the angels. Your destiny *as my son* is to govern your world, explore what's possible within us both, and travel on your own private rocket ship with your closest friends and family by your side into the Great Beyond. For an eternity. You can't do that on a leash."

Adam stared at his father feeling completely overwhelmed. He sit-uated his body so he could once again lean his head back on the lion and contemplate the revelations of the evening. His mind struggled to sort through it all. Made in his father's image, the first of a race called the sons and daughters of God. "Made higher than the angels," he heard his father's voice echo. But Adam and his future family had a target on their backs and the only thing standing between them was Adam's faith in his father and his father's faith in him. His head suddenly hurt.

Eventually the Lord stood up and walked over to the river to check out how the newest baby deer was getting along. Witnessing the tenderness with which he exhibited his thorough inspection of the fawn's gait, eyes, and ears, Adam calmed himself by wondering practically, just how long could such a loving father really allow his children to suffer, even if it was due to the result of their own choices?

Soon the Lord returned and indicated that his son should rise. God held onto the shoulders of the one thing on Earth he loved more than anything and looked him straight in both eyes. He wanted to take him into his arms, promise he'd never let anything touch even a hair on his head, that he'd never feel fear, sickness, pain, or loss. He wanted to promise him that above everything else he would never let him suffer. Not even the consequences of his own actions. He wanted to tattoo on his son's heart that nothing would ever, ever mean more to God than his family or their well-being. To remind him he was raising future heirs to the kingdom, and it was his responsibility to equip them. Not turn them into puppets. But instead, realizing there was nothing left to be explained, he simply said, "I need you to tell me, Son. Leave the Tree or chop it down. The choice is yours."

Adam wished he could turn back time and never have asked his father about the Tree. His dad would never hold him accountable for what he didn't understand was a sin. Now, the Tree, instead of a curiosity, had suddenly become a threat. To him, to his future family—and for how long, Adam had no idea. All until God decided Adam was mature enough to handle it. Who knew when that might be, he asked himself. For the first time Adam knew what it was to want something and be told no.

He looked at the ground knowing the Lord would give him as

much time to deliberate as necessary. To be fair, his father wasn't forbidding access to the Tree, he thought. He simply told him the consequences and let the decision be his. He could have been angry if his father had forbidden it. Now, it was his choice, but the warning certainly couldn't have been clearer.

Adam looked at the lion sprawled out on his back playfully batting a dragonfly that darted tauntingly back and forth. Suddenly his irritation melted as he remembered his father's words, "Nothing I love more than you. The apple of my eye. Anything you want I will transfer into your world. Glorious plans for the future. Heir of God, no one else, not even the angels can make such a claim."

Adam looked up and noticed the fawn and its parents had stopped and turned their heads towards him as if waiting for his answer. It was almost as if they knew that somehow his response would affect them. The wind ceased, the air was heavy with silence. A gray fox could be seen across the river. Adam watched him as he pounced on a chipmunk but missed, sending the chipmunk scurrying down a welcome hole in the ground.

Adam closed his eyes and rested his hand on his father's shoulder. Soon he looked up into the eyes of his Creator who was closely awaiting his son's response. Sensing the significance of the moment, the lion quickly and solemnly rose to attention and stood next to Adam's form as if to provide necessary witness to his vow.

God gazed lovingly at his son and Adam continued humbly, "I swear on this day that I will love, honor, and follow the Lord God Almighty as my forever king and leader and that I will guide and teach my family the value in doing the same. I will wait upon the Lord, seek his face in all I do, and acknowledge that all good things, including the very breath in my lungs, start and end in him.

"Passionately and with fervor, I will give God what only a human being can give him," he paused and then added, "the only thing God cannot get for himself." Adam looked meaningfully into his father's eyes. "A family who loves, trusts, and will follow him of our own free will."

He smiled into the misty eyes of his father, bowed his head, made a fist with his right hand, and pounded it into his heart. "I swear it!" The lion, looking from God to man, suddenly rose on his back legs, lifted his face to the heavenlies, opened his jaws wide, and let his verbal confirmation majestically fill the air.

Everyone at that moment, even those watching in the heavenlies, believed Adam would do it.

CHAPTER 8

THE PILOT WAS ON THE OVERHEAD SPEAKER ANNOUNCING they were changing altitudes again trying to avoid additional turbulence. Passengers out of their seats needed to return. The fasten seat belt sign chimed and illuminated. The couple playing cards temporarily stopped their game and put away their tray tables.

Grace stood by the side of the lavatory sink absently chewing a hangnail. She ignored the instructions. She replayed the conversation with Adam again in her head.

She'd analyzed and treated many patients in her career and was familiar with most forms of mental illness. Adam, or whatever his real name was, didn't fit the typical profile of someone suffering from a delusional disorder. *Most schizophrenics don't participate in cohesive conversation, engage in subtle banter, manipulate complicated software programs, and wear designer shoes,* she reminded herself. Yet his pain was real. He clearly wasn't playing a joke on her. *What's going on?* she asked herself. Certainly, he didn't believe he was the biblical version of Rip Van Winkle.

It wasn't long before Grace suffered a pang of guilt. It was evident Adam needed help. He was also right. She *was* anxious to analyze him. She had recklessly decided digging into the psyche of a good-looking stranger would be fun evening entertainment on an otherwise long and boring flight. She had shamefully encouraged him to share his concerns with her and get emotionally naked. When he did, she'd called him a religious fanatic and then practically ran him over trying to escape when the conversation slid out of control. *My license should be revoked,* she scolded herself harshly.

Besides recognizing pain in others, Grace was familiar with the demon of despair herself. *Where's my empathy?* she chastised herself harshly. Regardless of how uncomfortable the conversation turned out to be, she was responsible for prying open his Pandora's box. She needed to behave like a professional, not to mention a decent human being, and at the very least help him get the lid back on.

She left the lavatory and returned to her seat. She stopped Katie and asked for a cup of coffee. It was going to be a long night.

Adam stood up to let her pass but not before she noticed he'd pulled out his laptop and started working, indicating rather obviously he was done talking. She slid into her seat, and he went back to his computer.

Katie showed up with coffee and extra napkins. Grace thanked her and after a few minutes turned to Adam and said, "What are you working on?" She knew it was a weak attempt to re-establish rapport, but she had to start somewhere.

"A bid to build a bridge." He answered but didn't look up from his computer screen.

She tried again. "Well, I had something amazing happen while I was in the bathroom. God spoke to me and told me I was a poor excuse for a therapist and if I didn't march back out here and beg your forgiveness he was going to yank my credentials." A direct approach was the best she'd decided. "I'm sorry, Adam."

Although he was embarrassed, humiliated actually, Adam couldn't help thinking he still found Grace disturbingly attractive even though he could barely see her face under the dimmed cabin lights. Her shoulder-length blonde hair, bobbed just below her shoulders, had subtle streaks of red and gold that reminded Adam of summer wheat. Her eyes lit up like sapphires when she laughed but churned stormy gray when upset. She wore a simple ivory silk shell underneath her linen suit jacket. The end of a long herringbone gold chain disappeared somewhere underneath the shell. A small dragonfly pendant on another thin double strand gold chain, worn around her neck, accentuated a pattern of freckles scattered across her skin. He asked without smiling, "Are you sure you weren't having a psychotic break?"

"No. Not totally," she said disarmingly and then added, "Seriously, please forgive me, Adam. I am very sorry." When he didn't answer she added, "Even if you can't forgive me at least cut me some slack. You have to admit your story *is* pretty 'out there' to say the least. You said it would be difficult to understand but you didn't warn me it would be *that* unusual. You knocked me for a loop!" She studied him to gauge his reaction. "I thought you were just messing around with me at first."

He gave a heavy sigh, shut his laptop, and leaned his head back against his headrest. He closed his eyes. He'd already made up his mind any conversation between them was over.

Sincerely wanting to help, and not simply to ease her own

conscience, she continued, "I know you warned me, but I don't know anyone who could've been prepared for a story like yours." She looked at him again to make sure he hadn't taken offense. He kept his eyes closed and she added, "Honestly, Adam, I thought you were messing with me for calling you a religious fanatic. I didn't know how to respond." The couple across the aisle had resumed their card playing but paused, appearing curious at the unusual exchange between two strangers. Grace noticed the woman was obviously straining to hear Adam's and her conversation and lowered her voice. "But I realize you weren't messing with me. I won't pretend to understand but I promise you I want to try. Please, Adam. Put away your computer and talk to me."

Adam opened his eyes and released a long sigh. "It's not a good idea," he informed her honestly. "Let's just forget it. It's been a long day and I'm sure you're tired of listening to other people's problems anyway. Noah always did say I had a warped sense of timing." He gave a weak smile to let her know he was kidding but held no hard feelings.

Grace was unwilling to concede. She reached over and rested her left hand gently on Adam's arm and in the faint cabin light he noticed a slight tan line on her ring finger and wondered if it was from where a wedding band used to be. "Adam, you said you need someone to talk to. Regardless of how I acted I am a trained therapist and usually I'm a pretty good one. We have hours before we reach Honolulu. I'm not tired. And I promise you no matter what you say I won't run away or insult you again. Please, trust me," she smiled encouragingly.

Adam looked at her hand still resting on his arm. Her fingers were long and slender, her nails rounded, medium length with light pink polish. It had been a long time since a beautiful, intelligent woman had offered to talk with him about anything meaningful.

He finally decided it might be worth the risk of further humiliation. The hardest part of the story was behind him, and he'd probably never see her again anyway. He leaned down and pulled out his computer bag. Slowly sliding his laptop in he said, "Look, I know how weird this sounds. I stopped talking about it years ago. Frankly, I was tired of getting the look you gave me before you encountered the Almighty in the bathroom. But sometimes I forget how bizarre it all sounds and blurt out my woes to some unsuspecting stranger. Today was just your lucky day I guess."

He was self-confident, vulnerable, charming, and quick to let her off the hook. "I want to hear your story," she reiterated, and he gave her a cautious but grateful smile. "But I do need to ask," she ventured carefully, "you said you once took a bad fall. Did you hurt yourself? Is there any possibility there was a head injury involved?" She needed to understand the major aspects of his health, both physical and mental, and the ways he had previously sought treatment.

Suddenly the plane lurched sideways from additional turbulence and Adam went white and grabbed the armrest as if to steady himself. In a moment he objected defensively, "My problem is not physical. It's not emotional. It's spiritual, Grace. My fall was the mother of all falls! The world and all it's past, current, and future problems are a result of it," he said honestly. "My problem is between *God* and me, possibly because of it. I don't know. But I do know my issue is not due to a physical or mental ailment some quick shock therapy or series of injections can fix. I made a mistake that sent the world into a downward spiral it can't seem to recover from. I have centuries of memories. I can't take a pill and say, 'Oh well,' and just move on."

Not knowing how to respond, she carefully maneuvered around the coffee on her tray table, reached into her purse, and intentionally fumbled around until she pulled out a container of mints. She offered one to Adam who declined. "Okay, then let's start there," she said, trying to appear unruffled. But silently she was still leaving the door open to the possibility of an undiagnosed physical problem. There was a medical condition she'd heard about where some head injury patients live normal lives but have periodic regressions into a false reality caused by a chemical brain imbalance. Once he started telling his story she certainly would be able to pinpoint the holes and convince him something physical was most likely the cause. She had a plan. She relaxed a little.

"Alright, Adam, you're obviously articulate, insightful, and appear to be intelligent and gainfully employed. Tell me your story."

He smiled, aware she was trying to re-establish rapport.

"You said earlier you don't want me to give you any advice. I should just listen and ask sensible questions, right? Therefore, I'm going to try to suspend my belief of what I think is possible. I'll take at face value whatever you tell me and hopefully we'll get to the bottom of it. Deal?"

He stuck out his hand. "Deal."

He wasn't crazy, she decided. He was just sick. Her goal, she thought again, with the short time they had together was to get him to trust her enough to agree to seek medical treatment when he returned home. She could even help him get in touch with the right people in Dallas. That settled, she decided to get right to the point. "So, tell me, Adam, what happened?"

He looked into her eyes and answered sadly, "I lied to God, broke his heart, and trashed the house."

CHAPTER 9

K ATIE WALKED BY WITH A COFFEE CONTAINER AND GRACE
accepted a refill. She swallowed hard. Her training had taught
her when at a loss for words simply reformat the patient's
last statement into a question. "Go on," she encouraged, stirring sugar
into her coffee. "How did you trash the uh . . ." she asked awkwardly, "I
assume you are referring to the Garden of Eden?"

Adam picked up the empty sugar packet from her tray table and
handed it to Katie along with his empty coffee cup as she passed by
asking if they had anything they wanted her to take. A passenger a few
rows back in coach rang his call bell and told Katie the internet had
stopped working. She headed to the front to check on it.

Adam answered Grace's question. "Yes," he confirmed. "Eve and
I ate from the Tree of the Knowledge of Good and Evil, so we had to

leave the Garden. God warned us in advance of the consequences, but we did it anyway."

Grace tried to recall the story as outlined in the book of Genesis. "Yes," she said, "I remember." Feeling foolish for participating in a conversation rooted in impossibility she inquired, "You ate a poison apple and God kicked you out, right?"

Adam shook his head and chided her, "I'm not Snow White, for Pete's sake," he said defensively. "For the record, we chose to leave. We wanted to know what God wouldn't show us," he shrugged his shoulders and shook his head remorsefully. "As they say, hindsight's 20/20. We should've listened."

Adam paused and after second thought couldn't help but veer slightly from his story. "Leaving the Garden was never going to be permanent. We always knew it was only going to be temporary."

"What do you mean, temporary?" Grace furrowed her brow.

He crossed one leg over the other and adjusted his pant leg. Grace noticed his socks were black with colorful hummingbirds on them. "Remember your Bible? Angels only barred access through the gates. They didn't blow them up. God certainly wasn't going to scrap all his plans, turn his back on us all, just because Eve and I threw a monkey wrench into things. Oh no. He's still got a plan."

"Which is?"

"I thought you said you read the Bible?" he chided gently. "The gates to Paradise are opened back up, Grace. Wide open." When she didn't respond he added, "Thy kingdom come, thy will be done. On *Earth* as it is in heaven. Ring any bells?"

Totally taken aback, all she could think of to say was, "You think *this* is heaven?"

"Depends on what you're looking at. Heaven is anything or any place God inhabits. The more God you let in, the more heaven that comes with him."

She scoffed. "I don't know about that, Adam." When he didn't say anything, she said, "Okay, tell me why you think it's possible."

"Jesus, Grace. It's why he came. To fix what I messed up. Get us back on track. Because of Jesus people can operate on all cylinders again just like Eve and I once did. Anyone can have all the heaven he or she can handle. Right here on Earth."

The captain came on the loudspeaker saying they had reached a higher altitude and he was turning off the seatbelt sign. He assured them his radar indicated they were in the clear and there should be no future weather issues. Adam breathed a sigh of relief.

Grace reached out and laid her hand on his arm softly. "I understand why you'd want that," she said gently, "but it's just not possible anymore." She leaned her seat back and stretched her legs out. She unbuckled her seat belt and tried to get more comfortable. She turned in order to face him better. She wanted to be sensitive since obviously his illness had convinced him he was responsible for the world's problems, and she could certainly understand why he hoped it was true. Based on his perspective how could he hope otherwise? But she also wanted to be practical and help him see for himself the fallacy in his thinking. "Maybe in the beginning but mankind is a long way from any sort of paradise, don't you think? I'm pretty sure even God has conceded that ship has sailed." She thought but didn't say, *If there even is a God.*

He shook his head. "You're wrong. I have firsthand experience and the Bible clearly states otherwise. Jesus said heaven is within us. We have everything we need," he pointed to his chest, "right in here."

"You think heaven is possible on Earth? Now?" she asked again, this time less gently and more skeptically.

"Yep. Jesus is the fix."

"I remember the story," she said dubiously. "But I don't think Jesus helps anyone on Earth. Maybe after they're dead," she responded practically. "If there is a God, I might agree he's got a plan B but look around, Adam, the world hardly looks like heaven. And you gotta admit, the prognosis looks pretty bleak."

Adam cocked his head and studied her momentarily. Finally, he said, "So, then, what? Life's a bitch and then you die? How's that winning? My God's way bigger than that," he informed her.

"You said you were miserable. How's that winning?" she challenged.

"I am temporarily miserable, I concede. But God and I have been through way worse. We'll fix it. We always do," he said optimistically. "But notwithstanding my current but temporary troubles, my life's pretty awesome. So close to what I had before. And I know other people walking in Paradise, right now. Right here on Earth."

Worried, Grace asked him, "Adam, are you actually *seeing* people in the Garden right now?"

"Well, not as many as I'd like. And that's painful, Grace. I feel like I stole that from God."

"Stole what from him?"

"Relationship. Faith. Intimacy. People operating to their God-given capacity. Knowing who God created them to be. Seeing their own coolness through his eyes. In love with him. Empowered. Free. Excited about their futures." He also reclined his seat trying to get a little more comfortable.

Grace couldn't help herself and gave a slight snort laden with derision. Call bells of frustrated and bored travelers continued to ring as they demanded updates from Katie and Anna as well as the other flight attendants regarding the internet status. Many people got up from their seats and stretched their legs. Sounds of the opening and slamming of overhead doors could be heard throughout the entire plane as people searched for alternative forms of entertainment.

Grace asked, trying to appear a little less cynical, "Are you sure it's healthy to love or even believe in somebody you don't even know for sure exists?" She wondered if his illness was contributing to some form of delusional search for a missing love relationship somewhere else in his life.

Adam lightly laughed, "Healthy to love God? I'll have to ask and see what he has to say about that."

She inhaled slightly and asked gently, "Adam, don't you think talking to people who aren't there and hearing voices could possibly be an indicator of mental illness? Or a chemical imbalance . . . or head injury?" she ventured cautiously.

He cocked his head momentarily and said, "Possibly. But then again so is breathing."

She gave him a questioning look. "Sorry. You'll have to explain that."

"All people who have mental illness, breathe. However, all people who breathe do not have mental illness."

She said in mild concession, "So you're saying some people who are mentally ill hear from God but not all people who hear from God are mentally ill."

"You got it. God created Man in his own image. We've got his DNA. And for those of us who've accepted him, we have his Spirit living inside us as well. With expectation, practice and an increased sensitivity, we can tell when that Spirit moves. Recognize his communication signals. Then once we connect—well, not even the sky's the limit. We'll have access to everything we could ever need and most of what we could want. Forever."

She stared at him. "How?" she couldn't help but ask.

"Talk to God and do whatever he tells you to do," he said. "Talk to him about everything. If he tells you to do something, do it. His goal is for us to win. So have faith you're hearing right and hang in there. When you miss it, just don't give up. Keep trying until you figure it out. He'll help you. He wants the communication even more than you do."

She stared in disbelief. He talked about hearing from God like he was explaining how to turn on closed captions on the TV. "No way," she shook her head confused. "You're saying God talks to people? Communicates with them? And some people actually *like* it?"

He laughed. "Yes, Grace. People actually like it. And yes. God talks to people all the time. Through our spirits. Hearing him just takes practice," he elaborated. "It's like learning to speak a foreign language. But once we figure it out," he held out both hands, "it's a beautiful thing."

She shook her head again. "No way. That's why God gives people the Bible and maybe even preachers. He doesn't need to talk to people. Plus, he'd be too hard to hear anyway. Even if it was possible. And getting it wrong would definitely be too risky. What if people made a mistake and followed the wrong voice? Like, 'God told me to rob this bank. Jump off a bridge. Steal your car.' It would just give people license to make stuff up. As long as you call it God, do whatever you want." She didn't agree with Adam's theories, but she understood them well enough to point out the holes in them.

"The Bible is one way God talks to people," Adam agreed. "However, God talked to people directly more than 2,000 times in the Old Testament. He talked to Moses through a burning bush. He instructed Noah on how to build an ark. He called out to John in a voice like a trumpet. Before there was the internet God was the first to introduce communication through the airwaves. The Holy Spirit is like the great API—transmitting and receiving two-way communication. Why can't God talk to people if he wants—Spirit to spirit—and help us learn to hear from him? He loves us, wants to be involved with us, guide us. How's he going to do that if we can't communicate?"

She studied Adam and said, "I don't think the goal for humans is to have a relationship with some *god*. I think the highest goal for any human is to take care of yourself, make sure nobody screws you or your family over, treat others with respect, and do the right thing by the universe and everything in it. If it makes you happy to give your god a name, go for it. But I personally don't think it has anything to do with some white bearded guy hanging around out there watching how it all plays out. That just seems so religious and honestly, unevolved."

Adam looked at her calmly and responded, "How's that working for you?"

She started to feel uncomfortable. Adam was sick. She was starting to consider his arguments as something other than the ramblings of an unhealthy person. Grace decided to change the subject. "I think we'll just have to agree to disagree. Unless somehow you think it relates to your problem."

"Probably not," he conceded but immediately countered, "but maybe. It bothers me that so many Christians don't see the potential of what's inside them once they've accepted Christ and received the Holy Spirit within. Lots of people believe in God but how many really *partner* with him? See themselves through his eyes and what's really possible. Not to mention find the happiness that comes from the love affair you get when you finally connect with him. I hardly hear anyone talk about how good it feels when God unleashes his heart on them." His face darkened and he added, "Yeah. That's on me." He took a deep breath and said eventually, "I don't know. I thought I let go feeling guilty about it. Maybe not."

Grace raised her eyebrows. "A love affair with God?" An uncomfortable emotion started to rumble deep within. The young newlywed in front of her got up and pulled open the overhead compartment to get his wife's travel case for her. She grabbed something out of it and he returned the case and shut the compartment with a loud slam.

"They don't call Jesus the Bridegroom for nothing."

She stared at him and he continued, thinking she doubted the truth of his words. "The Bible, in the book of Hosea says, 'In the last days you'll call me my Husband." Adam raised his eyebrows and smiled enticingly at her, "He wants to marry you, Grace. Move right inside that heart of yours. "Yep," he leaned back and cracked his knuckles casually, "His hope is the two of you will build a beautiful life together. For like, the next zillions of years."

Temporarily forgetting the troubles of her patient, Adam's words incited an unexpected anger that started to rise within her and suddenly became impossible to contain. She held up her hand in protest and said hotly, "You think once people get all cozy with Jesus they live in some trumped up la-la land? You think Jesus and Christianity are some great panacea?" She had treated too many Christians in her practice and knew that wasn't true.

Adam shook his head. "Not without struggle along the way." He moved his arm to make room for Katie as she swayed past them checking people's needs for refills. He lifted up Grace's empty cup to Katie without being asked and said, "Love affairs are messy, Grace. Even God's. Eve and I were in love with him in the Garden. Anyone who chooses can end up in love with him there in the end. Nobody said the middle would be easy."

"Easy?" she scoffed angrily and her voice started to rise. "I'm sorry, Adam, but God doesn't *deserve* that kind of love. Any god who allows war, murder, sex trafficking of children," she spit out, "when he has the power to stop it and even if people *beg* him to and he ignores us, them," she corrected. "It's all bullshit!" she exploded. "And even if he is real, which I sincerely doubt, he certainly isn't any god I care to get close to or even believe in for that matter! Based on his past and present performance, or lack thereof, I wouldn't marry him if he were the last god on Earth!" she spat out fiercely.

Momentarily taken aback by her outburst, Adam looked into turbulent, stormy eyes and saw confusion, pain, and rage. In the cabin's faint light he could see Grace's face and chest were flushed with anger. He reached above him and opened the air vent allowing a pent-up trickle of cool air to escape.

"There is absolutely no justification," she continued chokingly, "for looking down from some holy ivory tower, at people who are suffering and doing nothing about it! And when traumatized people still cling to their illusions of a loving god," she paused for a breath, "and go to church, just a big frat house for mindless hypocrites, and *praise* him out of fear or false flattery or so their neighbors will think how holy they are," she spat the words out barely hanging onto her composure, "it just makes me want to *throw up*!" she hissed.

She stopped speaking and looked out the window into the night. She immediately felt remorseful and embarrassed at the eruption. *This was* his *therapy session,* she reminded herself. She took a drink of coffee wishing the cup was filled with vodka.

Adam closed his eyes and was surprised to feel the familiar presence of the Lord stirring within him. "She's in the desert, Son," was all God said to him. Adam was suddenly and acutely aware of the deep love and compassion God felt for Grace. He suddenly wondered, between the two of them, who God had sent to the other that night for help.

CHAPTER 10

WITH THE INTERNET STILL DOWN SEVERAL PEOPLE WERE milling around the cabin and Katie and Anna were kept busy with requests. Tops from beer and soda cans could be heard popping throughout the cabin. A few people were waiting to use the first class restroom. Still irritated but determined not to let Adam think she was fleeing again, Grace asked him calmly if he would please let her out to use the restroom again. She knew it was her third trip to the lavatory since she got on the plane, but she didn't care. She had consumed a lot of fluids. If Adam didn't expect to keep getting up he should've kept the window seat. She handed him her coffee cup, stepped into the aisle, sidestepped Anna, who was looking at more pictures of the elderly couple's grandchildren, and walked to the back of the plane.

She waited in the restroom line and tried to make some sense of the night. She focused on her own unexpected outburst. She chewed a hangnail and thought deeply. Why had Adam's words, his fantasy of some divine love, incited such anger in her?

For the second time that evening Grace found herself remembering the love she'd once felt for God. For Jesus. And the hopes she'd once had for a love affair with him. An intimate relationship. *Fairy tales,* she told herself staunchly. A mother holding a two-year-old stood in front of her. Big blue eyes stared intently at Grace.

Grace smiled at the child and considered her abandoned relationship with Jesus. He was no different than Santa Claus. Just an elusive, mystical, male parental figure who generated hope and excitement but, in the end, just a childhood myth. A fairy tale made up by adults in order to help children navigate between naughty and nice. Angels and elves secretly watched to determine heaven or hell, presents or coal. *Too many similarities to discount,* she thought. The child seemed to study Grace's face intently and they both stared into each other's eyes momentarily.

She let herself once again think about the relationship she once thought they'd had but written off as a childish fantasy. The one she'd had with Jesus before he'd turned from an obsession into an obligation. But did she really have a good reason for abandoning her spirituality? *Isn't everyone part spirit?* she asked herself practically. *Where does that spirit come from?* She decided to play devil's advocate. Her sense of open-mindedness demanded it. Was she possibly being shortsighted? Even narrow-minded? Did it even matter? *But what if God is real?* she persisted. Possibly not Jesus, but God? Any god? Buddha? Mohammed?

"Excuse me. Aren't you the woman sitting next to Adam?" she heard a man's voice ask her politely. She turned around to see another passenger from first class standing behind her also waiting for an available restroom.

"Yes. How do you know him?" Grace was shocked. *Who now, the snake?*

"He's my boss. The guy sitting next to me, Nick, and I work for him. We're going to Honolulu to make a pitch to build a bridge. He's also thinking of buying a software company while we're there. He's big into computers, technology, all that." He then looked at her curiously. "I saw the two of you talking. He's really bending your ear. He doesn't normally talk that much to strangers." He looked at Grace again. He didn't know much about his boss's personal life, but it wasn't too hard to imagine why Adam was spending so much time talking with this beautiful woman. "Do you want to switch seats?" he asked. "I need to talk to him about some of these numbers."

"You work for him?" she asked incredulously. "How long have you known him?" Her mind was having difficulty assimilating this new information.

"About twenty years. It's his company." He paused, noting her surprise. He continued as if he felt the need to elaborate. "He's a great guy. Best boss I ever had. He's afraid to fly though. He has a fear of heights, but don't tell him I told you." He chuckled good-naturedly at his boss's expense.

"Do you know what he did before he started his own company?" she managed to ask.

"Dunno. Guess he was an engineer somewhere else. That's what he does now. He's a civil engineer. We build bridges, overpasses, stuff like that. Ironic, isn't it? A guy who's afraid of heights builds bridges for people?"

He waited to make sure she could appreciate the irony. She gave a brief smile and nod.

"They say he's the best there is. He always comes in with the lowest bid but does a quality job and always finishes on time. He's got other guys that work for him that come from all over the country. A lot of them leave good jobs for a chance to learn from him.

"I like him because he treats everybody the same," he continued. "From the laborers to the design engineers. He's trained half the industry it seems," he chattered. "A lot of guys leave him to become his competitors. He doesn't care. He even helps the ones he likes get started. He makes a boatload of money and he's not afraid to pass it around. We're probably the only company in town whose office manager makes as much as the engineers."

"Oh, I see," she said absently, still trying to digest this new and surprising development. "Uh, has he always, um, seemed, well?"

"Well? Like in, not sick?" He looked confused.

She nodded feeling foolish.

"Well, yeah. He's pretty healthy. In fact, he never seems to age. We call him Dorian Gray and try to get him to tell us his secret, but he just laughs," he said and shook his head. "Anyway, best pitcher on our league softball team. We play a bunch of guys from around the area," he explained. "Adam's got a pretty mean curve ball," he added with obvious admiration.

"Has he ever mentioned a wife or anything?" she asked, feeling like a sneak.

A strange look passed his face, and he lowered his voice. "Yeah. That's the only kind of bizarre thing. His wife died about five years ago."

"What's bizarre about that? How did she die?" Grace was afraid to ask.

"Old age," he said and looked at Grace meaningfully. "She was probably about forty years older than him. Everybody thought he must've had some kind of mother complex to have a wife so old. Maybe that's where he got his seed money, maybe from a sugar mama.

"It doesn't fit him though," he continued after some thought. He shrugged and his voice returned to normal. "It's none of my business. He's good to me."

The door opened and it was her turn for the restroom. She went in and took her time even though by then there were plenty of others waiting in line.

Adam was an upstanding citizen with his own business. Plays softball like a lot of other normal guys. *Doesn't seem to age and held it together as he buried an old woman who was his wife,* she told herself. Grace stared at herself in the mirror and felt the room suddenly spin. She steadied herself at the vanity and wondered if it was the plane that was spinning or her world. She opened up the restroom door and Adam's co-worker was waiting for her in the aisle.

"Did you want to switch seats with me?" he asked on their way back.

"No, thanks." She quickly squeezed by him and muttered humbly, "I need to figure some things out. I may need to learn a few things myself about building some bridges."

CHAPTER 11

THE INTERNET WAS BACK UP, THE CABIN LIGHTS WERE turned down low, and passengers seemed to settle in for the evening. The couple across the aisle had stopped playing cards and the woman was sleeping as her husband flipped through a menu searching for something to watch on his computer. The young newlyweds had stopped watching their movie and were looking at wedding pictures on her tablet.

Suddenly a teenager from coach class came to the front and started talking to Katie. Adam couldn't hear what they were saying but he saw Katie shake her head. The boy began to argue and soon Katie raised her voice slightly and sternly but professionally asked him to return to his seat. He reluctantly agreed and as he stepped aside to let Grace pass in the aisle she heard him mutter, "I only wanted one beer."

Adam stood to let her pass. Grace slid by him to her seat and smiled kindly, thanked him for letting her pass, and gently touched his arm on her way by.

Once she got settled, Adam handed her back her cup and asked her thoughtfully, "Are you okay?" Grace turned to face him. It was her turn to see compassion in the eyes of a stranger sitting silently in the shadows next to her, eager to help a fellow traveler he thought might have a problem.

She apologetically smiled and shrugged her shoulders. Adam's focus was intense, and Grace equally returned his gaze. She studied his handsome face, his eyes full of such warmth and gentle kindness. She was confused where he was concerned she didn't mind admitting. She knew he wasn't crazy. She'd seen crazy she reminded herself. This wasn't it. She took a final swig of her cold coffee and sat the cup down on the napkin. She picked up the stir stick and twirled it repeatedly, in and out, between her fingers. It was a habit she indulged in when deep in thought.

Grace was aware of a growing revelation. No matter how deeply she dug into Adam's psyche she knew she wasn't going to find some hidden form of delusion, chemical imbalance, or head injury. Grace considered her findings. He was intelligent, well-spoken, and insightful. She may not agree with his views on God, but they weren't exactly delusional. Mentally ill patients ramble, she reminded herself. They jump from theory to theory and usually complain of continuous and unwarranted persecution.

Adam was a deep thinker, she told herself. He believed in justice and fair consequences for behavior. Grace detected Adam also valued structure, rules, and logic. He projected an energy that was stable, focused, and predictable.

She continued the assessment of her seatmate. Plus, she smiled internally, an observation irrelevant to their discussion but true nonetheless, sitting next to her in such a confined space she couldn't help but acknowledge she found Adam to be undeniably attractive. He smelled like leather with a faint hint of cinnamon. When he moved she noticed no shortage of muscles underneath his perfectly fitted shirt. She was certain Katie wasn't the only person to have found him attractive and to have set sights on him.

Grace gave her seatmate one long, last appraisal before she looked away. She replayed their conversation, turning it over in her mind and reviewing it from all angles. After some conclusion she determined, regardless of his bizarre claim of some freak immortality, not only did she not think Adam was unhealthy and find him attractive, but she *liked* him. His employees certainly seemed to as well. Under different circumstances she might even have hoped for a continued friendship. He appeared to be one of the good guys.

The realization came as a surprise. She lightly picked at a hangnail and made a decision. Considering all the facts, plus her recent outburst revealing her obvious bias toward God and religion, she couldn't in good conscience continue to view or treat him as her patient. "Adam," she said, "I have to tell you something."

He smiled expectantly. "What?"

"I can't help you as a therapist anymore," she confessed honestly.

"Why not?" he asked surprised. "Was my insurance denied?" he teased her.

"Because, big news flash," she said truthfully, "I'm mad at God. And I can't pretend to hold onto any emotional high ground where he's concerned," she confessed and grinned at Adam sheepishly but honestly.

He laughed aloud and she lightly joined in. She was grateful he could see the humor in it.

She spoke again, "I'm sorry but I think I'm going to have to change our arrangement."

"How's that?" He smiled at her again and took a sip of the new coffee Katie had just delivered, peeking out at her expectedly over the rim, the remnants of concern mixed with mirth lingering in his eyes.

"I said I would listen, and I'll still do that," she said.

"Okay . . ." he said cautiously.

"But instead of being your therapist tonight I'll just be your friend," she announced and explained. "I don't think you're crazy. I don't think you've got a head injury. I honestly don't know *what* to think," she said candidly. "But let's just let our guards down," she said, "without filters, without judgement. We're just two friends talking. Both who have hugely different and complicated issues with God. And let's just see where it goes. Okay?"

Adam sighed in relief. He knew she'd been analyzing him, moving him around therapeutically, perched and ready to pull out her prescription pad at any moment. It was liberating and exhilarating, he thought, to be able to talk openly without either side having an agenda. Altering the lyrics a little, he started to sing, *"Amazing Grace, how sweet the sound. That can't save a wretch like me."* Before she could voice her objections he said, "I'm teasing. Sounds great. You're fired," and they both laughed.

"But Grace," he inserted considering the force of her outburst, "I know we're focusing on me right now, but I've got to tell you, in my opinion you could use an updated perspective on God. In fact," he added, "I think you might just benefit from a spiritual do-over. What do you think?"

She smiled without humor and said, "Undoubtedly. But let's just focus on you."

"We could pitch a double," he offered. "It's a long flight."

She shook her head regretfully and said, "No, Adam, too much water under the bridge. I'm certain God really has lost my number."

CHAPTER 12

S HE KICKED BOTH HER SHOES OFF, LEANED HER SEAT BACK A little, and tucked one foot underneath her to get more comfortable. It was bound to be a long night and they needed to get started. "Adam," she asked in her best, non-therapist "friend" voice, "you mentioned you'd taken a fall and there were some devastating effects. What really happened?"

Adam sighed. He wasn't looking forward to telling that part of the narrative. He leaned down and pulled out his briefcase, fumbled for a minute until he found some gum. He offered her a piece and she shook her head. He slowly took off the wrapper, struggling to find a way to begin a painful and complicated story.

Where do I start? he asked himself. *Talking snakes, mind-altering fruit, daily walks with the Almighty?* It was a different time with unrelatable characters and circumstances. He decided to cut to the chase and condense. "Eve was the first to fall," he began, "not that it mattered, we both made the same choice ultimately."

"Yes, Eve," Grace agreed uneasily. She wondered how much she should delve into the subject of Adam's "wife" and how relevant she was to the story. She asked cautiously, "The legend goes," she looked at him cautiously to ensure he didn't object to the term, "that God put you to sleep, did some sort of major surgery on you, and when you awoke, she was just there. Um," she struggled for her next question, "did it really happen that way?" She looked up in time to see the large woman two rows ahead in the oversized multi-colored caftan get out of her seat and move towards the restroom.

Adam leaned back his seat, closed his eyes, and thought of his "legendary" wife. Grace had no idea the accuracy of her words. There'd never been, he surmised, a woman described, photographed, painted, or barely imagined that could compare to the true description of Eve; not Adam's woman he told Grace, but God's, given on loan to Adam only.

Eve was formed in the image of God the feminine. She was the original and perfect combination of humanity and Garden goddess. A lioness mane that spilled down her back like sheets of silver rain framed her perfectly symmetric features on her heart-shaped face. Luminous, almond-shaped, bronze-colored eyes that reflected safety yet belied the smoldering fire that continuously stoked her passionate soul. A soul that wrapped itself around every living being that was fortunate enough to exist even closely in the same proximity.

She had a full and generous mouth that Adam only knew to speak love, truth, hope, and encouragement to the Garden's every living being who possessively considered her their own personal muse and guardian. Skin that appeared to have been created without the benefit of pores and a color Adam was certain God stole from the moon. Her laugh fueled the breeze and ignited the wind; her anger, although seldom expressed, was an unexpected riptide that sharply drew the sand from underneath your feet, pulled you under, and then while praying for continued life, lifted you back up, set you upright somehow, feeling waterlogged but cleansed, refreshed, and ready to try again.

Her long slender legs she inherited from the gazelle, although she regularly lamented that God had forgotten her wings. Adam knew God had not given her wings intentionally out of compassion for her husband because had there been any chance of flight, Adam would have been a full-time bachelor. Eve's love of adventure surpassed his own and there had been many wee hours in the morning he'd gone looking for her to find her sprawled out in the fields, bidding farewell to the stars, with only her lion as companion.

Adam remembered the day the Lord revealed his plans to provide Adam with "the gift of all gifts." For Adam she would be companion, lover, partner, and helpmate. And due to the Lord's pomp and circumstance, gravity and excitement at the revelation of the planned gift, Adam knew there would never be another bequest given to any man, that the Lord esteemed any higher than the gift of a godly woman.

Adam looked at Grace from the corner of his eye and smiled. In all women, he thought secretly, he still saw pieces of Eve. Granted, not necessarily in physical appearance and although Eve was certainly beautiful to behold, it was never her physical attributes that bound him to her. Adam remembered it was not long after Eve arrived he was struck with a revelation accompanied by a mixture of deep fear and elation that the Lord's gift had become his immediate and unexpected addiction. The Lord had promised him a wife but what he gave him was an obsession. A "helpmate" and Adam smiled at the word because when she was present and turned her full attention and charms to her husband, he needed all the help he could get to find the strength to do anything other than exactly what his mate wished of him.

Adam relayed the incidents to Grace as if they had happened recently. "Yes, you are correct," he confirmed. "One afternoon the Lord appeared earlier than usual and led me to the area of the Garden that I loved the most, the area where the four rivers flowed. He instructed me to lie down. He told me he intended to remove a rib from my side and from that part of my body he would extract my future partner, lover, and soulmate, Eve."

Grace was uncomfortable but resolute to keep her vow to Adam. She would listen to his story and take his rendition at face value. However, she asked, "Why would he create Eve from your rib? Why didn't he just breathe into the dust? If she was your equal then why didn't he make her the same way?" She hesitated and then added, "I assume that part of the story, God breathing life into the dust to form you, is true?"

Adam nodded and said, "It is. But God didn't create Woman the same way he fashioned me because Eve was never second to me. She was distinctive in her own right. She had the right to expect the same in her creation. I was not God's master design, and Eve the follow up version. The Bible states that Man and Woman each are formed in the image of God. He made us male and female. Therefore, woman is not Man 2.0. I am Man 1.0; she was Woman 1.0. Each one of us an equal representative of God in the flesh. We were separate but totally equal."

He continued, "I will also tell you that God chose not to create Woman from dirt because of her unique loveliness. Women, created in God's image, share and mirror God's feminine qualities. God did not want to create Woman by blowing spit and air into the dirt. Even if that spit was divine. Adam took a sip of his drink and both he and Grace watched the woman in the colorful tunic return to her seat. Her husband stood to let her pass and tucked in the tag that was sticking out unknowingly from the back of her dress as she passed.

Grace frowned. "But if that was the case then why pull her from your body? Isn't that indicating that women are really merely subsets of men and less significant?"

Adam smiled admiringly at his late wife's memory. "That woman had qualities that never came out of me, I can assure you." He further contemplated Grace's question and said, "I can't say for sure what God was thinking but I'm pretty sure that by taking something necessary from my body and putting it into Eve's, God was signifying neither one of us was the end-all. We needed each other. The more we lived together, the more obvious that became. When I listened to her, my life was certainly better than when I didn't."

Grace suddenly remembered the story of the Fall and Eve's part in it. She said, "Well, I beg to differ, and I don't mean to rub salt in your wound, but it was pretty much her fault you got kicked out of the Garden." She waited and when he didn't answer right away she said, "Right?"

Adam shrugged in concession. He wore a plain gold band on his right hand and twisted it absent-mindedly. He leaned his head back and began to tell the story to his seatmate of what happened the terrible afternoon when life for everyone in heaven, hell, and on Earth changed in a fated instant.

❧

Eve had been taking a late afternoon stroll. Before long she encountered Lucifer coincidentally ambling along in the same direction. He asked if he might join her and together they strolled through the Garden. "Finally, to bask in your beauty without having to share you," he purred.

God had warned them often, and forcefully, not to trust Lucifer and had even gone so far as to strongly suggest they completely avoid him. He was a snake, a potentially life-threatening enemy, God had cautioned. But as Adam and Eve grew confident in their roles as stewards of all things in the Garden they began to lose their wariness of Satan. God had made them the rulers of the kingdom. When Satan was in the Garden he was subject to them. No one, certainly not Satan, had ever disputed this. Why should they avoid him? He knew his place.

Eve and Lucifer strolled silently in the sunshine, a beautiful spring breeze wafting through the trees. Soon they stopped to rest and sat on the ground. Eve looked up and saw they had chosen a spot under the Tree of Knowledge. She told Adam later she had not intentionally walked toward the Tree. Satan had discreetly led the way and had distracted her with stories which honestly she'd found fascinating. Stories of potential adventures Eve couldn't relate to or even imagine. She'd lost her bearings, caught up in new tales of which she'd had no knowledge.

As Lucifer continued to vividly project his narratives of wars, revenge, villains, and triumphant conquests onto the screen of her imagination, Eve, regardless of her growing wisdom and stature, started to feel naïve, ignorant, and childlike. She wondered for just an instant what it would be like if everything wasn't always so . . . she struggled for the word . . . predictable.

Eve's face and thoughts were transparent. Satan said simply in response, "You could have unpredictability," as he smiled at her seductively.

"I have enough adventure," she answered with practicality.

Satan nodded his head sagely. "Yes, I understand. God is so good." He arose indicating he was ready to go. She got to her feet and as they started to move away from the Tree he stopped, turned, and said in the tone of someone older and wiser, "You can always trust God to protect you. Keep you innocent. You know, pure? Set aside and holy." He watched for her reaction then continued. "After all," he looked around, "why else would he keep you sequestered in this boring prison?"

He watched as she narrowed her eyes, surveying him, striving to comprehend his motives. "But who can blame him?" he admitted. "If you belonged to me I'd protect you too. I'd lock you up so tightly you'd never get free."

"I'm not locked up and he doesn't tell me what to do," she said casually, ready to end their time together.

"Oh, no?" he challenged. "Can you leave the Garden? Explore what's outside?"

She ignored him and pulled an unexpected plant thorn from her heel. He continued, "Didn't he warn you about me? Tell you to be careful? But won't ever really explain why?" He cocked his head and smiled at her knowingly.

True, she thought silently, surprised Satan knew they'd discussed him.

"I thought you were the smart one," he said condescendingly and shook his head. Eve moved to walk away, and Satan jumped ahead of her temporarily blocking her path.

"Don't mind me," he said with sudden false self-effacement. "None of us knows why God does what he does. He's God. In the end we all just do what he says. What choice do we really have?" He gave a heavy sigh of resignation. He started to slither away but instead stopped, lowered his voice, and suggested, "Just between the two of us, I think he's scared."

"Nothing scares God," she scoffed.

"One thing does," he said knowingly. "Losing you. God's in love with you and Adam. I've known him a lot longer than you have. I've never seen him like this," he added truthfully. "It would absolutely cripple him to live without you," he suggested and his eyes gleamed.

"He'll never lose us," she said proudly. "He loves us, we love him."

"Yeah, yeah, I know. Nothing else matters," he stifled a bored yawn. "Still," her adversary continued, "didn't he say if you ate from the Tree of Knowledge he wouldn't be able to touch you anymore? You'd be unclean?" He was silent for a moment and let the truth of his words sink in. "Eve, if you go against God he'll leave you. He told you so."

She contemplated the half-truth of the enemy's words.

He smiled at her and added rakishly, "Don't be upset with him, honey. Like I said, if you were mine I'd keep you under lock and key as well," he promised truthfully. "But unlike him, if you belonged to me and you did something wrong I'd never leave you alone for a minute," he hissed.

When Eve made no further movement towards leaving, Satan quickly devised new and divisive tactics. "God's way is to keep everyone but himself in the dark. Keeping you in the dark is just his way of controlling you. I mean protecting you. 'Don't eat from the Tree, don't eat from the Tree!'" he mimicked like a parrot. In a falsetto added, "'It's too dan-ger-ous!'"

Eve became obviously agitated. "What's so dangerous about that Tree?" she demanded. She had asked both God and Adam the same question multiple times. The Lord had given her the same explanation he'd given Adam plus answered every additional question she'd had. But unlike Adam, Eve was never completely satisfied with God's answers.

Adam's nature was to seek out and experiment with Earth's elements and processes to improve and increase its physical structures. Adam spent his days with God primarily discussing four things: how to build structures that would last and serve future generations, how to best steward Earth, his future family, and how to keep his wife happy, not necessarily in that order. Adam and God spent their days happily building things and discussing their future plans. They spent their evenings walking, talking, and revisiting the topics of the day.

Adam was satisfied to easily enjoy the presence of the Lord, diligently seeking his heart and mind for guidance, meditating upon perceived answers, and then sharing face to face his adventures and achievements with his father in the cool of the evening. Adam loved the Lord with reverence and humility, always grateful for the goodness he provided.

Eve talked vociferously with the Almighty immediately upon waking until she fell asleep, sometimes even in her sleep. Whereas Adam loved God as his perfect and gentle, loving father, Eve considered God her best friend, playmate, and closest confidante. They talked happily and freely about everything that came into her mind. Eve and the Creator primarily discussed plant and wildlife care, her unborn children, concerns she had about Adam, what kids might do to their marriage, creative home and garden design, her hair, and whether God thought she had a nice singing voice. All before noon.

After their walks together at night, God and Adam looked forward to ending their evenings with Eve as she regaled them with her version of the day's events and getting her input on their discussions regarding tentative future plans. Their walks were enjoyable but spending time with Eve had become the highlight of the day for them both.

Adam was an intelligent, kind, brave, and righteous man with a keen sense of humor; a person who knew how to enjoy himself but also took his responsibilities seriously. Adam honored God first but admittedly, since Eve had been introduced, secretly wondered if he didn't love his wife just a bit more. He put his wife's needs above his own and was grateful every day of his life for her love, intelligence, wisdom, passion, and presence.

Eve loved Adam and as he was a good, loving, respectful and honorable man, held nothing back from him he desired. Adam and Eve's love for God, their commitment to each other's personal welfare as their own, their marriage, their future family, and stewardship of the Garden, in that order, was the balance and foundation they would build the future upon.

Eve was inclined to focus not primarily on issues of the physical realm solely but considered all branches of the physical, emotional, and spiritual spheres simultaneously when contemplating the best course of any action. Eve was equally as comfortable with her sixth sense as her husband was with the first five. Her skill at comprehending words that were spoken and meanings that weren't was exceptional. Adam acknowledged this and valued and respected her role as the one with the more keen spiritual and emotional insight.

Eve knew intuitively the Tree of Knowledge at some point was going to be a problem for her family. Anyone who ate the fruit from the Tree would suffer and eventually die. The Tree was not just dangerous, it was lethal. And it was in her backyard.

Her protective instincts went on alert every time she thought of the Tree. *Why did it have to be there?* she wondered. *Why wouldn't God and Adam chop it down?* She had asked God to do it and it was the only thing he'd ever refused her. *What if it was still there when her kids were born? What if one of them wandered into it? Adam could be absent minded sometime. What if he accidentally let them eat its fruit? What would happen to her family? To their future?*

God understood her concerns and repeatedly promised her, "In time you'll understand. The Tree is something you'll eventually comprehend but it needs to be a very slow reveal," he warned. "Please trust me and respect the process," he would ask. "It's important, Eve," he emphasized every time she brought it up.

Eve didn't want to understand in time. There was too much at stake. She and Adam wanted to get pregnant. Start a family. Anxiety was clearly written on her face. Her enemy took advantage of her concern and said, "I could show you now . . ." he offered.

"Show me what?" she commanded. If neither God nor Adam would provide a straight answer that would satisfy her maybe someone else would.

"Don't blame God," he offered, "He just wants you to experience flowers and butterflies, rainbows and unicorns, and nothing else." Lucifer started to sing an unfamiliar tune, "Not just posies and puppy dogs . . ." He danced around in a circle and lifted his head to the sky mockingly. "Let me show you love, love, love, baby, baby, please, I'm a bleeding disease, forced down on my knees . . . !" He jumped and twirled with exaggerated energy.

He looked at Eve and smiled gently at her shocked face. "See, Eve?" he said simply yet slightly disdainfully. "You don't have a clue what I'm talking about, do you?" And then as if taking mercy on her he said simply, "I'm just saying there's more out there than loooove." He rolled his eyes and made a gagging noise.

Eve laughed out loud, letting her guard fall, relieved the conversation was taking a lighter turn. "So, what do *you* know about love?" she teased companionably.

Satan leapt through the door she had casually flung open. Emboldened by her question and her familiarity, he made his play. The enemy suddenly advanced towards her, extended his height, and loomed over his intended prey. Yellow eyes aglow he stared down at her seductively, his mouth dripping with venom. "It would be my honor to show you," he ventured aggressively.

Eve gasped and recoiled in disgust, tripped over an extended tree root, lost her balance, and fell to the ground. Hurriedly, she backed away from her enemy.

Once certain he was not planning to advance upon her, Eve rose slowly to her feet, her blazing eyes never leaving those of her adversary. Her mind opened, she experienced sudden and full understanding: It was Satan, not the Tree, who was her real enemy. And not just her enemy, she quickly deduced, but the potential destroyer of her husband, their future children, and worst of all, all of God's kingdom.

Eve continued in the complete revelation. Satan wanted to be her god, to transform her into his image. To lead her, control her. He wanted to torture her and all she held dear and then watch her die. But more than anything he wanted to capture and rule what God wanted most, the apple of his eye, his pride and joy, his family. Satan wanted to revel in the pain he knew such a conquest would cause the Creator.

Lucifer, quick to react, immediately retreated and returned to normal stature. He struggled to think of something clever to say that might deescalate the situation. However, the horror and fury written on Eve's face revealed to him there would be no more civil conversation or banter.

Eve did not turn her back on him or run. Instead, she studied him slowly, intently, and boldly, much as a scientist would examine a strange and grotesque new specimen recently uncovered under a microscope.

Faced off, paces apart, enemy to enemy, Satan backed down and quickly resumed a more humble stance. He gave a self-conscious, nervous laugh and cowered as she stared threateningly at him, obviously contemplating what form of bodily harm she could inflict. "I think I forgot my place, madam" he apologized, obviously contrite. "Please forgive me," he said while bowing low to the ground. His skin turned clammy and pale. He looked more like a worm than a snake. He shook slightly.

The shaking was from true fear. He remembered a warning the

Lord had given him when the Almighty had first placed his family in the Garden. He told Lucifer if he ever touched them, even overtly threatened them, God would personally disembowel him.

Unnerved but unwilling to completely turn loose of his prey, Satan took his final parting shot. "I'm sorry, Eve," he said shakily. "I was just playing with you. I was foolish to think you would join me," he smiled and shrugged.

She turned to walk away and threw over her shoulder, "I will never join you, you snake!"

She had not gone far when she heard him answer, "I know. I'll have better luck with your kids."

And it was there on the edge of Paradise, on what should have been an ordinary, blissful, sunny afternoon, Eve turned the key, allowing hordes of demons eagerly awaiting on the other side to push en masse on the door that God had intended to stay permanently closed. The door to lies, sin, fear, pain, suffering, and hell.

God and Adam had both reassured her that one day God would show them what they needed to know about evil and forever get rid of any danger associated with it, but it had to be in God's timing. Eve decided they had both underestimated how much threat to her family she could tolerate.

With her action the door to the Garden was flung wide open and then torn from its hinges leaving a gaping hole. Pride and recklessness led the march that eventually captured and took possession of God's holy sanctuary. Eve leapt forward, raised her foot, and ground it into the neck of her enemy, bruising her heel in the process. She rushed to the Tree, lunged towards it, and pulled off the first piece of fruit hanging and bit.

"Just try it!" she bellowed in thunderous fury. She turned, prepared to hurl the remainder of the piece at her enemy as a gauntlet of challenge, as she readied herself for battle. Instead, she found Satan rolling from side to side helplessly laughing in wild, shrill, and uncontrollable shrieks on the ground, savoring the carnal sensations of his new domain.

Eve stood and stared as his posture and the sounds of hysterical laughter erased any assurance of the righteousness and wisdom of her call to war. Her challenge had been the final confident words she would ever speak.

CHAPTER 13

A DAM WENT FOR A WALK. HE WAS LOOKING FOR EVE. SHE hadn't been gone too unusually long as she was prone to long walks alone but something in him suspected who was with her and where they'd gone. Halfway through the Garden he saw a large shapeless object on the ground. *What is that?* he asked himself curiously. As he got closer he saw it move slowly, crawling along the ground aimlessly in a circle stunned and confused. Wide-eyed with horror he recognized his wife.

He rushed to her calling her name wildly. Eve was dull-eyed, moaning, and pawing the ground, not even aware of her husband's presence or his shocked and sickened gaze.

As he knelt beside her Adam understood there was only one thing that could have caused such a state. He screamed, "Please God, no!" to a silent but watching heaven.

Adam eventually got his wife home. He watched over her into the night. She finally stopped crying and fell into a dull stupor, hugging her knees and rocking back and forth.

Adam stared helplessly at the frenetic movements of his partner, soulmate, and only human friend. Panic set in. She was the most important thing to him. He could never lose her and live, he told himself. Adam could see Eve, smell and touch her. She was his beautiful lover, his security, his light, and his hope for a happy future. No, he reminded himself sternly, his Creator was his hope for the future.

A vision of the Lord flashed before his eyes. Adam contemplated their relationship. He loved God with all his heart, he assured himself. But Eve was certainly a close second.

But as Adam carefully studied his wife and realistically contemplated her fate his primary allegiance shifted. He'd once told his father, "Where you go, I will follow." He watched his tortured wife laying in the fetal position on the floor. He turned to Eve and thought that his vows to her now included "until death us do part."

Adam ran from the house and rushed into the night before he lost his nerve. He didn't need Satan to tempt him, and he didn't want God to stop him. He found the Tree in a matter of minutes. Adam looked on the ground, spotted the uneaten portion of Eve's fruit, picked it up, held it momentarily to his lips, closed his eyes, and finished it.

A host of the Lord's warrior angels led by Michael himself hovered in the atmosphere preparing for battle that would begin the moment Adam made the call for help. Divine assistance to keep the wrecking ball that had already knocked the door down from completely demolishing the house.

Adam and Eve had been appointed the Garden's magistrates. In the physical realm their will was supreme, and their authority super-seded that of even the angels. When Adam uttered no prayer for divine intervention each heavenly soldier stood by helplessly and watched God's offspring recklessly deliver both sets of keys to the Garden's new landlord.

The moment Adam ate the fruit the presence of the Holy Spirit left him. The force of the departure knocked him to his knees. The filter between all possibilities both good and evil disappeared from Adam's mind, spirit, and body and he was flooded with a smorgasbord of un-familiar thoughts and sensations.

A new and sudden panic released excess adrenaline throughout his body. Adam's DNA immediately began to re-configure, making room for new baggage hauled in by unhealthy and unwelcome tenants. Fear, despair, deep anxiety, and dread entered through newly opened doors and windows and quickly settled into their new home.

A nightmare of potential scenarios entered his mind, events that could have possibly transpired between Eve and Satan, and Adam was overcome with extreme fear, jealousy, and anger. Had Satan touched his wife? Forced himself upon her? Images of possible violent scenarios caused Adam to escalate into an uncontrollable rage that ended with a resolute decision to hunt down and slaughter his enemy.

Spasms racked his body and the earth around him began to spin. He pounded his fists into the ground as potential scenes of torture, death, and sorrow reeled through his mind like a series of horror films on an internal projector he couldn't unplug.

Somewhere in the distance Adam could hear uproarious and vic-torious laughter with intermittent shrieks of sheer exultation. The hilar-ity intensified until it became deafening in Adam's ears. The excitement was coming from Satan himself who had just received the latest update, hosts of unseen demons only too happy to deliver the news.

Adam's mind instantly conjured celebratory images of Satan and his dancing compatriots. Lucifer was on his knees lifting his hands high in the air in mock praise to a God he had just bested. Adam's pain was unbearable. Rolling around on the ground he screamed for mercy, desperate for the vision and thundering explosions of revelry to subside. But no mercy came.

He feverishly searched within himself for some new material that could act as a wall between his conscious mind and the new and terrifying supernatural visions he was being bombarded with. Anything that would block the window and stop the assault to his battered and crippled consciousness.

Eventually, Adam found new emotional devices that could help deal with his pain—unhealthy but effective power tools known as denial, projection, and blame. Adam deftly maneuvered them and constructed the first man-made emotional wall built for the purpose of self-preservation; a wall that generations later he and his descendants would constantly struggle to dismantle.

Adam crawled to the base of the Tree and managed to roll onto his back. *This was all Eve's fault,* he convinced himself. Laying on the cold ground considering his wife's flaws, Adam found the necessary strength to sit upright.

He conceded he might be partially to blame. He should have monitored her more. Insisted she be a little more forthcoming and accountable regarding her intentions and behavior. He and God both had warned her to be careful of Satan. *Once she's well we need to have a discussion,* he decided sternly. Without the Lord to guide her she would certainly require more of his firm hand.

Leaning against the base of the Tree Adam became aware of a great void within him in the place the Lord had previously inhabited. Adam was spiritually alone and knew he was destined to stay that way.

For the first time in his existence, he experienced what it was to live without the divine well of love, joy, peace, approval, purpose, and easy comradery the companionship of his father had provided. Adam wept bitterly for his loss.

With his defenses down, the demon of shame came charging in, commanding the room. Of all sins, shame will never stay in the background for long. Self-doubt, insecurity, and feelings of unworthiness also introduced themselves as replacement tenants for the empty spaces his father had previously occupied.

Channeling new inner demons Adam chided himself. *In the end who am I really?* he questioned. God had called him his son created in his own image. *Was that all a lie?* Adam felt bile rise in his throat and he struggled to keep from throwing up.

"Why would a deity create and raise human beings and then lower himself by living inside them?" the new voice of deception questioned him. Adam forgot "love and relationship" would have been his answers yesterday. "*You* as God's *temple*?" the demons added tauntingly. "Effectively imprinting his ways on your heart and mind to help you become like *Him*?" they scoffed in complete derision. "Why would any god raise potential competitors?"

Adam couldn't have been created in his father's image, he finally conceded. After all, how could a son of God lay tear-stained, retching, blaming his wife under a tree, unable to even stand up let alone walk home? Tears continued to stream down his face and his sobs overcame him as he became convinced not only was he not created as a son of God, but his father had probably never even loved him. Distrust, abandonment, and blame installed a hook into Adam's heart and were gleefully dragging him through the unfamiliar realm of the dark side of his unconscious soul.

Spurred on by new and unfamiliar demons, Adam cried aloud

bitterly to anyone in the spiritual realm who might still be listening a dire warning to the Lord's unsuspecting subjects. "Don't trust God! He doesn't really love anybody!"

Any hope Adam nurtured that God was planning to redeem him, Eve, and their terrible situation had completely dissipated. Still unable to stand, Adam pulled himself around and began the long crawl towards home.

Suddenly he remembered his father's warnings about the Tree of Knowledge that included a conversation about the Tree of Life. God had told him, "If you eat from the Tree of Knowledge you will die. The only thing that could save you would be the Tree of Life. And if you eat from the former, I will immediately send angels to cut you off from any chance of living on Earth forever until the struggle between good and evil is finished, and I come to redeem you myself."

The memory gave Adam the strength to rise. Filled with a new independence in thinking he was convinced of what he had to do. He and Eve had brought destruction into their lives, but Adam would not die for it. God had said the Tree of Life could save him.

The thought of death terrified Adam and he became aware of a new sense of power and autonomy that sprung from the desire for self-preservation. *We will not die!* he decided. Adrenaline coursed through his veins, and he found the strength to run.

From heaven's portal, still distraught from the sight of his beloved son and daughter's downfall, God saw Adam's determination to reach the forbidden Tree of Life. He saw his son had not only lost his faith but also his judgment and was planning to further challenge him.

Warrior angels under the archangel's direction sped towards the Tree with swords drawn, but Satan's minions had already been dispatched and had reached the Tree just seconds before. The two teams battled for the first time on human soil. The mission of heaven's angels was to obey their God and ban the Tree of Life. The mission of Satan's angels was to seal Adam's fate as their captive.

Eden was center stage as a cloud of heaven's witnesses collectively held their breath. In all of history there had never been a scene such as this. As Adam approached, he saw both groups fighting for territory. Momentarily surprised and dismayed, he stopped and debated the wisdom of his plan. He knew who had dispatched the angels and why. But guided and strengthened by a new and strangely compelling force he made his decision to continue.

He sprinted until he saw the Tree of Life ahead, clouded by the dust of battle. Suddenly he collided with a very young angel.

Quickly assessing the situation, the angel lunged at Adam in an attempt to stop him from accessing the Tree. God's orders were clear. That particular fruit was no longer an option for Earth's inhabitants. A shortened life was an act of God's mercy in a world filled with sin and misery. Adam had to be stopped.

But Adam's determination prevailed. With the smaller angel jumping at his heels, Adam maneuvered, dodged him, leapt into the air, grabbed a piece of fruit and bit.

Swallowing, he landed both feet on the soft, green, and lush earth below him. Immediately he felt the fruit strengthen him. He stood up straight and remembering his young nemesis turned defiantly to face him. Instead of the expected anger on the young angel's face he was shocked to see love, compassion, and pity in his tearful eyes.

As the enormity of Adam's actions swept over him, shame and condemnation filled his entire being. He threw the partially eaten fruit to the ground. Adam shivered as a cold new wind blew across his face and naked body.

A partial view of heaven had always been open to Adam and Eve and through the portal of their spirits they had been privileged with visions of much of the activity within heaven's gates. Through spiritual eyes many of the secrets and mysteries of God's universe were available to them.

At the first taste of sin a wall had begun to block Adam's spiritual view. He tentatively glanced upward, guilty but curious as to what he still might be able to see. As the portal to the spiritual world began to close, God's human son was given one clear and lasting image. To Adam's shock and horror, he saw the two realms his father had once explained to him that existed. Adam saw heaven but for the first time was introduced to its evil counterpart, the realm and domain of God's enemy, Satan.

Adam was neither spared the scenes of weeping angels in the throne room or the continued uproarious, almost insane, celebration of the demons of hell; evil, pale-looking creatures dancing and stomping the floor of their own domain feverishly with delight. Adam fell to the ground unable to watch either scene.

Angry clouds opened and harsh, cutting rain began to fall to the earth in torrential sheets. Looking upward, Adam shielded his eyes, desperately searching for his father's face. As black clouds connected, shutting out the remainder of heaven's light, Adam's and his father's eyes met for one last time. Once filled with love and pride, Adam's final tormenting memory of the day was his father's eyes filled with pain, loss, inconsolable grief, and disappointment.

Darkness completely separated heaven from Earth. God's son rolled around in the mud, convulsive sobs wracking his body—sobs full of new awareness, the knowledge of both good and evil. Adam had received all he had requested and at the same time the damning revelation of what once was and would probably never be his again.

Soon, from the solitude of an empty room, Adam's father leaned his head back against his throne. When he was certain the last of his scribes, advisers, and attendants had cleared the room, tears fell in torrents as he slowly closed the drapes on the windows to the scene of his bereft and deceived son crawling home on his knees, about to find his beloved wife in the middle of a nervous breakdown.

The Lord hung his head and continued to let his emotions flow. He knew Adam's shame, his decision to never completely trust God again, and his vow to survive in the world using his new and unhealthy tools, had just constructed the veil that would separate Man from God for centuries to come.

CHAPTER 14

ADAM FINISHED TELLING HIS STORY AND BOTH HE AND GRACE were quiet. She rang her call bell, Katie approached, and she asked for a glass of water. So did Adam. Katie picked up their old napkins, coffee cups, and trash and soon returned with their waters. They thanked her as she set them on fresh napkins on the available trays between them.

Grace took a long look at Adam. His story told in logical sequence so filled with vivid detail and emotion could no longer be mistaken as the byproduct of a head injury or chemical malfunction. Not only in word but in sincerity she decided to suspend her belief in what was and wasn't possible for the remainder of the evening and take Adam's story at face value. Once the night was finished, she would re-visit, re-assess, and re-evaluate. But all at a later date. For the night, Grace promised herself, Adam was *the* Adam.

"Did you ever see God again after you ate from the Tree?"

Adam's voice was dull. "For a while," he unhappily continued. "But his presence made us even more miserable. When he'd visit Eve and I stood around nervous and embarrassed. God just seemed so sad."

"Sad?" She never imagined God having emotions. In fact, as an adult when she considered him at all, she always thought if there was a God, he, or maybe it, was probably some sort of higher power, collective consciousness. A mindless, personality-less, emotionless cosmic force whose only function was to keep the universe in order. "Are you sure you aren't giving God human characteristics?"

Adam considered her words. "When God laughs, cries, celebrates, he's not stooping to the level of experiencing human behaviors. We're made in his image. Our emotions make us like God. Not the other way around."

He continued, "So why wouldn't he be unhappy? He'd lost as much or more than we had." Then added, "Once we discussed the merits of additional rings around Saturn. After we fell when God asked us a question we'd hang our heads, dig our toes into the ground, and stammer like two ten-year-olds. We felt so guilty."

"Did he come to the Garden to personally escort you out?"

"Not right away. But eventually, yes, he came looking for us. We were afraid to see him at first as you can imagine. When we heard him coming we took off and ran into the Garden like a couple of scared rabbits and hid. Of course, he came after us."

"What happened?" Her curiosity was genuine.

"Once we saw his face and that he wasn't mad, believe it or not we thought maybe he would just forget about it and help us find a way to return to normal."

"But he didn't. He made you leave home, didn't he?"

Adam stared at Grace momentarily, took a hard swallow, leaned his head back on the headrest, and closed his eyes. Feeling her eyes upon him he said, "Give me a minute."

❧

God had come that day for a purpose. Adam recalled the troubled yet determined resolve on his father's face and remembered how he'd been unable to meet his eyes. It was obvious Adam and Eve had not been the only ones suffering.

The Lord found the young couple hiding in the Garden ridiculously covering themselves using leaves from the trees as some form of camouflage. Seeing their pale, thin, and fearful countenances he simply stared at them sadly and thought again about his plans to best protect them from the full force of the fate they had chosen.

The Lord simply motioned for his offspring to follow. Wordlessly, God led them towards the southern gates of Eden. Adam and Eve tailed their father nervously. They hiked through the Garden silently and Adam wondered if they might just keep walking until someone got the nerve to broach the subject. When he saw God was looking for something he was relieved. Maybe he was searching for an item with which he would make the point that Adam and Eve should have obeyed him.

Adam was sure their father would tell them how badly he was disappointed in their choices. However, it had never been the Lord's way to speak harshly or criticize them. When their father wanted to teach them something he simply showed up and suggested they go for a walk. Eventually they would discover a new plant, animal, or force of nature he would use as a teaching aid.

But on this particular day there was no new bird, insect, or animal to observe that would teach them what they had opted to learn. The landmark God was looking for was the south exit out of the Garden.

Spotting the gate in the distance, he stopped, turned, and faced them both. His silence and painful expression caused his beloved son and precious daughter to know the awful truth. There would be no lesson that day that ended in smiles and congratulations for seeing a new and superior way of living. They had told God the lessons they wanted to learn. They wanted to know what choices were available to them without him as their filter. He was there to personally see them off to school.

Adam and Eve panicked and desperately tried to save their own skin. Adam lost his temper. Eve began to cry. Neither took responsibility and in the end blamed each other and the devil.

God watched and listened sadly, further convinced of what needed to be done. They knew the one rule and the consequences for breaking it. However, no one but himself knew how desperately at that moment he wanted to turn back time and start again.

Adam opened his eyes, took a drink of water, and explained to Grace their exodus into the world. "No," he confirmed, "there was no do-over. God showed us the door."

"What did you do?" Grace asked with concern obvious in her voice. "Did you fight back?"

"What could we do? Tackle him?"

"But what did he *say* to you?"

"He gave us his best fatherly advice and sent us on our way." Adam remembered and recounted the conversation to his new friend.

꿍ᴕ

"You've opened a door you can't close," God explained carefully to his wide-eyed and anxious children. "You want to know what I know, and you didn't wait for me to show you." As he spoke they never noticed how often he looked away to avoid the pain and panic in their eyes.

God prophesied over Adam, Eve, and all future generations. He started with Adam. "When our minds were connected you knew how to receive from my table effortlessly." He looked at his son closely. "Now it will be by the sweat of your brow you will eat, find clothing, shelter, and protection.

"Adam, love and cherish your wife more than your own body. Protect her and provide for her. If you don't you'll lose her in this harsh environment." Eve suddenly burst into fresh tears.

The Lord waited until her tears had subsided and said gently, "Watch over your husband. There will always be enemies trying to steal your livelihood. You still have your woman's intuition. Help him tell the difference between his friends and his enemies.

"Daughter, soon you'll be mother to the world. However, you and mothers after you will suffer greatly during childbirth. In losing access to my mind, you no longer understand how to manage and control pain.

"Eve," he continued emphatically, fully understanding her nature, "resist the temptation to possess your husband, manipulate him, or drive him too hard. Remember, he's not me. Try not to make him your god and then resent him because he can't be."

God's face clouded as a vision of the future flashed before him. Sadly he studied his children. "You will both fight the urge to dominate the other. Remember, love is not a weapon. Don't withhold it to get your own way. You'll have to work together as a team if you're going to survive.

"Help each other," he advised as they stared at their feet, over-whelmed by the ominous tutorial. "Overlook each other's flaws when you see them. Don't exploit the weaknesses of your partner, cover them.

"Remember to put each other's needs above your own," he continued. "If only one of you follows this advice your marriage will fail. However, if you both commit to giving more than you receive, rarely ever at the same time, you can maintain a successful partnership. Don't keep score.

"Be prepared to deal with scarcity, hardship, and unexpected trouble. You will come to understand self-sacrifice. You'll have to if you want to keep your marriage and family together."

At this Eve buried her face in her hands and cried, "How will we live?"

He looked at his weeping daughter and his heart melted. His voice softened and he answered mercifully, "When you have a decision to make you can still ask me for help. Pray out loud together. You don't have access to me anymore through our spirits, but I can still hear you when you pray. I'll still help you," he promised. "Just try not to lose any more faith in me." His voice was so tender two sets of hopeful eyes looked at him wondering if the Almighty might be changing his mind.

But the Father's stance was firm and he shook his head resolutely as if speaking as much to himself. "You opened this Pandora's box. I wasn't ready but you forced my hand," he reminded himself. "Therefore, the door is open. You and your heirs will see ALL good and you will see ALL evil before this season is complete."

"What?" Eve cried out in dismay.

Adam's voice was barely audible. "For how long?"

The Father turned to his son and said gravely, "Until everyone in your family for many, many generations to come has looked, seen, and made his and her choice. Who will bow their knee to me and to my

Love and Truth as part of my family and who will try to dethrone me and become their own god. I was going to introduce the effects of evil gently and in my own timing. You changed that for you and your family. We'll deal with it now."

He continued, burdened, "Every person born will experience the consequences of both good and evil, each deciding for themselves how they want to live and who or what they want as their god. When every inhabitant destined to be on Earth has seen and chosen we'll end this. Once and for all."

"Everyone must see and choose?" Eve stammered, already afraid for her unborn children.

Her father turned to her. "There's more than one way to live, more than one way to govern your household. I have great plans for our future, plans that have not changed based on your recent choices. These long-term plans do not include worlds and governments where suffering, pain, death, and destruction are allowed by you and your heirs. I won't provide supernatural resources to people who would use them to aid an enemy.

"Justice demands," he added, "and my family, the sons and daughters of God, deserve the respect to be allowed to choose and demonstrate who's with me and who's against me. *Before* we move into the next chapter of eternity."

He pointed to the open door and they numbly stumbled through it. Two large angels appeared. They stepped in front of the entrance, pulled out their swords and crossed them. The weapons barring the way immediately burst into flame indicating clearly the eviction was non-negotiable. The banished tenants stood staring at each other unsure of what to do next.

CHAPTER 15

G RACE CONSIDERED HER COMPANION'S WORDS AND ASKED, "Did you ever see him again?"

"He came to my baptism," Adam answered. When she didn't respond he said, "But no. Not really. Sometimes we suspected he came incognito to watch and check on us, but never another face-to-face conversation. Eventually we made up, but he stopped coming to see us in person." Katie came by and offered to top off their water glasses. Both nodded and thanked her. She smiled sweetly at Adam but eyed Grace. Katie knew Adam's intentions would not include her that night, or any night for that matter.

"Do you miss him terribly?" Grace asked empathetically.

Adam smiled, the love he felt for his Creator evident in his eyes. "Oh yeah," he affirmed. "Over the years we've gotten close again. In fact, my life looks very similar to what it once did in the Garden. I was dead for so long." He paused for a moment and reflected silently while taking another sip of his water.

"God forgave you? He let it go? Gave you your old life back? After all that?" she asked incredulously.

He answered dryly, "Yes, Grace. After all that. God's my best friend. I don't think I could even get out of bed without knowing he's with me. Normally we talk all the time. He's closer than any foxhole buddy I've ever known. The blessings in my life are too many to count. The hole in my soul forever gone. The longing for something I want but can't put a name to, gone. I'm not ashamed to say it. I love him. He's everything to me."

Grace stared at him and thought momentarily about what Adam had done to God's world. The devastation he'd caused. Adam and Eve together were responsible for every heinous crime ever committed against Man and God and yet God forgave him. And even more unbelievable, Adam called him his best friend.

She studied the hangnail and tried to resist chewing it. Instead, she picked up a stir stick and absent-mindedly twirled it between her fingers like a baton. She thought, *All I really did was dump God. I didn't ruin his world.* Then suddenly thought of several things she'd done she wasn't exactly proud of, was maybe even ashamed of, really. But still, if God could forgive *Adam* . . . She looked at him sideways.

Her mind wondered. *I wonder if God would take me back? Or would he slam the door in my face and call me a traitor if I even called?* She looked out the window and thought, *But would I even want him back? What would I have to give up? Or worse yet, face? What would really be in it for me?* Grace was a woman who was true to herself. She wasn't about to give in to a notion based on an airplane ride with a good-looking, mysterious stranger just because he claimed he lived on Paradise Lane. No matter how empty her life seemed.

"You actually had a bromance with God?" she asked instead.

He laughed a little. "I *have* a bromance with God," he corrected her. "We're in a hiccup. That's all."

Grace sat and stared at the naked love and longing only someone can feel for another worthy of such adoration. She experienced a sudden pang and couldn't help being reminded again that she had once felt about God that way. The baby behind them started to cry and Adam and Grace stopped talking momentarily until the baby could be soothed.

Grace looked out the window and suddenly realized that regardless of the plausibility of Adam's story one thing was certain. In spite of any commonalities there was one major difference between them. Grace had intellectual theories about God while Adam worshipped and adored his Creator. When he talked about his God his eyes gave away all his heart contained. Grace had never known a man who was so willing to express such naked passion and adoration for anything in this world, let alone for someone who wasn't. Remembering a little how she once felt about God, for the first time since meeting Adam, Grace actually felt a little bit jealous.

"Did you pray when you first left the Garden?" she asked curiously, when the baby had stopped crying.

"Not much at first," he answered, "and before too long we lost all communication. Eve and I stopped talking to God and he stopped answering us. We were so busy we didn't have time to notice much though. Feeding and clothing ourselves was a full-time job."

"What'd you do to survive?"

"Farmed," he said. "All the time."

"Why all the time?"

He laughed. "Because I was terrible at it," he said, remembering.

"I would plant the crops. If the seed was good and there was enough rain, we might have had a decent harvest. However, I didn't know how to keep the animals and insects away. Keeping food on the table was a constant struggle."

"We learned too late outside the Garden walls that trees and other food producing plants go dormant in late fall. Once we realized this, we gathered all the fruit and nuts we could find and stored them in a small storage hut I built. But when autumn was over and the first freeze came upon us we almost starved."

Adam remembered the first time he intended to kill an animal for its hide. His face went dark at the memory.

ৡৄ

Eve had just gotten pregnant with the twins. One wintery evening he came home to find his wife lying on their pallet on the floor, shaking from fever and chills.

He lay on top of her hoping the warmth of the fire and his body would be enough to make her stop shaking. They didn't have any wool blankets or animal hides. Eve had used some hemp to tie large leaves together that served as a makeshift blanket, but the leaves kept tearing, leaving gaping holes. Adam went outside into the howling wind to search for additional firewood.

Up to that point, no matter how cold and hungry they were, both Adam and Eve agreed all life was sacred. God put them on Earth and gave them dominion over everything, plants and animals alike. Their job was to safeguard life, nurture and protect it. They did their best, even in harsh conditions, to maintain as much of their original purpose as possible.

But Adam had to face reality, he told himself. The only way he and Eve could make it through the winter would be to kill anything he could catch. Animal hides could keep them warm, and the meat would give them strength. The lakes had frozen over. There would be no fish available until spring.

Kill an animal? He was appalled and repelled at the thought. *I'm here to protect them!* he argued with himself. He just couldn't take the life of another living creature. He knew that level of savagery would be the final nail in the coffin of his already disintegrated self-esteem. Murder would take him to a new low from which he was sure he could never recover.

Adam returned inside to sit with his wife and pray to a distant God whom he hoped was still listening for intervention. Eve passed in and out of delirium. For a while she would talk as if they were still in the Garden. Then she would remember, cry, and berate them both. Eventually she called out to God that he would end her life and rescue her from her misery.

Adam remembered his father's deep compassion and special love for Eve. He would want to save her from pain and if she asked him, he might just take her. Adam panicked. As her fever continued to rise, he knew death was very likely to occur soon with or without God's help.

Adam envisioned his life without Eve. He couldn't exist in a worldly jungle by himself, and he knew it. The couple was miserable, taunted by the memory of what they had thrown away, but it was a tolerable misery because they had each other.

If Eve were gone he'd have nothing left. He irrationally wondered if God might take Eve and leave Adam alone to punish him. Eve could die but Adam could not, he reminded himself dejectedly and berated himself for his rash choice the day of the Fall to eat from the Tree of Life without being able to capture an additional piece for his wife. *What was*

I thinking? he chided himself again. He watched Eve writhe deliriously. Suddenly and without warning tidal waves of fear washed over him. The pain of losing her would be unbearable. He began to fear insanity.

Adam searched his mind for any solution. All he could think of was she needed instant food and warmth. He couldn't wait until spring. Eve would be dead that night. He needed an immediate remedy. He heard a familiar sound outside and opened the door. About a hundred feet in front of him, a lion walked through the woods. The lion saw him and sent out a minor roar of greeting.

Adam had known the lion since he was a cub. He'd named him Simeon, and among his peers Simeon was the most noble and regal of all. Projecting full majesty, he had once stood still and proudly allowed Eve to add rainbow highlights to his mane. He was the only thing she had ever called "pet" and they loved each other fiercely.

Adam had always thought it comical that when he would make his rounds through the Garden Simeon would push his siblings aside to take his place next to Adam. It was obvious he considered himself Adam's personal aid, friend, and bodyguard.

Adam remembered resting his head on Simeon's back at night when gazing up at the stars. Immediately he remembered the heat that had radiated from his flesh. His eyes filled with tears. His wife dying with no hope of salvation, Adam knew he had no other choice.

He could still see the look in his friend's eyes as he stood perfectly still, silent, without defending himself, as he waited to willingly submit himself in sacrifice.

With tears rolling down his face, Adam lifted his instrument, ready to strike a lethal blow, when suddenly Eve appeared at the door and called his name. Adam turned to see his beautiful wife, pale and weak, but obviously in the early stages of recovery. He fell prostrate on the ground and wept.

CHAPTER 16

I

T WAS ADAM'S TURN TO STAND UP, STRETCH, AND USE THE restroom. Grace noticed in the dark cabin most of the other travelers were sleeping. A few still played games on their computers or watched movies. Adam came out of the restroom and noticed his employee was awake and watching a movie. He walked back and they talked for a few minutes before Adam returned to his seat.

"Dean said he talked to you earlier," Adam said with a smile. Grace nodded her head in acknowledgement. With a glimmer Adam asked, "Did you ask him if I was married?"

Tempted to lie, Grace admitted sheepishly, "It might have come up."

Adam laughed out loud and said, "What'd he tell you?"

Embarrassed, Grace said, "Not much really. He just said you had a wife, but she died."

He looked at her knowingly and said, "Umhmm . . . That's it?"

Grace opted for the sin of omission. "That's all," she said, hoping Adam would drop it. She quickly changed the subject. "So, how'd you and God make up? Was it a long time later?"

Adam must have asked Katie for another cup of coffee because she showed up with a cup and a miniature bottle of Irish cream. She returned to the galley to retrieve a forgotten stir stick. "It was after the birth of Cain and Abel. Kids will make anybody cry out to God," he said, only partially joking.

"That's right," she said slowly, watching him stir cream into his coffee. "Cain and Abel were your sons. I'd forgotten about them." Then asked cautiously, "Um, so Cain and Abel were real people?"

Adam tested his coffee and asked, "Why would you think otherwise?" while adding more cream.

"Well, I don't know. I thought maybe they might've been, um, you know," she faltered, "symbolic or something."

"Symbolic? Maybe, but those boys were definitely real." At that Adam began to recount to Grace the story of the incident that helped Cain and Abel's parents heal their relationship with God and each other.

੭ਤ

Eve rallied from her illness and eventually both she and Adam became somewhat better at dealing with the hardships of life outside the Garden. Adam became a better farmer, Eve learned to turn wool into clothing, became a decent cook, and together they struggled but somehow became accustomed to their new lives.

At first as a couple they had clung to one another, devoted and empathetic partners providing companionship and assistance through the many new and continuous hardships. But within time the process of constantly evaluating, deciding, and coping with new and strange thoughts, desires, and emotions, their own and each other's, became overwhelming and exhausting.

Every single idea, emotion, and decision had to be analyzed and evaluated for merit. No perceived course of action could be depended upon to produce the desired result. No comment or motive was taken at face value. The assessment process was tedious and seemed never-ending.

Over time both partners grew overly sensitive, anxious, frustrated, angry, and prone to emotional outbursts. Eve found it easier to complain about a problem than to look for its solution. She grew passive, forcing the majority of responsibility for decisions onto Adam. He was frustrated by her lack of involvement and became domineering and critical.

He openly belittled her for her lack of initiative. She rolled her eyes behind his back and told herself the monkeys made better decisions than he did. Both suffered from bouts of hopelessness and depression. Intimacy waned, leaving both feeling isolated and lonely.

But when Eve got pregnant with the boys the couple rallied. The promise of the next generation filled both parents with hope. "This will be a chance for a new start!" they told each other. The second generation of Man would erase the mistakes of the first. In their children they would start anew and through them Adam and Eve believed they would salvage the fate of future generations.

Their sons would be smarter, wiser, and better prepared to live in a world with so many choices. Their daughters, more creative, intuitive, and ingenious. Their children would be like their parents had been before the Fall—perfect. Before memories, poor choices, disappointments, and disastrous failures had changed them.

Their children's births, new adventures, and success stories would produce a family bond that would never be broken. They would prove to God they could live outside the Garden even without his help.

Eve and Adam determined their children would thrive, not just live to survive like their parents were doing. They would work hard to reproduce a Garden-like environment for their kids, but unlike their father, once they'd created it and put their children in it, they would secure it. They would eliminate any threats to their offspring, certainly never intentionally leaving access to anything that might harm them. They would improve upon God's parenting skills they assured one another.

Adam and Eve devised a plan. They would teach their children about the differences between good and evil by giving them clear rules and boundaries. Strict rules their children would obey. There would be swift, harsh, and immediate punishment for any non-compliance, Adam had decided. God had given them too much freedom. Obviously, freedom they couldn't handle. There would be none of that free will nonsense trickling down to the next generation.

Their children would be smart, they promised themselves, and highly evolved. They would understand and learn through their parents' experiences and be grateful they didn't have to learn life's lessons the hard way. Thankful someone else had travelled the hard road ahead of them.

But as a precaution the young parents decided they would always be present to effectively serve as their children's overseers. They planned to expand their dwelling space as the kids grew and had families of their own so they could always be present to point out the mistakes their kids and grandkids might make. It would be their jobs as patriarch and matriarch of the world to make sure everyone remained compliant, happy, and safe. The future of their family and the world depended on it.

Cain was born first and shortly thereafter came Abel. As they grew, the new parents soon realized their intentions, although noble, were ill-conceived. Their boys convinced them through ongoing escapades, Abel's usually innocent, his brother's not so much, if they were going to maintain their sanity and unity they were going to need outside help.

They needed God desperately they agreed simultaneously after, in a fit of rage, Cain intentionally started a fire outside the shed where they stored the grain. Adam had refused their sons' request to build a makeshift boat out of a hollowed-out and rotting tree trunk. Cain and his brother planned to try some white-water rafting that would include a last minute dive to avoid plummeting over a thundering waterfall.

The fire was put out in time, but the event was the catalyst for the couple to drop any pretense they knew how to control their sons, especially the older who proved to be wilder and more rebellious than his parents had imagined possible. They needed the divine help only the Lord and his watchful band of angels could provide. He might not walk and talk the same with them anymore, but certainly God Almighty would be able to keep their children from burning the house down, they assured one other. Adam and Eve decided to make the call.

But once the decision was made, Adam nor Eve knew how to re-establish a relationship with God after years of ignoring him. They had left God, not the other way around. They were the ones who needed to take the first step.

They couldn't see God but knew they could still talk to him, that he was listening. He told them the day they left the Garden to keep him involved in their lives; he would always be around to help them. He said they'd have to learn new, external ways to communicate with him and follow him. It would be more complicated, but they could still have a relationship. But they had gotten busy, prayers for much needed help didn't seem to always provide immediate relief, and eventually they just stopped trying. They each admitted any faith they possessed was hanging by a thread.

"What if he won't take us back?" Eve asked Adam fearfully. They looked at their boys. "What if he won't help us? Show us what to do?" They had to try, they told each other. If their children were to follow God, they would have to understand him and his ways. Adam and Eve knew it was their responsibility to teach them how.

Also, they admitted to each other late at night talking together in bed, partners again, they missed God. They still loved him, each confessed. Neither had ever really stopped. But both were upset with him, even angry. They knew the responsibility of their situation was theirs, but they believed if he really wanted to, God could have saved them from their fate.

Eve said God should have been more specific and told them exactly what would happen to them if they disobeyed him. He should have explained more graphically what the sin and its consequences would be. Adam didn't feel the need to come to God's defense and remind her that he had explained the consequences. Instead, he agreed and added that God should've never let the snake or the Tree into the Garden in the first place.

Still, they admitted they had stopped communicating with him. They knew he was watching and listening, but they'd mostly ignored him. Mainly because they didn't want to deal with the whole big, messy separation and dissolution of the relationship.

The main problem was the shame, they finally concluded. They simply hadn't been able to overcome the humiliation of what they'd done, what they had willingly thrown away, and what they'd become. It was hard to talk to God openly and candidly, they decided, when they felt they had fallen so low. Real or imagined, they'd always thought if they'd been able to see God's face when they talked to him, his eyes would only reflect grave disappointment. Maybe even anger.

What they didn't realize was that God longed for reconciliation even more than they did. He had never stopped loving them and missed them terribly. They were his children. He had poured all his love and creative energy into designing and constructing the perfect world for them. There was nothing he wanted more than to reconcile with them, celebrate their victories together, and eventually lead them back to full Garden residency. But he was determined to wait for an invitation. He wouldn't force the relationship. The call came none too soon.

It turned out to be Eve who repaired the bridge. One day she was walking with Abel by the side of a nearby river. They were there to wash clothes. Adam needed both boys in the field working with him that day, but Abel wanted to go with his mother instead and Adam had agreed. Abel was his mother's special joy, one of only a few remaining, and she loved spending time with him.

Abel insisted on carrying the makeshift basket of laundry. He was about thirteen and although not as sturdy as his brother he was healthy and strong. He carried the clothes trailing slightly behind Eve who carried her washing tools inside another basket.

There had been plenty of rain and the river rolled slightly below them as they treaded carefully on the path. Adam had warned his family to be careful when the water was high and moving swiftly. He had seen more than one animal swept to its death in the currents, especially after the spring rains.

Eve and Abel approached the landing where they normally washed. Eve decided it was too dangerous to stop there. The river was too high and the ground too soggy to give them solid footing for their task. Eve knew of yet higher ground slightly ahead and they walked carefully along the water's edge to reach it.

Eve saw Abel struggling with the basket slightly too big and heavy for his small frame. Again, she tried to take it from him, but he insisted on carrying it. She stepped over a protruding tree root and called out a warning for her son not to trip. Too late, Abel's toe caught the root. He lost his balance and tumbled over the edge into the river. Eve watched horrified as her son, unwilling to let go of the basket of clothes, was carried away by the rushing waters.

Eve threw down her load and ran stumbling along the river's edge, screaming for her son to release the basket and catch a branch. He couldn't hear her. The sounds of the rushing waters muffled her terrified cries. The river turned and soon she lost sight of him. Without waiting she dropped to her knees in the mud, lifted her hands to the sky and cried, "I love you! You love me! You said nothing would ever change that! Come back then and save my son!"

She looked around wildly hoping to see God storm onto the scene. She saw nothing. She couldn't wait. She jumped up and ran forward, desperate to save her child. She saw something ahead in the water. For a moment she thought it was a beaver's dam. Her eyes cleared and instead of a dam she recognized the basket Abel had been carrying. She raced forward and got close enough to see that a large branch of a fallen tree had reached out and caught the basket Abel had refused to release. There in the rushing water her son clung for his life to the basket miraculously hung up on a tree branch.

Praying loudly all the way, Eve cautiously made her way down the slope. She ventured toward the fallen log. Frantically calling out to Abel with instructions to hang on, she checked for sturdiness and carefully made her way onto the branch where her son struggled to keep a grip on a slipping basket.

With more strength than she possessed, she grabbed his one free hand, and lifted him and the empty basket out of the rapids and onto the branch. Eventually, they made their way together to land and safety. When they returned home she ran to the fields to find and tell Adam the story. That night, Adam, Eve, Cain, and Abel got down on their knees and prayed to God for the first time as a family. Adam and Eve apologized for keeping him at arm's length for so long and vowed to do better seeking him, and not just when their lives were a mess.

Each parent was emotional as they thanked God for saving Abel's life. The four family members held hands. The parents asked God to receive, love, and protect both of their children for as long as they lived. They asked him not to hold their previous sins against them and to start afresh with these innocent children.

God heard them and gently sighed. He watched and listened as Adam and Eve encouraged their sons to talk to the God of Love they hadn't been introduced to yet. He thought of another son. He reminded himself he had reason to feel optimistic.

CHAPTER 17

I T WAS A LONG FLIGHT AND THEY WERE PROBABLY ONLY A THIRD of the way there. Katie was back offering fruit and cheese trays for anyone awake and looking for a snack. They both accepted and she set down individual trays with packages of crackers, brought Adam a fresh cup of coffee and Grace a cup of tea.

"Is the story about Cain killing Abel really true?" she asked, hoping it wasn't insensitive to ask.

The question didn't seem to bother him. "It's true."

Grace stirred a little sugar into her tea while Adam poured the rest of the cream into his coffee. "I'm sure it was hard to have a child you loved so much kill his brother."

Adam thought about the early days with his children. "I'm not sure I ever loved Cain after he started to talk," he answered truthfully. "Eve and I both loved Abel so much but his brother was a terror and difficult to love, even though I can say we both honestly tried."

"His temper was his downfall," Adam explained, taking a drink of his coffee and setting the cup down on the napkin, "and a constant threat to us all." He remembered the difficulties they'd had raising Cain. His wrath surfaced unexpectedly and almost daily without provocation. Adam told Grace once he'd made Cain a toy shovel. One afternoon Cain attempted to walk for the first time. Adam had taken the shovel Cain was playing with and walked a few paces away. He'd held the toy in his hand and told Cain if he wanted it he'd have to come get it. Cain stood up, fell down, once and then again. When he saw no one was coming immediately to rescue him he screamed and pounded his fists on the floor in frustration.

Adam, seeing he was not going to try again, walked over and leaned down to pick him up. As he did Cain grabbed the shovel out of his hand and angrily hit Adam in the face with it.

Adam remembered crying over the event. To have his child strike him was all the evidence he needed; rage lived not deeply but close to the surface within his son, hardly more than a baby. The species of Man was corrupted, ruined, and irreparably tainted he concluded. And he and Eve were responsible.

Through no fault of Cain's, Adam knew the sins of the father had been passed genetically to the sons. When Cain hit him, he seemed more like an animal than a descendant of God. Adam felt shame and horror for the innocence they'd stolen from the world.

Even though Adam had vowed to rule his children with a strong hand, guilt reversed his position and he and Eve became the first, however certainly not the last, overly permissive parents. As many of their descendants would experience, they didn't know how to battle the angry demon that possessed their son, so they fed it. When Cain threw a tantrum, they gave in to his demands. They learned to reduce the number and severity of outbursts by anticipating his every desire even before he expressed it. When they fell short, they moved out of the way until the storm passed.

"You had the original problem child," Grace sympathized.

"And the original good child. Abel was as good as Cain was violent. He bore Cain's outbursts with patience and love. If Cain took his wrath out on his younger brother, Abel forgave him immediately, even making excuses for him. Abel never once retaliated.

"I was always afraid one day Cain would kill Abel. Abel just would not defend himself against his brother. Watching Abel's passivity is when I seriously began to worry for the future of all mankind. What if all the future Cains eventually wiped out their more passive brothers?

"When Cain fulfilled my fears and murdered Abel I lost all hope for the world's future." Adam pulled the grapes from their stems. "At that point I was sure God would admit he'd lost the war. 'Let it be written' on the seventh day God rested, on the eighth he stood in shock, and on the ninth he pulled the covers over his head."

"What did he do?" Grace took a bite of apple slice.

"I know what I wanted him to do," he said, twisting his ring again. "I wanted God to call in the author for a script rewrite. I wanted him to give in and give us a bath in some holy water. Fix us. I wanted my family to be pure again. I begged God to give us a flesh transfusion, trade in our hot-headed, despondent, pessimistic, passive, manipulative, and depressed ways for our old clear-headed, healthy, passionate, optimistic natures. To forgive us and make us whole again. More than anything I wanted us to be free. Away from the constant badgering and torment of the enemy. God assured me that he had a redemption plan. But all he would say is, 'He's coming.'

Shortly after Abel's death Eve became pregnant with Seth. She had severe morning sickness. The birth was hard. When I realized God was moving forward with an imperfect creation, one so easily prone to anger and violence, I fell into a great depression."

"Because you thought Cain or one of his heirs would do the same thing to Seth as he did to Abel?"

"Sure, who could stand up to Cain or any son he was likely to sire? His goal was to bully, intimidate, control, or destroy anything and anybody and he certainly was equipped with the weapons of destruction to make an easy task of it."

She asked, "Maybe God kept going because he saw such goodness in Abel?"

"Possibly. But because Cain's violence was so commanding, so dominant, we didn't believe anything good could survive in the wake of something so brutal," he admitted. "Good people, more passive in nature, wouldn't stand a chance, we thought. We were sure the world would be overrun by the Canaanites."

Grace inwardly shuttered. Who wasn't worried about the possibility of that still? Adam continued, "Later when I was on better speaking terms with God, we talked about it and he told me that Cain and bullies like him were a threat to Seth and good people like him, but Cain was certainly no threat to God.

"We learned as a people that God shows up in the same measure as what we turn over control to him. We give him a little, he takes a little. We give him a lot, he comes in with guns blazing. It didn't take us long to figure out in the end we were no match for Cain and his tribes. His ways turned out to be nothing short of evil. He didn't fight the powers of Satan, he embraced them, tried to corral them, and use them to his advantage. We saw that and it scared us almost to death. But soon we realized the Lord was our strength. As long as we relied on God to fight our battles with us, to go before us, he always somehow managed to protect us from Cain and his band of terrorists."

"Do you think he's still willing to do that? Now?"

"Things are no different today than they were then. Our enemies no less formidable, daunting, or scary. What we give to God he handles. What we keep, we handle. So, what do you think a good strategy would be?"

She said, "Well, a growing population of both sides seem to be loading up the arsenals and I'm not sure how much God's been invited to either party. I think lots of people, like my mom, are still praying but they think in the end the bullies will have the day. Don't you think God's just going to stand back and watch the whole thing implode?"

"What? That he doesn't know how to put a plan together? What he builds anyone can come in and just destroy? Won't guarantee what he starts he can finish?

"No," he insisted. "That's the point, Grace. He's God Almighty. And all that power, everything we need to restore our Garden fortress, is available to us through him. God hasn't left us here defenseless without his resources. Jesus is the door and the way back and the Father's storehouse is open to anyone who partners with him through the Holy Spirit.

"We can win, Grace. Nothing of this world or below can defeat us if we, not just pray to God, but *partner* with him. Talk to him. Listen and do what he says. Know that he'll do his part. Don't break ranks. Stay connected and know that if God is for us then who can be against us? No matter what happens in the land of the Cains."

"But are you sure God's paying attention? He's still interested and working on a plan? He didn't lose interest? Not going to let the devil destroy us all?" she asked dubiously. "How do you know he hasn't checked out? Said 'I sent you Jesus, what more do you want? You take it from here. See you when you're dead. Or not.'"

Adam gave her a look and she felt a little like the chastised unbeliever that she was.

He took a drink of his coffee and after a moment continued with his story. "Whereas Cain was the child that poured salt into my wounds, Abel was the balm that soothed them. To the degree in which Cain acted out, Abel made up for it."

Adam remembered something he hadn't thought of for years. Cain had been sick in bed with the flu. During brief periods between retching, he had screamed at his mother and father if they'd never sinned, he wouldn't be sick.

As he vomited, Eve held his head and prayed God would heal him. God didn't respond. Cain berated his mother and Adam. As they each silently mouthed their prayers he cried, "Fools! God's not going to help you. You're wasting your breath," he hurled at them. Both were devastated because they thought he was probably right.

Cain eventually recovered but his parents didn't. Each replayed their son's cruel accusations repeatedly to themselves. Eve silently withdrew, realizing the futility of hoping for family unity or consistently answered prayers. The devil whispered to her in the night, "How can you love a God who ignores you? Can't be counted on to come to the rescue? He's gone, Woman! Your life is never going to be what it used to be." Her faith further waned as she started to fall out of love with God again. Her hair started to fall out. She gained weight. She and Adam started to quarrel again regularly.

'Abel noticed the change. One afternoon he came crawling into the house screaming in anguish. He claimed he'd fallen out of a tree and broken his leg. He bellowed with pain as Eve attempted to examine him. He watched his parents as they stood by helpless, not knowing how to help him.

"Pray for me!" he commanded.

Adam and Eve stood unsteadily in the middle of the room watching their son writhe in pain.

"Pray!" Abel insisted.

Adam and Eve looked helplessly at each other. Both knew the other was remembering their last unanswered prayers and Cain's taunts that followed. They were hesitant to try again.

But Abel would not be denied his prayer. Finally, Eve and Adam knelt in front of him. They offered up a short prayer asking God to heal their son and take away his pain.

Before the prayer reached God's ears, Abel jumped up and began dancing around the room. "I'm healed!" he squealed. Abel praised God and his parents loudly. He hopped around on one foot gleefully wiggling his healed leg in the air as witness to God's faithfulness.

Adam and Eve stared open-mouthed at the obvious ruse. Adam swore later to Eve he'd heard God laugh.

Cain was not so astute and did not detect the deception. Instead, he became incensed at God's blatant favoritism.

Neither parent knew how to handle the situation. Eventually they left the room, allowing both boys to believe a lie. One son angry and bitter, rejected by God. The other believing in his ability to save his downtrodden parents.

"Cain abused us. Abel rescued us," Adam said.

"What eventually happened to Cain?"

Adam shook his head sadly. "Our weariness for his bad boy behavior grew. Eve and I decided to stop placating him and tried ignoring his tantrums instead. His rage only increased."

"I finally lost all patience with the outbursts and the havoc he wreaked in our home. He was too big to throttle but I did what I could. I used threats, sanctions, and bribery."

"Did any of it work?"

"Not a bit. He got worse. It was like he was working up to a show-down." He took another drink of his coffee. "Periodically we had cele-brations, sort of like Thanksgiving, where we gave God presents. Thank you offerings for what he'd done for us. It was a big deal and everyone spent a lot of time preparing special gifts for him. But when God saw Cain's present, he ignored it. Yet highly praised Abel's. It was the last straw for Cain."

"Why did God do that?"

Adam tried to remember. "A couple of reasons, I think," he said. "Cain gave God an offering in order to get something; Abel, in order to give something. Abel loved God out of a place in his heart none of us quite understood. His gift to him, his favorite first-born lamb, the best from his flock, was motivated by that love. Cain's gift was also from his trade as a farmer, but nothing more than an elaborate bribe."

He took another sip of coffee. "Cain actually worked night and day and his presentation to the Lord was really outstanding. But his motive was clearly to one-up his brother. Abel put together a much less showy offering, but it was one he gave God from his heart. Abel was grateful for everything God gave him. Cain would have stolen God's wallet had he left it out in the open. In fact, at the last minute he held back part of the gift intended for God for himself."

"How did God respond?"

"He wasn't impressed," Adam answered dryly. "Cain considered God good for one thing, a means to an end. If God wasn't going to co-operate then Cain wanted no part of him. God knew Cain would even-tually dump him. God calls himself 'I Am' not 'I Do.' He's alive, he has feelings. The creation of his family is his love gift to himself. His greatest desire is to give love and receive it, both without conditions. He was and is opposed to simply being used for his power."

Grace remembered her earlier blowup when she told Adam God

didn't deserve to be loved because of what she considered his poor performance. But Adam said God wants unconditional love just as people do. That was hard for Grace to grasp but remembered Adam saying that Man is created in God's image. But what does that actually mean? Is it an emotional resemblance? Spiritual? Moral? Intellectual? All of the above? None of the above? If God wants to be loved unconditionally and most people only want him to answer their prayers wouldn't there be a big disconnect in the relationship? Wouldn't both sides, Man and God, undoubtedly have unmet expectations? Not being a religious person, she didn't have a clue. She went back to Adam's story. "So what happened?" she asked Adam curiously, taking a sip of her tea.

"Cain blew up at God like he blew up at the rest of us. God, being God, didn't respond. That's when Cain decided to punish us all."

"By murdering his brother?"

Adam nodded. "Vengeance and jealousy. When God confirmed what Cain already suspected, that Abel was more pleasing, he lost it. He bludgeoned his brother to death." Adam was silent for a moment remembering the pain of the event. Eventually he said, "After the murder, Cain did what he had wanted to do for a long time. He left."

Grace tried to visualize the events Adam described. "I thought God chased him away," she said.

"Cain wanted to go but it was out of mercy for us all, especially Eve, that God drove him completely out of the land."

"Why out of mercy?"

"He probably would have killed us all eventually," he said. "He was so verbally abusive it was only a matter of time. Finally, God said, 'Enough!' and made him leave us alone."

Grace pulled her own grapes off their stems. "Poor Eve," she said empathetically.

"Yes. It was too much for her. She cried as we stood in the doorway watching him pack. One son dead, the other his murderer. There were no police. No juvenile detention where we could send him. We weren't strong enough to deal with him. It took God to make him go.

"He broke a favorite piece of his mother's pottery on his way out, a vase full of water and flowers left over from the Day of Offering, as he swaggered out the door. Instead of apologizing, he picked up a broken piece of pottery, cut his own hand, and let the blood fall onto the floor and wreckage. He kicked the broken pieces out of the way, told us the blood of the world was on our hands, and told us to keep the pieces around as a reminder of what we'd done to him, our family, and to all of creation."

Adam looked at Grace and waited for a comment. She said nothing. He leaned back in his seat and they both sat in silence until finally he said, "I kept a piece of that pottery with his blood in a box until Jesus snuck into my house like a thief in the night and replaced it with something I still keep on my mantle today."

CHAPTER 18

G RACE WAS STUNNED. "YOU HAVE SOMETHING IN YOUR house that Jesus gave you?" Adam nodded and she sat and stared at him in the dark. As ridiculous as it sounded even in her own head, she thought, *You should give that to the Smithsonian. Or to the Vatican.* Overwhelmed and thinking that for the sake of her own sanity she needed to get back on stable ground, and not knowing what else to say she asked, "Then is it Seth's descendants that are God's family now?"

"We're all God's family, Grace. However, at that time it was Seth's offspring who continued to follow God, have faith in him, and who benefitted from his presence. Cain's family never acknowledged him. They rejected him. Sided with the enemy. Told God to take a hike. They didn't pray, couldn't care less what God wanted, took whatever they could plunder, left the rest in shatters. They cultivated their own strength relentlessly, their goal to capture their weaker brethren, enslave us, and dominate the Earth. Their motto: 'Survival of the fittest. The rest be damned.'"

Grace suddenly felt sorry for God. "To be so rejected and have your children turn on you, almost declare war against you, that must've been hard on him," she said, suddenly empathetic towards an Almighty just hours before she doubted even existed.

Adam continued, noting the change. "No doubt. But to further answer your question, we're all the sons and daughters of God. But spiritually speaking, every person who walks upon the Earth from God's perspective is either a Seth or a Cain. A person who wants him or a person who doesn't. It's that simple.

"But God tells everyone we must choose. Pick a side. Commit. In Cain, he saw first-hand not everyone would want him. One of the natures of Love is that it doesn't force itself on anyone. We might all be his by blood, but if we don't want to be with him then, like Cain, he's not going to make anyone call him God. Let alone Father, or Savior, and certainly not Friend. We can choose him or not. It's up to us. But he does want to know. And in the end, he's still responsible for us all."

"Can you still go to heaven if you don't want anything to do with God?"

He said, "I don't know." Then added, "Probably not."

"Why not?" she scoffed. "Certainly he wouldn't send people to hell just because they don't care for him."

"I didn't say anything about hell. But in order to have eternal life we have stay connected to God. Through Jesus. The Bible says we can't get to the Father except through the Son."

Grace interjected, "Why Jesus? Why not Buddha or Mohammed or any other god? Who cares what we call him?"

It was his turn to scoff. "Uh, God cares. Jesus isn't just one of a smorgasbord of gods for people to pick and choose from. He's one-third of the Trinity. The Alpha and the Omega. Alive from the beginning. He's as much God as is the Father. So is the Holy Spirit. All three are God, just different expressions. Also, it was Jesus, our big brother, who came in the flesh and who paid the price and won the world and our futures back from the enemy. He came because the Father asked him to and because we need him. Buddha, Mohammed, or any other god cannot save us, transform us, or save our planet. Only Jesus can claim that honor.

"Also, heaven isn't a hotel for nice people," he added. "It's God's home. It's not a person's right to live in the castle if they don't care much for the king but simply don't like the alternative housing choices. That's called trespassing. Let those people find someplace else to rest their head at night. God's under no obligation to provide for them if they reject him. Why should he be? Especially since there's no upfront fee to move in. It's just making a choice before you actually hit the gates whether you want God or not and acknowledge it's Jesus that got you there."

Grace never thought of it like that. Even though her mother and sister made it clear they thought she was booked on a one-way flight to hell, she had adopted the theory that when a person died, based on their karma, good or bad, they'd go with other people of like mind. Based on what Adam said she wondered if that was true. "Is there anything else you have to do besides choose God to live in heaven with him after you die?" she asked aloud. "What if you never consulted him a day in your life about, well, anything?"

"We're all God's children, whether a biological Seth or a Cain, the invitation to come home extends to everyone. Jews, Gentiles, prodigal sons and daughters alike. No matter what you've done. Or didn't do. The only choice that really matters is whether you want to be in his family or not. Just send a reply accepting the offer. However, if you want your life to significantly improve, if you want to manifest heaven on Earth, fully walk in God's greatest plans for you, you've got to get in the game."

She asked, "If salvation is a free gift you get by accepting Christ, why do I need to 'get in the game?'"

Adam replied, "I said if you want all God has for you here on Earth. To do that, you've got to put in some effort. But your salvation *is* free. Heaven after death costs you nothing but the choice. However, achieving your full potential while you're still alive? Now that takes dedication. And a lot of it."

She said doubtfully, "But are you sure about what it takes to get into heaven after you die? My mother says the gates of hell are wide open but the gates to heaven are narrow. Hardly anyone gets in. She says people have to toe the line or you're out!" She motioned her thumb strongly towards the window.

Adam replied, "Personally, I think that's why so many people have so much angst about God, religion, and sin. And why God's intentions towards us get so misrepresented. It's because that passage in the Bible is misunderstood by so many."

"How so?"

"Jesus says in the Bible 'The gates of heaven are narrow and only those who enter through the narrow gate will find life.'" She nodded and he continued, "But what many don't realize is the term 'heaven' in the Bible has more than one meaning. Jesus wasn't talking in those verses about our eternal salvation. That's free to everyone who receives Christ. John 3:16 promises it. He was talking about heaven's narrow gates as a holy state of being."

"Not the place you go after you die?"

Adam shook his head. "No. The kingdom of heaven in this passage means God's full expression within a person's life. The state of that rare person's life who's actually given up everything to follow Christ."

"How could anybody do *that*?" she asked aloud but thought silently, *Or even want to?*

"That's why Jesus says the gates are narrow. It's not easy at all but it's the only way to find complete peace, power, purpose, rest, joy, and honestly near euphoria so much of the time while you're still alive. It's perfect love. A life without fear. It's Paradise. Eden. Heaven. On Earth."

She teetered between disbelief and fascination. "Seriously? That's all achievable? On Earth?"

He nodded. "Yep. But you've got to be willing to give it all up in order to get there. Most people will never do it."

"What's that actually mean? Sell all your stuff and move to Zimbabwe?"

He laughed. "Not hardly. Giving up everything to follow Christ," he replied, "doesn't usually mean becoming a missionary or a monk or living in poverty. Finding life, by entering through the narrow gate, in plain English means being 'all in' with Jesus. In practicality, it means that you give God full authority to transform you and your life from who you are to who you have the potential to fully become. You put everything you are, everything you think, and everything you have on God's altar and you let him decide what stays and what goes. You don't pretend you didn't hear him or rationalize it away when he asks you to give something up or tell him to stop when the transformation gets painful. Based on how entrenched you are in your current life depends on how painful the remodel."

"Yowsa," she said. "Like I said, who would do that?"

He nodded emphatically. "Right? But it's why Jesus said, 'Pick up your cross and follow me,' and why Paul wrote 'Run your race like you're the only one to win the prize.' Both knew life through the narrow gates is fantastic and worth the effort. They were both talking about Paradise."

"Full self-actualization?"

"Umm. Something like that. But more on God's terms."

She considered that. "So Jesus wasn't telling people to actually die?"

He shook his head. "No, Jesus was challenging people to die to 'self,' the flesh, by becoming 'all in.' He was challenging people to let God give them a total makeover. Giving God permission to pluck everything out of their lives that was holding them back from being everything he created them to be."

"Hmm," she said thoughtfully, "it sounds good but I bet in reality that would hurt like hell."

He chuckled again. "I've done it. It does hurt like hell at times. But the reward is certainly worth it. The result, if you don't quit, is that you make it into Eden, the land flowing with milk and honey. On Earth. You become all you're destined to become and your world reflects it."

"But you have to give him everything?" she asked unbelieving.

He smiled. "If you want the grand prize at the end of the race you do. Everything. Your thinking, emotions, circumstances, relationships, religious theology, finances, self-reliance . . ."

She was confused. "So if you don't have to be poor to make it, why did Jesus tell the rich guy in the Bible he couldn't get into heaven unless he gave away all his stuff? You can't be 'all in' if you're rich?"

Adam smiled and said, "I'm rich and I'm in. But that rich guy's money occupied God's throne inside his heart. Money was his god. Jesus knew it. So, when he asked Jesus what it would take to become a full believer, 'all in,' Jesus said, 'Give up your money and come on!' The guy couldn't do it. That prompted Jesus to say, 'It's almost impossible for a rich person to enter into the kingdom of heaven.' Some things are harder to let go of than others. Money is definitely a big one."

She nodded. "I can certainly see that."

He continued, "Giving up our idols, and their trappings, is tough for anybody. It takes a lot of faith and desire to stay the course. That's why Jesus said the gates to the kingdom of heaven are narrow. He wasn't saying you have to meet a set of requirements to get into the physical heaven when you die and it also wasn't a criticism of the rich man. He knows that people are human. The kingdom of heaven, total inhabitation of God in your life, is like the Superbowl for Christians. It's worth it but you've got to have the stomach for it along the way."

Grace asked, "I don't think I'd ever want to try that hard, personally. Why would anyone?"

He answered, "Most people don't and that's perfectly okay. Like I said, the narrow gates are the Superbowl. Usually at the end of a Christian's life they end up someplace in the middle. Not at the starting gate, but not exactly turning water into wine and raising the dead."

"That's for sure," she muttered.

He continued, "But the more a person turns over to God, the more their life and being start to look like Christ's. And the soul you develop on Earth, the one Jesus saves, is the one you'll keep for an eternity. Give it the care and attention it deserves."

"Care for my soul because it stays with me after I die?"

He responded, "The Bible says, 'Don't lay your riches up on Earth.' You will prosper as your *soul* prospers, *eternally*. People are going to live for zillions of years, Grace, after they leave planet Earth. Who wants a weak soul as your engine? So I like to suggest that people at least try working on themselves. Evolve. Strengthen your spiritual muscles. Partner with God, become as Christlike as possible and gain access to the greatest gifts imaginable. Power, Authority, Love, Truth. Things on Earth don't last. Be a long-term planner, Grace. Don't just live for today. Think about the next zillions of years. Use the time here wisely. You've only got so much time at Gym Earth. Get in the game, girl!" he commanded encouragingly.

She felt a little convicted but at the same time amazingly encouraged. She took a moment to consider her options and soon asked realistically, "What if you only want to make the playoffs? Not make it all the way to the Superbowl? Can you do just a little work?"

He smiled. "Absolutely. Just know that whatever you turn over to God he will transform. Whether it's a little or a lot. It's totally up to you. But in the end, your eternal salvation is guaranteed if you accept Christ.

"John 3:16. Everlasting life is a free gift to all and requires absolutely nothing but accepting the invitation. No work is required. But if you want to help run the universe while hanging out with Jesus and some other heavy hitters, well, that's an option too!"

Grace looked out the window into the darkness, listened to the hum of the engines, and thought about all Adam had said. Her head was spinning as her paradigms split under the nuclear light of her Adam bomb. "I thought getting into heaven is about being a good person. I thought it's all about following the rules and sliding in through that narrow gate. I thought I had to let God and the church control me. Tell me what to do. I didn't think being with God had anything to do with simply wanting him. I certainly don't want to play in any spiritual Superbowl, but I might like to 'get in the game' a little. Play in the shallow end. Do you think God would be okay with that?"

"Sure. Like any good dad God's more interested in your willingness to come home, not how hard you play the game. Prodigal son, Mother Teresa, or anything in between. It's your choice. And no one's perfect, Grace. God's not expecting it, so let it go."

CHAPTER 19

G RACE WAS THOUGHTFUL FOR SEVERAL MOMENTS AND THEN thought to ask, "But what if murderers, rapists, and drug dealers choose God? Will he take them?"

Adam was trying to get Katie's attention who was talking with the passengers in row two. He answered Grace absent-mindedly. "If in their hearts they want him, he does."

Katie saw him, approached and asked sweetly, "What can I do you for?"

"Do you have any chips or anything?" he asked. "I'm still hungry."

She laughed like no one had ever asked her that before. "Sure! Let me see what I can find."

"But how's that fair?" Grace protested once Katie had retreated to the galley.

"How's what fair?" Adam tried to remember her original question. "Oh right. Murderers and drug dealers." He answered, "What's fair got to do with love? With family? If Cain walked in the door I'd buy him a drink. Try to get to know him again. If he apologized, I'd take him back into my life. Carefully at first, but I'd try. He's still my son. Why wouldn't God do the same?"

Katie returned with a bag of SunChips and a bag of Fritos. "Will these work? I stole them from my private stash."

Adam snatched them from her enthusiastically and smiled broadly. "These are perfect. Thank you, Katie!"

She winked at him and said, "My stash is your stash!" He laughed appreciatively and ripped open the Fritos as she swayed back toward the galley.

"But don't people get in trouble for what they've done?" Grace asked, shaking her head at his offer to share his snack.

Adam shrugged and said between bites, "There's a lot about that we don't know, Grace. A lot. However, just because God wants his family home and forgives our sins doesn't mean justice isn't served. If you kill someone God doesn't just sweep it under the rug and say, 'Don't worry about it and if you do it again tomorrow, well, that's okay too.' Society couldn't survive that sort of justice." He dropped a Frito on the floor, leaned down to pick it up, and placed it into the empty bag. He crinkled the bag and stuffed it partially into the seat pocket in front of him. He ripped open the bag of SunChips and once again offered to share them with Grace who declined.

He continued. "God tells us to forgive others but knows people can't just forgive someone who's abused them unless we have the assurance that somehow the scales get balanced," he elaborated. "As the King of Justice, God promises us he'll make sure that justice is served.

Justice is the very *foundation* for forgiveness, Grace. Real forgiveness is only possible if we can be comforted knowing justice is not blind."

"So a person might go into spiritual rehab or something if they die still planning to murder somebody on their way to heaven?"

He chomped on a few more chips before answering. "I don't know. I just know in the end it's made right by God for all parties concerned."

Grace contemplated the ceiling then said, "But, however it's dealt with, if you're the abuser God doesn't throw it up to you anymore once it's over?"

"Your mother might, but God won't," he said, finishing the bag. "Nobody knows exactly what happens during a person's day of atonement. It's a mystery. But whatever the outcome," he assured her, "if we RSVP each person ends up at God's dinner table resting comfortably knowing justice has already been served and we're all moving on to dessert. Because he loves us and if we love him," he held out his hands palms up, "then in the end nothing else is more important."

Adam handed Anna his two empty bags as she passed by. Grace remembered a recent shopping outing with her mother and sister that ended badly. She was grateful they had come in separate cars.

They were at the mall trying on shoes and a young teenage boy and his girlfriend walked by. The girl had on a crop top with her belly button pierced. She had on super short shorts and the boy couldn't keep his hands off her. After they walked by Grace's sister said under her breath, "Slut."

Grace looked at her sister and said coolly, "Better than being a cold fish."

Her sister retorted smoothly, "Oh, that's right. You probably have a pair of shorts just like that you wear to work at night, don't you?" And they were off. Grace's mother ended up in tears. Grace stormed out of the mall and left her mother and sister in the shoe department at Nordstrom with the salesclerk as witness to the entire encounter.

She said to Adam, "And you're sure it's not all about the sin? God's not clicking his tongue at those of us who color outside the lines from time to time?"

He smiled. "It's about the choice and the journey. Living responsibly, morally, and yet at full throttle. Embracing your God-given potential. People's sins still need to be dealt with because they get in the way. You deal with your crap because it's the healthy and moral thing to do. Not just because of a religious mandate."

Grace looked out the window into the darkness and listened to the hum of the engine. "I thought it was about following the rules. I didn't think being with God had anything to do with wanting him. I honestly didn't think there was anybody out there who really cared that much."

"Yeah, well, you and a lot of other people. Like I said, God's a person with feelings. Connect with him and you'll find out. He's love in person." He suddenly had another thought and said, "For just a second, Grace, forget what you think you know about 'God' and envision what you think Love would look like as a person instead." He paused and let her think for a moment. She closed her eyes and in a minute she smiled and a look of peace washed across her face. "Yeah," he said. "Go with that guy."

She frowned. "Somebody should've told me this years ago. I feel stupid. Duped. I thought sin was center stage and everything God related revolved around that. Thinking heaven was only for the elite few who could somehow miraculously squeeze in through the narrow gate but knowing it would never be me. I thought love from God was something I had to achieve. The better I am, the more love I deserve." She said to herself, *I didn't know he already does. Why didn't somebody tell me this? Look what I've missed!* She suddenly felt renewed anger at her mother, the overall church, society in general.

The Texan had fallen asleep and was snoring loudly. She chewed on her hangnail absent-mindedly and in a few minutes had second thoughts. She asked tentatively, "He may not be mad, but don't you think God should have a reason to want to be with us? I mean there's so many of us. Why wouldn't he just choose the best from the herd to hang out with?"

Adam laughed out loud. "I would. But I'm not God."

"I would too. Why do you think he doesn't?"

He thought for a minute before answering. "He's not a man, Grace, but he is a father. We're made in his image, but we can't really grasp all the moving parts. But this is what I do know. He loves each one of us because, like any father, there's a unique part of himself he's placed in each one of us. He gave every single person something special he didn't give to anyone else. Something that makes us each irresistible to him, touches his heart in a way no one else can." He closed his eyes and added, "It's like having an itch only one kid can scratch. No matter how everyone else tries, no one can satisfy it but that one kid. That's the love of a highly devoted father."

Grace asked, "But what if that one kid's beyond hope? A disappointment? Maybe even a real loser? Hit bottom so many times it's finally become his ceiling?"

Adam looked at Grace in the filtered light of the cabin and decided he needed to give the answer some real thought and not just offer an off the cuff response. For reasons he could not fathom, the question seemed important to her and possibly even a sticking point in her seeking a relationship with God. He finally said, "Tell me someone in your life who you really love. A lot."

Immediately she said, "My best friend, Charice."

"Why? Is it because she's such a good person? Never gets it wrong?"

Grace laughed out loud. "Well, she is a very good person, but she smokes like a chimney, she's got every shoe ever made, I'm afraid to ride in a car with her, and she finds the devil in a bottle of tequila," she laughed joyfully. Finally, after considerable thought she said a little more seriously, "She has a way about her. Nothing I can really pinpoint. It's just her way. Maybe her smile. Maybe her laugh. Probably her brutal honesty." She thought again and said, "Honestly, I really don't know. It's just how she makes me feel when I'm with her, I guess. I just love her."

Adam nodded in understanding, then asked again, "Got any nieces, nephews, or family members you really love?'

She quickly jumped in and said, "Oh my, yes. I have a niece I'm crazy about. How she came out of my dipshit sister, I'll never know." She paused and added, "Excuse my French."

He asked, "Did you tell her mother that before you'd accept her into the family you'd have to wait until she was old enough to display her character and moral compass? That you'd decide how much you loved her once you'd seen her report card? Wait until you found out if she'd ever lie, cheat, steal, get drunk or high and end up in jail? Before you'd let her into your heart?"

"Well, of course not," she said definitively. "I loved her as family even before she was born. Her 'belonging' has never been a question. Our whole family loved her with all our hearts once we knew she existed in my sister's womb. My mom, my sister, my dad. She's ours. She could never do anything to change that."

Adam looked at her and asked, "And what if she became a murderer? A thief? A prostitute? Slept with every guy in town? Got captured by some pimp and did unspeakable things because she'd lost all her self-worth? Maybe she didn't have any money and did what she had to do to survive. Didn't have anyone to help her. Would you dump her? Shame her?"

Grace shook her head in the dark and answered truthfully, "I'd bawl my eyes out."

"But she was raised in such a good family. It would be her fault, wouldn't it? Wouldn't it be because of some almost unforgiveable flaw in her? Wouldn't you roll your eyes behind her back thinking 'What a loser'? Throw up a wall around your heart, keep her out, and only let her back in once she'd gotten her act together?"

"No," she said slowly, thinking. "I'd save her."

"How?" he asked.

After a moment she said, "First I'd try to influence her while she was still a child to keep that from happening. You know, help teach her the right way to live. But God forbid, if it did happen, I'd do anything I could to appeal to her and get her some help."

"But let it be her choice, right?'

"If I could, otherwise she'd probably go right back to what she was doing and probably resent me for the intervention," she nodded. "But I think eventually," Grace's eyes teared up, "if she were trapped and couldn't get away, or just couldn't see the light, it would be too much for my heart to handle. I'd probably go in with guns blazing and make her come with me."

"Even spend a bunch of your own money to help her get free?"

"All I have," Grace vowed.

"Hmmm. That just seems so unfair," he parroted her words. "You know. To your other nieces and nephews who possibly could have always behaved."

"Well, if you're making a comparison to God," she said, "I would never threaten to send her to hell for her sins. No matter what she'd done."

"Because she'd already found it, right? You'd just do everything you could to free her. But eventually, if she wouldn't come willingly, would you take away her free will? Isn't that what you said?" He paused until Grace slowly nodded, then he questioned, "So let me ask you, Grace. How long would you wait before you told her you didn't think she has what it takes to turn it around? One year? Two?" He let her think of all possible scenarios and finally said, "How long would you let her stay in hell before you kidnapped her, broke her leg, if necessary, to keep her from running and took away her free will? Went to court and took guardianship of her?"

"Is that what God's going to do in the end?"

Adam shrugged and said, "We're made in God's image, Grace. If we couldn't stand to lose a family member who knows what God's going to do. The Bible says in the end every knee shall bow and every tongue confess that Jesus Christ is Lord. So no one, regardless of what they claim, really knows how it will all play out in the end. But the Bible does say that if we believe we are assured of eternal life. It also says, 'It's better to believe without having to see than to have to see to believe.' So for me and my house," he claimed passionately, "we believe!"

She turned back to Adam and said, "People like me need to hear this stuff in plain English. Have you ever thought of writing it down?"

CHAPTER 20

KATIE SUDDENLY SHOWED UP WITH MORE WATER AND AN extra teabag for Grace. She looked at Adam and said, "You two certainly have found a lot to talk about. Are you having your own little slumber party? Are you still hungry?"

Adam smiled, shook his head and complained, "Too much coffee, Katie. This is your fault." Katie laughed and made her way back to her jump seat in the front, where she and Anna were keeping each other company. After just a minute the seatbelt sign was illuminated, and the co-pilot came out of the cockpit to use the restroom. He spoke to both attendants. Immediately Katie stood up and entered the cockpit, allowing the co-pilot to continue into the lavatory.

Grace asked, "Do you know why when a pilot comes out of the cockpit a flight attendant always goes in?"

Adam answered, "In 2015 there was an accident involving an aircraft when the captain entered the washroom and the co-pilot, left alone, crashed the plane. Nobody knew what really happened. One theory was the co-pilot intentionally crashed the plane, another was he passed out, but regardless, the cockpit door was locked, and the pilot couldn't get back in. After which the airlines regulated one pilot should not be left alone in the cockpit if the other one steps out."

Grace asked, "How do you know that?"

Adam laughed and replied, "Don't ask." And she didn't.

Dean, Adam's co-worker, tapped him on the shoulder and said, "Hey, do you have a minute? There's a problem with this bid."

Adam turned to Grace, excused himself, and stepped into the aisle to talk with his co-workers. She leaned her seat back a little further and moved her purse slightly, giving her a little more room to stretch her legs. She closed her eyes and took the opportunity to think about all Adam had revealed.

Grace thought about Cain and Seth and how every person born after them falls into one spiritual camp or the other—those who choose God, and those who don't. Adam didn't seem to be too distraught about his sons' or the world's choices any longer even though it was obvious he was on a mission to let people know Eden was open for business again. He seemed to have at least reasonably accepted that every person has free will and what happens from here is out of his hands. God loves us all, has a plan, an open-door policy, and people can enter or not. Our choice. If we put some spiritual muscle into it, our worlds can look like Paradise. That seemed to be reasonably good enough for Adam.

Grace had agreed to stop acting as his therapist that evening but helping people is not something a trained analyst automatically turns off, she told herself. Adam said his dilemma was a sudden and unusual loss of contact with God. He'd said he'd lost his rudder and he felt lost. She planned to subtly put him back on the couch.

But suddenly she had another thought. Adam had asked her earlier about her relationship with God and she'd brushed him off. Said she was beyond hope. The night wasn't about her. It was his therapy session, she'd told him. However, she wasn't his therapist anymore. Just his friend. And after a thorough evaluation, she had to admit honestly to herself that she was actually probably in worse emotional shape than he was. Hadn't just a few hours ago she'd wondered about the plausibility of scoring some legalized pot to help deal with the onset of depression?

She looked out the window into the gray clouds and for a moment tried to remember what it felt like to love God. And even more so, what it felt like to think he loved her back.

In a moment of impetuousness Grace decided to throw caution to the wind. *Go for it,* she told herself. *I'll sober up in the morning.* She let her mind wander towards new possibilities. Could God have orchestrated this plane ride for her? Did he want her back? She chewed on the problematic hangnail. Should she consider it? She reminded herself that she'd already fallen over the cliff of supernatural speculation in agreeing to suspend reality and consider Adam's claims. Why not venture a little further in? Consider what else he might have to say on the subject? If there was any merit to it at all, couldn't it just possibly give Grace what was missing in her life? Something that could fill the empty place in her heart nothing else was equipped to do? Give her some hope? A sense of true purpose? Something healthy and lasting? *No,* she thought suddenly, *someone healthy and lasting.*

But she needed to be practical, she thought, wobbling on her spiritual surfboard. She would wake up in the morning and have questions. After the night was over, she'd probably never see Adam again. If she opened Pandora's box, who did she have who could help her sort things out? Where could she go?

She did a mental scan of friends, colleagues, and acquaintances and found the list wanting. *Certainly not my mother*, she thought. And definitely not her sister. Who else was out there and could help separate fact from fiction? Where could she go? Who could she talk to? Did they have clinics somewhere? Who were the experts? Who knows how to fall in love with God? Certainly she couldn't go back into organized religion. Surely they didn't know anything about falling in love with Jesus, did they? Had the church of her mother moved on from hell and brimstone, walking the tightrope of sin, and graduated to teaching about the nature of the Bridegroom, the God that falls in love? Did they have classes on how to have a relationship with God the person, how to discover his will for your life, the challenges of faith, and how to deal with disappointments in the relationship that were bound to come? Were there guest speakers who knew about Jesus, the door to everything? Who taught how to find Eden on Earth? The role of the Holy Spirit in guiding us back there and how to access God's resources? And no one had told her?

She remembered a recent dinner conversation with her mom and sister. Her mother was complaining about a new song they were singing in their church. It talked about the kisses of Jesus and feeling his breath upon her face. They were still thinking of switching churches over it.

Were there some churches or people who knew about the things Adam claimed were actually in the Bible? Were they mysteries? Fantasies? Heresies? In the Bible God says to be hot or cold towards him, because lukewarm he would spit out of his mouth. That sounded like the statement a lover might make. The Bible says John the Beloved was the disciple that Jesus loved. Didn't he love them all? Doesn't the title denote maybe it was a deeper attachment? A two-way devotion built on a deeper love?

The Bible calls Moses a friend of God, she remembered suddenly. Adam said Jesus was better than a foxhole buddy. He said the Bible says in Hosea that in the last days we'll call God our husband. He was certain that Jesus is the eternal Bridegroom. Wanted to find his rest within her. She'd about had a meltdown over it. *Why?* she asked herself. What was so threatening? Isn't that what she actually *needed*? If it all turned out to be just a fantasy, wouldn't she actually find out pretty quickly? How long could a well-educated, intelligent, logical, not to mention highly cynical person fake an attachment if God didn't participate?

That's when she realized something that had been hidden in her soul since she'd left Jesus, the church, left her dreams, really. Whatever that feeling was she'd had on the balcony as a child dancing with Jesus, had in Sunday school, had at church camp, whether it was right, wrong, truth, or fantasy, Grace wanted it back. She wanted to feel that sort of "in love" again. Not with a mortal man, but with God.

Grace did a quick mental health check on herself. Could it just be that something was so missing in her life she was willing to grasp at straws? Jump at the first solution other than drugs, shopping, sex, or a new book with promising international speaking engagements? Hadn't she already had all that?

She looked out the window again and reminded herself that going to Sunday school then church camp was the happiest time in her life. The love she felt there was the only thing that ever seemed completely *solid* to her. The only relationship that had ever made her feel truly wanted, safe, and complete. But who could help her figure it all out now as an adult? She couldn't go back to Sunday school or church camp. She resolved to google Mrs. Paulus once she got off the plane.

Still, she told herself. She'd had enough conversations with her family, friends, and patients to be fairly certain that the mainstream church was not the place to fall in love with God. Maybe find out about his history, maybe even hear his plans for the world's future. But fall in love? Find out what it means to be his Bride? Love him with her whole heart? Trust him and put him first? Like when she was a child, she wanted to have a *relationship* with God, not just be filled with head knowledge about the logistical principles of faith and morality. *Those you can get from a book,* she told herself. *But what could you get from the author himself?* she wondered.

She listened to the hum of the engines and vacillated again. But even if there was someone out there, did Grace really want to delve into it? Care about God as a person? Have someone or something else making demands on her time? Did she really want to remove him from arm's length where she had him like the Great Oz behind some forbidden celestial curtain? She studied her hands and had not noticed before how much they actually looked like her mother's. She asked herself practically, somewhat fearfully, *What if he asks me to do something? Won't answer every prayer? Or worse yet, makes me battle the wicked witches and bring him their broomsticks? Sends in the flying monkeys if he takes offense at my over-familiarity? Maybe even hurts me for it?*

Then Grace considered her professional career and scoffed internally. She sighed and shook her head. *Forget it,* she told herself regretfully. It would never work. Who was she fooling? She was certain she'd never publicly announce her faith. It would certainly be the death of her reputation as a well-grounded, rational, objective, mental health professional.

Admit publicly she talks to God and *hears* from him? She almost laughed out loud. From internationally respected psychologist to crazy lady fantasizing about a love life with Jesus. Writing Mrs. J. Christ in big cursive letters with hearts and butterflies on her notepad as she listened to her patients ramble on about their childhoods. She took a sip of her cold tea. *Oh, well,* she thought ruefully. *It was a good fantasy while it lasted.*

CHAPTER 21

ADAM CAME BACK A FEW MINUTES LATER AND SAT DOWN. Grace was once again thinking clearly, and she congratulated herself silently on her pragmatism. She'd been open-minded, more than open-minded, she corrected. She had evaluated Adam's arguments, challenged herself to consider another's opinions, and then made an educated decision that fit her lifestyle. Although she would probably never think about God and religion the same way, and her perspective on the Lord had considerably softened, she thought it best to accept that as enough spiritual growth for one night.

Her temporary dive into fantasy abandoned, she gave a slight frown and asked, "This probably doesn't have anything to do with your story, but I want to know something. You obviously are a person of faith."

"I'm a Christian man, yes. What's your question?"

She studied him as if she were observing an unfamiliar and newly detected species. "You appear to be very intelligent, kind, and, frankly, a pretty interesting person. By claiming to be a Christian how can you associate with such a traditional, often times fanatical, order of conservatism?"

Inwardly pleased with her at least partial compliment he coaxed, "Give me an example."

"My parents and their friends don't drink, they don't dance, they don't swear, they're prudes, and they consider themselves superior because of it. They shy away from acknowledging any 'carnal enjoyment' except when it comes to food. And they make these stupid religious jokes suggesting God amuses himself by casually and regularly threatening us." She mimicked, "If you think it's hot *here . . .*" and rolled her eyes. "Who could fall in love with *that*?" she questioned him. "I haven't heard a belly laugh from anyone in my family in my entire life. In fact, I'm pretty sure they lost their affects in the 70s." She added, "They don't do anything with wild abandon. After I told my mother the only thing I missed about my husband was the crazy sex I thought she was going to pass out."

She continued, "You seem to believe in freedom and in *living*. Why would you want a Christian label on the resumé of your life when you know what they stand for is so boring, uptight, and *flavorless*? I heard a woman say once she'd rather go to hell after she died than live in heaven because at least hell would have a happy hour."

Adam laughed out loud. Partially because he thought it was funny, partially to let out the emotion over the crazy sex comment. "Why don't you stop mincing words and tell me what you really think?"

"And I should have included shameless," she added and quoted a popular TV evangelist. "Send money now and God will give it back to you in ninety days, money-back guaranteed! Put your credit card payment on hold! Who would you rather have mad at you for not paying your tithes, Visa or Jesus?"

Adam waited for her to finish and, when she was done, looked at her steadily and pronounced definitively and without reserve, "I'm not just a Christian, Grace. I am a devout, dyed-in-the-wool, to the marrow of my bones, to the Nth degree of my quarks, Christian. I believe in God the Father, the Son, and the Holy Spirit and that they are all that is good in the universe with every fiber of my being and will follow them as well as promote and defend Christianity with my last breath. But just because I'm a Christian doesn't mean I, and many of the Christians I know, fit your stereotype. You're sort of blonde. Yet you have an advanced degree. Shocking!" He laughed as she punched him in the shoulder.

"Do you go to church?"

Adam replied, "Not currently."

That surprised her. "Why not?"

He shrugged loosely. "The primary goal of the churches in my area is to help people avoid trouble. Not to fully live. They say that can only happen once you get to heaven. The goal of life is to avoid the roadblocks they say."

"Isn't that a good thing?"

"It's a very good thing if you don't already know how. But because of Christ, my life has become pretty much reinstated to where it was originally. I don't benefit much from the sermons in my area because I've already incorporated the basics. I live on the shores of Paradise. I don't need to look back at where I've been. I like looking to the future."

"Tell me what living on the shores of Paradise looks like."

Without one ounce of pride Adam gave Grace a thumbnail sketch of himself as a fully restored and redeemed man of God. "I take full responsibility for my actions. The Holy Spirit lives within me and convicts me when I mess up. If I hurt someone, I am quick to apologize and change when necessary. I love God with my entire heart, talk to him unceasingly, receive from him bountifully and know how much he adores me."

He continued, "I exercise good boundaries yet emotionally support and deeply care for those close to me. I keep my expectations of others low, my faith and hope in God high, and accept people where they are in their lives and spiritual journeys without attempting to exert influence over their decisions or lifestyle choices unless invited. I don't offend easily, am not angry with the world, and don't blame others for any misfortune.

"I am also mentally, physically, financially, and spiritually healthy. I have lots of passion in my life yet virtually no drama. I hope to fall deeply in love again and want to pledge myself to that woman's happiness, promising to put her needs and desires above my own. I am happy and productive in my work, have more money than I could ever spend, treat my customers and my employees hopefully better than they expect, don't expect anything for free, pay my taxes without much complaint, and provide resources wherever the Lord leads. I don't benefit from church services that remind me how to live with the assumption I'm not already doing it, but I recognize there are others who need the help."

She looked at him and in her head she heard, *Whatta man, whatta man* ... but said nothing and was careful to keep a straight face and steady gaze. She nodded, urging him to continue. She was thoroughly enjoying his self-evaluation and couldn't help but think how wrong she'd been about him earlier. Adam didn't have a head injury or chemical imbalance, of that she was certain. Honestly, with a complete pendulum swing she was thinking about nominating him for Man of the Year.

He summarized by saying, "I also don't care for the way many churches dishonor women. Many limit their leadership roles and overtly or covertly suggest women need men to spiritually cover and/or lead them regardless of the circumstances and who the stronger partner is. It is also especially bothersome how many doctrines suggest Eve fell because she wasn't strong enough to withstand temptation when instead it was her she-bear instincts kicking in protecting her family. And I especially don't like the subliminal, if not overt message that our local churches convey, which is 'Life's a bitch and then you die.' I've seen what Jesus can do. It only makes me mad when the bar for what we can achieve through him is set so low. So instead of being agitated and wanting to grab the microphone away from the preacher, I pretty much sleep in on Sundays."

Grace chewed on her nail absent-mindedly, surprised yet strangely proud a man of God would stand up for her sex. "Still," she added, for lack of anything else to say, "can't you find a leadership role there and help others who need moral guidance? Don't those churches need help doing community work? Supporting missions? Helping widows and orphans? Leading people to Christ?" She surprised herself by flipping sides so easily and arguing the merits of organized religion.

Adam folded his napkin into a smaller square. "Don't get me wrong. Those are all valuable services and communities need their local churches."

"Doesn't the Bible also say not to forsake gathering with other believers?" she asked, parroting her mother.

"I have a few close friends and we support each other in our spiritual journey. However, I'm taking a break from church, which is not the same thing as taking a break from God, until he leads me to the right place."

She studied the air vent above her head, wondering if it was still open and then said, "I always thought God and the church were sort of the same thing."

He half-smiled and said, "Not at all. The church is God's Bride. Not the Bridegroom. And not all of its spokespersons are chosen or sanctioned by God. I heard an ex-preacher once say he was called to preach not by God but by his mother. He said he came to the eventual conclusion both he and God wished he would have become a dentist. So, if you're planning on joining a church you need to be careful whose lead you're following."

"So, who's his best mouthpiece?"

He responded earnestly, "That job belongs to the Holy Spirit, God's one and only true Matchmaker. Whose job is to continuously fan the flames of love between Man and God."

"But the official church still has an important role in the lives of Christians, don't you think?"

He nodded. "Most certainly. I believe it is the church's role to help the spiritually young learn to avoid life's pitfalls and warn of the enemy's tricks designed to entrap us. And then if they have the resources available, provide as much meat as milk."

"But you would personally attend a church if it focused on the heart of God? Told the whole story. How it all got started. Where it went wrong. How Jesus fixes it all. How we can get back on track. Like you were in the beginning. How people are really meant to partner with God and win and not just wait until they're dead to receive their rewards?"

"Exactly," he slightly nodded. "I'd attend any church and

practically fund their entire budget if their mission statement included teaching people to live with passion. Kicking the crap out of the enemy and taking our gardens back. Not just leaving the world to our rival, hoping to make the best exit possible."

"And helping those who want to be 'all in' create as much heaven on Earth as possible?"

"It's too late once you're dead, Grace," he said practically.

She pondered before commenting. "Maybe you can't find a church because people can't teach what they don't know. I would guess many preachers can help people get God on the phone but few who know how to actually have an honest, two-way conversation with him. Let alone marry him, become a living temple, and be together 24/7."

Upon further consideration she added, "Maybe what we need are river guides. You know, specialists who go from river to river as they're called and help others negotiate the deeper spiritual waters you're describing." She continued thoughtfully, "I mean, where's it written how to fall in love with God? How to hear and follow his voice? Where's the manual for having God as your roommate?"

He shrugged and added, "There is no step-by-step manual. But don't worry, Grace. God is completely capable of working out the details of each person's destiny with that person individually. There doesn't need to be a cookie-cutter cheat sheet. Because no preacher, no speaker, no author, not any Bible study can deliver you into a satisfying relationship with God. No one has the power to do that but the living Spirit of Jesus Christ himself."

"But they can give pointers and encourage people, right? Teach people how to become more sensitive to their spirits so they can actually hear from God? Know what's possible?"

He nodded. "Of course. I think it's the primary role of the church to encourage people to find God and build a relationship with him. Help dismantle, not perpetuate, the outdated image of the white, bearded scary guy. Do that and God will take it from there. Because no matter how good any author, speaker, or preacher is, the only person who can tell you who you are in Christ, what God has planned for you, how much he loves you and what you mean to him . . ."

Grace nodded, finishing his sentence, "Is God."

CHAPTER 22

ADAM'S OTHER EMPLOYEE, NICHOLAS, SITTING NEXT TO DEAN, got up to use the restroom and walked past them. He paused when he reached their row, glanced at Grace, and said to his boss, "You'd better get some sleep, buddy. You've got a big presentation tomorrow."

Adam laughed and said, "I can't sleep. She won't be quiet," tilting his head toward his seatmate. His co-worker looked at Grace appreciatively, smiled at his boss, and said, "Yeah, I feel for you." He nodded to Grace, shook his head at his boss good-naturedly, and walked on.

Adam unbuckled his seatbelt, sat his coffee cup on the center console between them, and pulled a file out of his briefcase. "Hang on a minute. I forgot to give Dean this file." He stood up and walked back to say something to his co-worker pounding away on his computer.

Grace looked out into the night. She was surprised to find herself inspired by Adam's passion and noticed something rising within her heart. It was hope.

She hadn't experienced hope for too long. She felt herself reconsidering her choices again. Regardless of the potential risk to her reputation she did want to be part of something bigger than herself. Maybe a group or movement that stood for something important, potentially life, even world-changing with an actual chance of success. She was tired of listening to the news anchors and podcasters who poured a steady stream of gasoline on the current raging social fires and who made it clear no help was on the way, just the promise of more fires.

Adam returned to his seat and asked her if she was warm enough. She nodded, adjusted the window covering and said, "If God wants people to fall in love with him, he needs a better social media campaign, don't you think? There seems to be more people who think his main goal these days is to come down here and rip into the wicked."

"Maybe ripping into the wicked is an act of love. Did you ever think of that?"

She nodded and shrugged a little. "Still, a lot of people think he's pretty scary because of his 'smiting' reputation. I don't think people know what might set him off. So maybe it's just safer to steer clear of him than take the chance of upsetting him." Since Adam and God were on good speaking terms she thought they could have a discussion about it sometime. "In fact," she added, "I used to have a friend. She named her three cats Surely, Goodness, and Mercy. She used to say her goal in life was to stay under the radar of both God and the devil and maybe they'd both leave her alone."

Adam smiled but didn't answer her right away because he too was thinking about God's ongoing relationship struggles with his family. However, his perspective was much different than that of his seatmate.

For those who have never allowed God to touch their heart, the feeling is unimaginable until he does. God and his family had relationship issues that could have been avoided if only he had been able to touch or lead them from within. One tiny mustard seed of faith that falls from the Tree of Love has the power to move mountains and provide wings that allow mere mortals to soar to unimaginable heights. Following God based on head knowledge about him alone will never have the same impact as being led by someone you can tangibly feel in your heart who loves, cherishes, wants to spend time with you, and only wants the best for you. And has the power to do it.

But without God's Holy Spirit gently guiding and empowering his family from within, due to the sin virus they'd inherited, the Lord was limited to external signs, wonders, and the voices of the prophets he had raised up to speak for him the best they could. But even with those resources, it was almost impossible to fully empower his children to successfully battle against the enemy that raged within their flesh and waged war against them in spiritual, not just the physical, realms.

He reflected on the various hardships and challenges both sides endured and wondered how it was possible that the relationship between God and his children had survived such highs and lows over the centuries. He marveled at the desire and commitment from both sides to fan the flames of love when the enemy did everything he could to forever destroy them. His mind drifted to what he considered the lowest point, a time when he was certain the enemy had won and God and his family had parted ways. For good.

It was the time the Israelites told God officially they didn't want him as their king anymore. The devil scored a major victory and shot an arrow into the heart of God the day his children asked him to leave.

Adam thought about King Saul, the first appointed king of the Jews. He hadn't actually known Saul, but he did know the prophet

Samuel who'd been God's mouthpiece and prophet and spoke to Saul on God's behalf. Adam thought of Samuel, whom he'd met long after Eve died. His heart flooded with gratitude for the relationship that had been his salvation, the relationship that came at the most opportune time during one of the low points of Adam's life—on the anniversary of Eve's death.

Abel's murder and Cain's disappearance had been more than their mother could bear. When Cain left, Eve survived but she never lived again. The birth of more children and then grandchildren revived her somewhat. Yet none of them ever saw the fiery passion that, had it lived within her, would have been the legacy she'd left to all her future daughters. One day Adam came in from the field and found her laying lifeless on the floor.

With Eve gone Adam had no one with whom he could share his secrets. His true identity became no more than legend to his heirs, his story too wild even for the youngest imaginations.

Of course Adam had chosen to remain with Seth and his family, the godless ways of Cain far too intolerable and unbearable. Seth's family continued to grow and as it did Adam's leadership position diminished. As Seth became father, grandfather, and great grandfather, Adam became known as an obscure distant relative. Not long after Seth's death Adam became totally lost within the extended branches of his family tree. Meeting Samuel, Adam remembered the joy and relief he first felt realizing the Lord did not intend to leave him alone and friendless forever.

Samuel had been chosen for service when he was still a small boy living with the priest Eli. Samuel's mother Hannah had taken Samuel to live with Eli in the temple as fulfillment to a promise she'd made to God.

Adam had left farming and become a merchant. He'd set up house in the hill country of Ephraim. As a trader he exchanged goods with

Elkanah, Samuel's father. After some time, the two men developed an easy friendship and could often be seen talking in the marketplace or in one of the shops discussing the business or politics of the day.

One night Adam, Elkanah, and Samuel shared a meal together. Samuel could see Adam held a secret. That evening in a dream the Lord revealed Adam's identity to him. Revealing men's secrets to Samuel was one of God's favorite pastimes.

Intrigued and sympathetic, Samuel quickly befriended Adam. He sought him out at his shop one afternoon shortly after their dinner together. "Adam, I have a word for you from our Lord. Will you hear it?"

Adam knew Samuel was not only a seer and a priest but also a judge and military leader. He was highly respected in all of Israel. Adam knew Samuel was a credible prophet and his message could indeed be depended upon to have come from the Lord. Still, he was not prepared for the message his friend's son gave him.

"The Lord says to tell you the road you have chosen will be a long and rocky one. However, you will not be alone. I will stay with you until my end and be a confidante and brother to you," he said as he smiled at his new friend. "Stay faithful to God and to your heart. If you persevere and don't quit, God promises all that was yours in the Garden, including complete peace and restoration, will be restored to Earth, to you, and to your heirs."

Adam remembered the shock and the tears that followed. Could he believe his ears? The son of his merchant friend, this widely acclaimed and respected prophet of God, *knew*? Adam was overwhelmed with gratitude. Finally, someone with whom he could speak openly and share his past and current burdens. Not since Eve had he enjoyed a true friendship.

He welcomed and made room for Samuel in his life and his friend reciprocated. God blessed the relationship for many years and there was hardly a day the two men did not share a meal and meaningful conversation.

Adam thought again of Samuel. Both were men of God with different but equally painful tales of woe. Each chosen for significant destinies, each consumed by fears of completely botching the job.

Adam remembered Samuel's story. Raised by Eli in the temple, just three years old when he was handed over to God by a faithful mother. A child whose education God personally supervised for the purpose of molding him into his holy mouthpiece.

Seth's descendants, then Abraham's, followed God and he accompanied them on their earthly journey, guiding and helping them through their many trials. Through famines, floods, incarceration, and desert nomads, God shepherded his family through their unceasing personal and tribal battles in both the physical and spiritual realms.

Israel loved and was faithful to God as their king. Even as they toiled as Pharoah's prisoners in Egypt the Lord assured them he would someday lead them into the Promised Land, and even though their bondage lasted for several centuries, the Jews remained faithful. And God delivered. Through Moses he freed Abraham's people and delivered them into the land flowing with milk and honey. The problem was they couldn't stay there.

The enemy raged strong against God's people. His only goals were to destroy their faith, take them as captives, and steal their inheritance. Satan wants to rule the world. He needs man's reliance on self, not God, to do it. The enemy already had partnered with Cain's family and taken control of most of the territory. However, he wouldn't rest until he had it all.

The enemy's primary strategy was to destroy the Israelite's faith by planting doubts in their minds about God. He continuously barraged them with accusations about the Lord's lack of predictability, his multitude of laws and traditions, his demand of sacrifices for payment for their sins. He accused the Lord unceasingly in the hearts and minds of any family member who gave him an audience.

Over time personal, religious, and societal conditions became increasingly compromised. Although prohibited, several Jewish males married Canaanite females who introduced false idols and other godless ways into the Israelite tribes. Discord was sown and many people's faith waned.

The Lord, silently watching, was concerned that his family would self-destruct before his very eyes. As a potential remedy he had planted, trained, equipped, and ordained Samuel to function as mediator. At the time when the relationship between God and Seth's descendants seemed completely undermined by the enemy, the Lord rested his hope for restoring good familial relationships and purity squarely on the shoulders of his young prophet.

God's plan was to speak through Samuel, and he was certain through this appointed and specially trained translator Israel would hear his heart and remember him. Through Samuel, they would gain the strength to stand up to the growing rank of godless rebels, a minority of members but mounting in strength and influence.

Through his new and highly anointed orator, God hoped his family would remember that he loved them and was there to protect them and keep them from dying off as a race. He was sure that once his family remembered his faithfulness, but that he simply couldn't produce a rabbit out of his hat for every problem, they would understand, love, and follow him more easily.

But it didn't work out that way. Spurred on by the enemy, the strength and influence of the discontent increased. Rebel publicans stood in the square and demanded their opponents explain what made God a worthy king. They wanted a new and different king. A king who represented all the people. A king for the times, an inclusive king, not the one of their past who insisted they follow the letter of an overabundance of laws that had turned out to be impossible for them to comply with and who made them pay for their weakness by sacrificing their very livelihood.

But mainly they wanted a king who would send in flesh and blood armies to protect them. They wanted a king who they could trust by sight, not by faith alone. Because for people uninhabited by the power and presence of the Holy Spirit, living by faith instead of by sight in a world filled with terror is an impossible, unreachable ambition. Even when those people love and believe in God.

Through caucus, opposing arguments, resistance, and finally concession from the majority of believers, Samuel was instructed to tell God of their nation's decision. They didn't want an invisible God as their king anymore. They wanted a godlike man whose human strength they could see and depend on. A king who would recruit and rely on the strongest males of the tribe. Armies they could see, not simply trust by faith to protect them. They wanted God to step aside and send in a replacement. They officially told God to leave. They didn't want him anymore as their sovereign king.

Through Samuel, God argued and objected. He told them in detail what a human king would demand of them, how little provision and protection they could actually expect. He said a human king would treat them like animals, not children. He would enslave them, steal their daughters, take the best of their lands, and give them to his friends.

"A human king won't love them," the Lord told Samuel. "Won't care for them. The Israelites aren't *any* people," he argued from his heart, "they're *my* people!" The Jews are God's chosen people, set aside, favored. Unlike Cain, Seth, then Abraham and on down the line, had committed themselves to God. Made covenants. Dedicated their children to him. Sacrificed the best of their livestock as proof.

The Jews were God's only dedicated family left on Earth. The only family he walked with, guided, shielded from the enemy. Protected. God loves all his family but holds deeper in his heart those who love him back. He has hopes and plans to someday lead his children back into the Promised Land. Yes, he'd been angry with them at times for their blatant disregard of godliness and their rebelliousness against him, but he always forgave them and was faithful, wasn't he? God did not want his children to leave him. They could work it out, he'd insisted.

Many of the Jews were heartbroken as well over the tribal decision to abandon God as their official leader. God was their God. They were his people. They wanted his ways. They didn't want a human king. They wanted God on the throne. They complained bitterly amongst themselves, and many gathered to pray that God would return as their king. But instead of standing firmly together and defying the godless minority, they let the enemy disunite them, leaving the new leadership in control.

Leaders speak for the people they represent. God honors the process. Reluctantly and remorsefully, Samuel went to the Lord and delivered the official news. The Israelites had agreed to petition God for a human king. They would risk being enslaved, gamble their lands, cattle, and daughters. They wanted a king like other nations. They wanted God to be quiet. Send help, when the requests came in, but stop talking.

Samuel relayed the conversation he'd had with the Lord tearfully to his friend Adam. He told him that after he'd delivered the news, wounded and distraught, God had been silent for several moments. He finally responded flatly, "Cain's family doesn't want me. I'd hoped Seth's would. I guess they don't."

Samuel knew at that moment the Lord was thinking nowhere on

Earth did he have a people to call his own anymore. No family who loved and wanted him for his person, not just his power.

The same family who'd witnessed and heard the stories of their father's overwhelming provision, protection, love, and faithfulness for generations. Hadn't he delivered them from Egypt? Fed, clothed, and protected them in the desert before delivering them to their Promised Land, flowing with milk and honey?

Hadn't he tried to understand them and make allowances when they complained against him? Had them set up altars of incense so they knew he was present there? Sent thousands of angels to demolish their enemies and helped them claim new ground against tremendous odds? Samuel, aware of the Lord's overwhelming disappointment and sadness, sat down on the ground and cried for his king's loss.

In his kindness the Lord said to Samuel, "I don't know why it's you crying, Samuel. It's me they're rejecting." After a contemplative moment he added, "They never really wanted to follow me anyway. When I helped them escape from Egypt they complained and questioned me every step of the way. Asking me to justify my actions to them like I was their servant, not their God."

Samuel later sobbed knowing his comfort to the Lord had proven so woefully inadequate. He was ashamed that in the Lord's sadness he had stopped and offered consolation to Samuel when Samuel should've been the one offering empathy to his Creator.

Adam remembered his sense of panic that night after leaving Samuel's. What if God had truly lost his family? The world was turning into a godless planet of Cains and it was Adam's fault. These were his heirs, and they were rejecting God! His heart broke for the father he loved so much. Not to mention he would forever hold the title as his tormentor.

Full of grief, he voiced his concerns to his friend after dinner one evening. "How will God and Man ever make up?" he cried desperately.

Adam remembered Samuel fixing his steely eyes upon him. He was, after all, the Lord's mouthpiece. "Once again, Man and God will take the long road." Samuel's eyes shone as he prophesied, "God will give his family what they wish.

"He will stand back and watch as we re-elect leaders who rob and abuse us and legislators who give us rules they themselves won't follow. A few loud, angry voices will muzzle the outrage of the silent majority and become the writers and enforcers of public opinion and law. Our police will end in shackles, while the thieves and robbers run free with the keys, protected by the outrage of their champions.

"The enemy will send a strong spirit of deception to confuse and silence the righteous, giving power to the wicked. Children will be killed the day before they are to be born for reasons no greater than convenience. And as the world debates the rights of the unborn, living women and children will be allowed to wander dangerously into foreign lands without accompaniment, provision, protection, education, or healthcare, captured by enemies, raped, stripped from their families, and sold for profit by merchants who barter in the desperate. And the people will allow it, but cry and stomp their feet and say the weak and corrupt leaders they elected are to blame.

"Darkness will cover the Earth. When we allow the truth we rely on, instead of divine, to become artificial in nature based on stolen records constructed by the unaccountable, unreliable, and ungodly, we will have reached the end of the age of complacency. Because at that point, Mankind will completely lose faith in anything we see or hear, even the obvious. And without the ability to trust one another, the only outcome is complete tyranny or anarchy, which the enemy knows the human soul cannot survive and was his plan all along.

"At the appointed time, the Spirit of the Lord will rise up inside His people and command us to action because God, and not Satan, is our Father and our Leader. And in our hearts, the majority of us not only acknowledge this, but desire it. And one day we'll gather together with one voice and announce that no other god, other than the God, will ever lead us again.

"From the heavenlies, God will rise and call to his family, 'Heaven is my Throne! The Earth is my footstool! In whom will I find my rest?' And all God's children, his individual and beloved temples, even those asleep thought for dead, will rise and respond, each according to the Father's timing, will, and purpose for their lives."

Samuel concluded, "In the eleventh hour, when every other god has been introduced and exposed as false, untrue, self-serving, and unreliable, God's family will remember the One who loves us. And together we will call out in unison and pray, 'Our Father, who art in heaven, hallowed be thy name. Let your kingdom come and your will be done on Earth as it is in heaven.

"Give us this day what we need to live and forgive us for the wrongs we have done to one another. Repair the damage we've caused and help us forgive those who harmed us along the way even as you have forgiven us. Heal our wounds and make us whole again.

"Keep us from chasing after false gods and save us from the trouble they've already created. Because, Lord, this is your kingdom, the power to save it is yours alone, and it's you who deserve all the glory, forever. Do this in the name of Love because you are merciful and for better or for worse, we are your family!"

Adam picked up his coffee cup, turned to Grace, and said, "God's strong suit is patience and his plans and promises do not change. In Genesis he lived with us in a Garden. In Revelation he promises to do it again.

"Over the years he's stood by and watched me grapple with the life Eve and I said we wanted. He let me and all my descendants, Cain's and Seth's, Jews and Gentiles, see, taste, smell, and roll around in the gutter because at first we could, but after a while we couldn't find our way out. For centuries mankind has struggled and many of our lives have been a living hell. But even then, not all of us have learned.

"We the people continue to struggle as our elected officials speak to God on our behalf. Through our leaders, the people of the nations continue to tell God we want gods we can see, not the One we can't.

"Most governments and many individuals still deny God as our king because he refuses to show his face and power, won't always respond the way we expect, is not always compliant or chatty enough. Some say 'I won't follow a God that doesn't make us behave. He's probably just a collective consciousness jerk who doesn't care about any of us anyway.' Those people don't realize God is writing his laws on our minds and hearts so we can live freely, successfully, powerfully, eventually without intervention or supervision. Not running a daycare."

Grace raised her eyebrows. "Without supervision?"

"The Bible says God's goal is that we all grow into the head which is Christ. Christ the head means we are designed to be self-governing. Because people made in God's image don't always like to be told what to do. And once we fully share the mind of Christ, have new and glorified bodies free from the influence of the enemy, and have his Spirit within our hearts gently guiding us, we don't need to be."

"And that's why Jesus came? So people could be free? Because we don't always know or have the power to always do what we want without the Holy Spirit inside to help us? Help us to be healthy and holy not because we're told to but because we want to?" Grace asked.

"Yes, Grace. Sin almost destroyed the race of Man. My family boarded a train of self-destruction, and it was careening out of control.

It nearly crashed and burned, killing us and forever crippling the heart of God. Just in time, he sent a Savior who paid the debts for our mistakes, took the teeth out of sin, and restored our dignity, inheritance, and position as the sons and daughters of God.

"The Father knew," he continued, "that sin is the barrier between him and his family but trying to follow the letter of the law as a method of restoration turned out to be impossible for humans, and the judgements for failing to do so only lead to death and condemnation. It turned out to be a catch-22. Man cannot redeem ourselves or restore our relationship with God through good behavior and sacrifice. In Second Corinthians, the Bible clearly states that the letter of the law kills. Paul and other followers of Christ realized the law, judgment for not following it, and condemnation for sin does nothing but imprison and eventually destroy us.

"But God breathed *life* into me in the beginning. His living Spirit is what keeps us alive. Eternally. Death was never meant to be part of his agenda. So, he took care of it. Jesus is the antidote to the sin virus that separates us. Now that we're clean, God can touch us again. The Holy Spirit can enter us and lead us back to God and into the magnificent future he has planned for each one of us. We are no longer shackled by the constraints of following the letter of the law, old ritualistic traditions, the need for sacrifices, and our old sins cannot destroy our lives unless we let them. We have Jesus and the Holy Spirit to guide us home and kick out the bad guys along the way. I tell you this, Grace, because the God of the Old Testament is not a jerk. He's just a very good dad who for a while has had a problem with some of his kids."

CHAPTER 23

ANNA WALKED BY AND GRACE ASKED HER FOR A BLANKET. IT had gotten cold on the plane and she was uncomfortable. The young flight attendant informed her they didn't carry blankets for passengers anymore but sweetly said she would ask them to turn up the plane's thermostat. Grace hadn't been the only one to mention it.

Once Anna walked on, Adam stood up, opened the overhead compartment, took out his coat, and handed it to his seatmate. Touched by the gesture, she thanked him. The garment she noted smelled like its owner and she inhaled the mild scent of leather, peppermint, and cinnamon. She laid the soft camel-colored wool coat over her legs and immediately felt warmer. And happier she couldn't help but notice.

Suddenly she had that déjà vu feeling again and wondered where she'd seen Adam before. She searched her mental archives, decided she was wrong, and returned to his story of Samuel. "When I was young, my mother and her friends talked about the same things you said Samuel predicted. The world's infrastructure, democracy, order, the money system, would all eventually collapse. My mom believes God's finally going to get fed up and give the whole world over to the devil, letting him have his way with us. But she isn't worried about it because she thinks all the Christians will be gone, raptured away before it happens."

Adam nodded. "It's a common Christian belief."

She continued, "They all get together every week at my mom's and pray to be raptured because they say the world is at the breaking point. They claim it's unfixable. Do you believe in the rapture?"

"I have no idea," he said. "However, I do know this. The Bible says Jesus returns to Earth when the Spirit and the Bride say 'Come.' Not from their seats in heaven where they say 'Go.' So probably not everyone gets raptured if such a thing exists."

"I guess that makes sense," she nodded slightly. "Then why do so many people believe in it?"

"The Bible makes reference to people leaving Earth the same way Jesus came, and many interpret that to mean collectively ascending into the heavenlies, two in the field, one taken, one left behind," he quoted. "In the early 1800s a young Scottish girl named Margaret MacDonald had a vision and came up with the rapture theory. A theologian from America was there and brought the concept to America. It's only one of four main theories on the subject and is called dispensationalism. It is most popular in the United States but certainly not everywhere."

Grace nodded. All she knew was that her mother and her friends were adamant the rapture was coming, leaving the ungodly behind to face the consequences. Once Grace's father had gone missing. He went to the hardware store with the neighbor, left the car in the garage, and hadn't left a note. He'd been mowing, changed his clothes in the laundry room, and left them on the floor. Grace's mother saw the clothes, panicked, and called the preacher to make sure the rapture hadn't come and she'd missed it."

She told Adam the story and he laughed out loud. After a while he said, "It doesn't really matter to me if it's true or not. The rapture."

"Why not?"

"Because my behavior wouldn't change, regardless. God's told me my part and I know I'll be here when Christ returns. And even though I don't know what will happen to everyone else, sometimes I think focusing on the rapture other than giving some people comfort often does more harm than good."

"How's that?" Still cold, she pulled his coat up a little.

"Jesus said in the last days we'll do even greater works than he did while he was on Earth. Lots of people think we're in the last days. But how's anyone going to do the miraculous if they're just praying to get the hell out of Dodge?" he asked with emotion. She listened thinking the issue seemed personal for Adam and then remembered he claimed God gave the world to him. He still felt at least partially responsible for what happened to it.

Grace studied her seatmate and thought in the semi-darkness with his dark eyes packed with indignation he looked more like a warrior than professional bridge builder and softball player. Suddenly she thought she might know where she'd seen him before. She studied him, remembering a magazine ad featuring a cowboy in a hat holding a cigarette, leaning on a fence post next to a beautiful blonde in a pencil skirt and cashmere sweater. She said, "This may be a dumb question, but were you ever in a magazine ad for cigarettes in the early 60s?"

For a moment he was speechless. "Why do you ask?"

She eyed him more curiously than suspiciously. "My mom and my aunt used to smoke together when I was little, before my mom turned religious. Mom had a stack of old magazines in the attic that I used to go through periodically and look at the clothes. I pulled them down once and had them scattered on the living room floor. I remember seeing the picture of a cowboy, his horse, and a beautiful blonde who was sitting next to him on a fence, and they were each smoking a cigarette. My mom and her sister were in the room and my mom pointed out the picture to my aunt and they both started to laugh.

"My aunt said they'd both started smoking because of the ad. They wanted to look like the woman and have the man. My mom said only a woman who looked like that could attract a man so good-looking. I tore the whole picture out and put it in my dresser drawer. I had it in there for years. I pulled it out occasionally to see if I looked like her." She waited for an answer.

Adam turned his head to face the aisle and Grace was convinced it was so she couldn't see his expression. Momentarily he turned back to her and said, "They thought he was that good-looking?"

An involuntary laugh escaped her. She shook her head and decided to let the subject drop. The night was crazy enough, she decided, without diving down any more rabbit holes. Instead she thought of Adam's views on the fate of the world and possibly her mother. She asked, "But couldn't some people get raptured before it all hits the fan?"

"Anything's possible. But like I said, I have no idea. And no matter what anybody else tells you, unless they've heard it directly from God himself, they don't know either. Many of the Jews are still waiting on the Messiah because Jesus didn't come the way they thought he would. I have found that God doesn't always like to show his hand before he plays it. Therefore, I'm not placing any bets. However, the Bible clearly says to 'run the race set before you, heaven is within, in the last days some will do greater works than Christ did when he was here and to pray for the establishment of God's kingdom on Earth.' So that's what I'm doing and expecting, not for anyone else, but for myself."

Grace thought about her mother and her praying friends. She hoped the rapture was true, at least for them, and her mom could be whisked off to heaven leaving her troubles behind. She was getting old and didn't want to witness or be a part of any worsening mayhem. She was a good cheerleader and even though she and Grace didn't always agree, Grace loved her and wanted her to be happy.

Sensing her concern, Adam said reassuringly, "Rapture or not, I think your mom and her friends will be thrilled with the outcome."

She poured more hot water into her cup from the small pot. "But really, Adam, what's the point of hoping for more? Doing all that work just to enter into some potential narrow gate? Isn't the devil you know better than the one you don't? Couldn't you just give God the stuff that doesn't really matter just to be on the safe side? You might not find Paradise, but you might find a better parking space," she offered.

"That would be the title of the enemy's website if he had one."

She nodded in concession. "What would be on God's?"

Adam shrugged and quipped, "I don't know. Maybe, 'Not my way—but Yahweh!' Or 'Bored again? Try born again!'"

Instead of laughing she scoffed derisively. "Oh, please! *Born again?* Ugh!"

Adam was silent. Momentarily, he asked, "Do you care to explain that last comment?"

She sighed heavily. "'Born again Christian' makes me think of the 'holier than thou' label people give themselves who insinuate if you aren't born again you're somehow substandard. And who constantly want to tell you about their future crowns and other people's reservations in Hotel Hell," she said sarcastically.

In a moment Adam said, "I get it. However, would you like a different perspective?"

She hesitated, sighed, thought, *Not really,* but said, "I guess."

"When I was in the Garden the Holy Spirit lived inside me and made me a pure conduit, an unblocked receptacle. Whatever God wanted to send me, whatever I asked him for, was mine. It was a clean transfer, no restrictions."

"What's that got to do with being born again?"

"I'm getting to that. In the Garden, there was no pain inside me created by abuse and no lies telling me God had created me with any significant deficiencies. No lies, garbage, or emotional blockage. No teachers, friends, parents, social media convincing me that I needed to do or be something different to be loved, safe, or powerful. No enemy standing over me ready to steal what was mine. I didn't lock my doors at night, worry about cancer, or fear that my kids might do drugs. God's Spirit was in me, and his Truth assured me that as long as we stayed connected, my future was nothing but bright. I had no reason to doubt him. I functioned at a level no human being, other than Eve, has ever experienced."

She nodded, "Okay . . ."

"But as soon as I ate from the Tree of Knowledge, the demolition began. Once God's presence left me, I found myself completely alone and vulnerable, surrounded by a battalion of enemy forces launching lie and insult grenades into my mind at machine gun speed. I didn't have enough God inside me anymore to withstand them. Within minutes I turned from a confident, holy, regal, and high functioning son of God, fully aware of my destiny, into a dysfunctional, self-absorbed, neurotic, semi-verbally abusive, wife-belittling, emotional cripple with literally no self-esteem. I once asked God if I was a deity. Once he left and the enemy planted his flag, I felt more like an animal than even human.

"Satan's primary strategy was then, and is today, to guard, clutter, and obstruct that same bridge that connected me to God then and connects every Christian to him now. His goal is to completely shut down our access to God and his resources. The enemy can't keep the Holy Spirit from entering a person, but he can keep the lines clogged if a person lets him. If he can do that, he can keep us from reclaiming all the territory God has designated for his daughters and sons."

Grace shuddered slightly from the cold. "How does he do that?"

"He lies," Adam said simply. "Constantly."

She picked up the stir stick and twirled it in between her fingers idly. "What's he say?"

"Anything that destroys our faith because it's faith that turns God's invisible resources into our visible reality. Without prayer and faith God's hands are tied."

"And then we stay trapped?"

Adam nodded. "The enemy's strategy is to separate Man and God. First, by discrediting God and saying he can't or won't help us. Second, by saying we're not worthy of help. There's something wrong with us. Out of one side of his mouth and depending on his audience the enemy says, 'People can't communicate with God. He can't talk to us directly anymore. He's unpredictable. He's busy. He's mad. He's too far away. He's too holy to talk to us. We can't know his will. He doesn't want to be understood. God is cold. Unfeeling. Detached. He's easily offended. We'll only be free once Jesus gets back or when we get to heaven.' I could go on endlessly."

He continued and Grace realized he'd been paying close attention over the years to his enemy's strategies. "Out of the other side he shames and discourages people with their previous failures while arguing with still others that failure is God's way of keeping us humble and absent of pride. He often quotes the Bible and says, 'Don't lay your treasures up on Earth. Wait and let God reward you in heaven.' That's one of his favorite twists on the truth to Christians because if he can keep us from partnering with God, walking in Christ's power and authority, and reclaiming his kingdom . . ."

"Then we'll give up and leave the world to our enemies?" she suggested.

He nodded and she said, "So again I ask, what's this got to do with the rapture or being born again?"

"Born again means we get a do-over, Grace. Born again means that in God's eyes we're perfectly clean. We get a fresh start. We start our race without any spiritual baggage holding us back.

"Once we receive Christ, the Holy Spirit is free to move inside us and begin the restoration process, helping us become all we can be and receive all God has for us. On *Earth* as it is in heaven. There are no limits. How far we take it is up to each individual. Our advancement has nothing to do with following the rules. It has everything to do with how much God we take in.

"But more than anything, Grace, being born again means we are clean, free and empowered. We have the chance to win. Pursue the life God has for us with a real chance of being successful. As humans we don't have to settle for the scraps. Defeat at the hands of someone stronger. We have God on our side and if he's for us, who can be against us? We don't have to leave the Earth in order to find happiness. Because of Christ and through the power of the Holy Spirit, we can walk in victory, *now*."

"How?" she asked suddenly transfixed.

"We make an exchange. God takes out of us what's not him and puts in us what is. He exchanges our lies for truth and our pain for gladness. Because as a therapist wouldn't you agree that it's the pain and the lies in our lives that create most of our prisons? Keep us from seeing and receiving what's possible? And so many of our beliefs we inherit as children, are often deeply imbedded, and without Christ impossible to get rid of?"

Grace carefully considered Adam's claims. She slightly nodded, silently acknowledging that she still grappled with her own early programming. Her mother had effectively role-modeled for her that people in general, especially women, should do whatever they found necessary to avoid confrontation. Grace's mother mastered the art and subtleties of keeping others from becoming upset and had passed the skill to her daughter.

Mrs. Jackson never told Grace directly but had intimated to her that she wasn't very smart, although she should be okay in life because she was so good-looking. In the sixth grade, Grace's science teacher had derisively laughed at her in front of the class when Grace said God made it rain instead of explaining the process of precipitation when asked. The teacher, an older single woman, told Grace that maybe with her looks she could grow up to be the weathergirl on Christian TV because she certainly would never make it as a scientist. The class laughed and Grace earned the nickname "Weathergirl."

She was extremely humiliated by the event and the nickname. The incident solidified her suspicions that she was stupid. Mortified, she came to the erroneous conclusion that she deserved to be humiliated because she had a hidden, yet material flaw—she was pretty but dumb. Grace was certain that a lack of intelligence wasn't something a person could keep secret for long and eventually everyone else around her would find out. Fear and shame entered her heart. Did she have other flaws she couldn't see?

Completely embracing her demons, and certain the flaw would be the death of any future hopes and dreams, her child's heart and mind decided if she were to survive, she'd better learn to fake it. She either had to pretend it wasn't true or that she didn't care. Because as any pre-teen can attest, publicly acknowledging one's weaknesses and shame is the stake in the heart of popularity.

Grace was a quick study and learned to mimic the behavior of the girls at school she admired in no time. She donned a haughty, overly confident demeanor, became critical of others, and badgered her mother to let her wear makeup and update her wardrobe with the latest fashions; any device Grace could find that helped deflect others from judging her by anything beyond her looks. She became obsessed with mirrors.

But in the end Grace turned out to be very smart. For Halloween, she went as the Morton Salt Weathergirl icon dressed in a flattering bright yellow dress, yellow shoes, and matching umbrella with the words "Morton Iodized Salt" written neatly on a sign her mother pinned to her front. The dress was short, and she wore white tights under the outfit that accentuated her long legs. She twirled around her friends as they admired her beauty and wit.

The nickname turned into a badge of honor. At Grace's high school graduation ceremony, the valedictorian gave a rousing and motiva-tional speech about the need to work hard to ensure a good future. She ended it with, "Because we can't all be the Weathergirl," and the class laughed in unison.

Until she got to college, Grace stopped voicing her opinion on al-most any subject of debate. She stuck to facts of which she was certain or obvious to everyone, or simply agreed with whomever was speaking. She didn't trust her debate skills because she was sure if challenged by others she would be exposed.

As she matured, her conscious mind finally accepted she was highly intelligent. She also knew she was a good person. She realized her looks couldn't and shouldn't always be depended upon to get her what she wanted. She earned more than one advanced degree, partially because learning was so enjoyable, but also as a subconscious means to ensure she never felt ashamed again for appearing ignorant. Or vulnerable.

Her mind knew she could trust her intellect but fear and shame, still lodged in her heart, often reminded her she was not enough. Not consciously but subconsciously she believed she could possibly have yet another devastating flaw currently undiscovered just waiting for the most inopportune time to surface. She feared she could face humiliation at any moment. Grace could hardly recall the initial shame of the Weathergirl genesis, but the heart has a long memory and sleeps with one eye open.

Grace grew in age and confidence and received many public accolades and gained respect. Her professional career blossomed. Her colleagues and patients regularly complimented her skills. Her practice was overflowing, and she often had to turn away new clients. She was published in many industry journals, had written a book, and was a favored speaker at national and even some international conferences.

Yet when tired, vulnerable, or sick, Grace was tormented by emotional baggage. If threatened, she immediately became overly confrontational. Even when others around her voiced opinions that had nothing to do with her yet differed from her own she often grew angry and felt the need to argue.

Grace had entered and participated in more than one dysfunctional relationship. Setting boundaries was a problem for her because even though she could often tell when she was wrong, she had difficulty knowing for sure when she was right. If she made an upsetting comment or if a confrontation ended with the other party experiencing hurt feelings, Grace invariably felt guilty, beat herself up emotionally, and often overcompensated the recipient of her wrath.

She sometimes allowed others to act as her barometer for how she should be treated and too often allowed close friends and family members to treat her unkindly or with too little respect. Too many had taken advantage of Grace, did not reciprocate equally in relationships, took more than they gave, and yet Grace refused to distance herself appropriately from them.

She lived with an internal pendulum that swung between bitch and doormat. She wished she could develop a healthy, internal plumb line as her guide when there were relationship troubles.

Regardless, Grace was still a very good therapist. She recognized the power of subconscious beliefs and could help other people deal with old wounds and identify unhealthy patterns and the lies associated with them that often resulted in real change. However, no matter how hard she tried, Grace could not seem to always exorcise her own demons.

"Yes," she told Adam, "I understand the concept of garbage in and garbage out."

"I knew this guy one time," he said. "He lived in the time of Jesus. His name was Nicodemus. He was super smart and very well-respected but had some emotional issues that spilled over into his relationships.

"Jesus told him he could be free and healthy, but he'd have to be born again. Nicodemus replied, tongue in cheek, 'What am I supposed to do? Climb back inside my mother's womb?' Obviously meaning he couldn't just start all over again and reprogram himself."

Grace was intrigued. "What'd he say?"

Adam answered, "Jesus told him he'd have to be born again not of the flesh but of the *Spirit*, meaning the Holy Spirit of God. It's a do-over, Grace. Our old garbage, and no one else's either, can hold us hostage anymore. We can be free. And the more people who actively partner with God to become free, raise their expectations of happiness on Earth not just after, the healthier and more empowered we can become."

Grace said thoughtfully, "A do-over. Forgiveness for past, present, and future sins and the resources and power to win. Even while we're on Earth." She twirled the stir stick again thoughtfully.

"Yes, and the best part is God wants us to win. He's willing not to just cheer for us from afar but roll up his sleeves and provide some real help," Adam insisted. "He sent his innocent and beloved *son* to die for it, Grace. Do you know what that cost him? How much more invested can he be? And here's the best kept secret yet. God's dreams are much bigger for us and his plans and opportunities far greater than we ever could imagine for ourselves."

Suddenly, and almost with a hint of desperation in her voice, she asked, "Do you really think this could work, Adam, for anyone? No matter who they are or what they've done? No matter how much they've blown God off in the past?"

Adam was staring at her and again she thought he looked more like a warrior than a business traveler. He said definitively, "Satan's a spiritual squatter, Grace. The Earth doesn't belong to him. It never did. Regardless of people's differences it's time we work together, partner with God, submit our lives, and let him transform them and kick that son of a bitch enemy out of our world." He raised his right hand and vowed, "Yes, Grace, it can work for anyone."

CHAPTER 24

G RACE'S BACK WAS TIRED FROM SITTING SO LONG IN ONE position and her right foot had gone to sleep. She tapped the ball of her foot on the floor several times. She looked up and saw Nicholas talking to Katie near the galley. Out of respect for the sleeping travelers they spoke in hushed tones but every once in a while one of them laughed out loud.

"Is he a good guy?" Grace asked, indicating his traveling companion.

"Very," Adam answered. "I wouldn't be travelling with him if he wasn't. I don't travel with anyone I don't like."

"It's nice you have the luxury. How long will you be in Honolulu anyway?"

He answered, "Just two days. We're in and out. How about you?" he asked. "Got any big plans?"

"Maybe," she said undecidedly. "I'm staying for five days because I thought I might like to visit some of the other islands, but I haven't totally decided yet."

"What's your presentation about?" he asked.

"Head injuries," she answered sheepishly, and they both laughed out loud.

She thought about the story Adam told her about Jesus and his friend Nicodemus, "Did you ever meet Jesus?"

Adam took a drink of his coffee and said, "I did. We were good friends, introduced by his cousin John."

Grace stared at him. "You were friends with Jesus and John the Baptist?" Adam smiled and nodded. "For a guy who's got a pretty big secret, you've certainly had a lot of heavy hitting friends," she said.

"God connects people committed to the same cause. Restoring his kingdom is obviously mine," he shrugged. "It makes sense, really, that he connected me with them."

After Samuel died, Adam walked a long time without a true friend. *It's hard living alone with such a secret,* he thought, giving Grace a sidelong glance.

He could still hear Samuel insisting, "God will *never* give up on his people!" He'd heard him shout it from the mountaintops and whisper it from his deathbed. God would restore heaven on Earth. Not just his people, but Earth itself would be redeemed. Adam needed to feel he wasn't alone, wasn't the only mortal still praying for the Garden, his original homeland, to be reopened and reinstated in the lives of God's family.

Still, years went by and instead of closer, God's people grew further away from him. Although faithful, many of Seth's descendants had come to see God as an unyielding and unforgiving policeman, judge, and jury, a distant being more concerned with rituals and traditions, someone to be feared instead of worshipped and adored. With no internal presence of the Holy Spirit, restoration of the world looked farther away than ever to Adam.

He thought of the Sadducees in Jerusalem, wealthy men who used their political and religious influence to their personal advantage, strolling through the streets headed to their Temple posts. It was painful for him to listen to their public addresses. In their most official voices, they claimed to channel God's moods and will for his people. They represented their own plans, opinions, and judgements as if they were God's and couldn't have been further off in their characterization of him.

Holding the majority of political seats in the Sanhedrin, the Jewish ruling class, the Sadducees left no room for any beliefs that didn't come strictly from the Torah, the first five books of the Old Testament. They told the Jewish people there was no life after death and most lived by the principal "you can't take it with you when you go," and so devoted all their efforts to building and protecting their political power and wealth. They told the people God demanded primarily three things from them: strict adherence to the Torah, submission to authority, and money.

Adam remembered a particularly egregious gathering when he'd heard them "relay" God's demands during a large temple service. He left desperately wanting to hit something. When he got home the chair leg was the unfortunate recipient of his wrath, and his shin supported a large ugly purple bruise where the chair had fought back.

It was during this time Adam had become extremely depressed. His descendants seemed so dispassionate about God and their religion. *But who could blame them?* he thought realistically. God's so called appointed mouthpieces burdened and disheartened the people, insisting everyone would be excluded from any form of heaven, on Earth or after. What hope for the people was left? Some Pharisees and most Sadducees did exactly what they preached against once they left the temple stairs, making them the greatest hypocrites of the day. At one point Jesus had called them vipers and compared them to Satan himself.

Adam was dismayed and greatly concerned by God's silence and lack of "smiting" those who misrepresented him. It almost drove him to a breaking point. "Why don't you intervene? Say something? Do something?" he demanded. God remained silent and Adam started to panic. Had God checked out? Had the rejection been too much for him? Was he leaving Man to his own devices? Never to return?

Adam desperately wanted God to show up in a cloud of fire and burn down the house, so to speak, while announcing to the world he was still on the throne, watching, and caring about the well-being of his family. Why would God ignore the blatant misrepresentation of his word and the hypocrisy of the religious leaders? Had he given up on the idea of redeeming the world? Making people behave?

One evening after attending temple services, Adam staggered home, heartsick and desperate. He reached his yard and saw a stranger nonchalantly leaning against his front door, eating a strange concoction out of a makeshift bowl. The man had a strange familiarity about him, but Adam couldn't place him.

"Can I help you?" he asked politely as he stepped into the yard.

"I doubt it," his guest retorted. "But you look like you could use a little."

"A little what?"

"Help."

"Who are you and what are you doing on my doorstep?" Adam asked, less politely this time.

"Dying of curiosity," was the answer. The stranger leaned over and with his foot opened Adam's front door. He moved aside allowing the owner to enter.

Who was this person? Adam eyed him suspiciously as he passed across the doorstep. Dark, tough, thin, untamed. A heavy camel skin draped over his tunic was tied to the waist with a leather belt to keep it from falling off. His hair, black and wiry, not only fell in strands below his shoulders but in equal distance fluttered upwards. One side decidedly shorter than the other appeared to have been either caught, cut, or burned off.

Wild, raven-colored eyes constantly darted back and forth, scouring Adam's bushes on the lookout for nefarious criminals or worse yet, Roman soldiers. His eyebrows were heavy and thick and almost met in the middle, giving him the appearance of someone either angry, suspicious, or, most likely, both.

Something else caught Adam's attention as he passed his guest. The contents of his bowl. What was that *smell*?

Adam regarded the fellow distrustfully. Without an invitation the stranger followed him into the cabin and seated himself on a small wooden chair. He still held the bowl but pulled out another chair from underneath the window with his foot. He motioned for Adam to sit.

Adam made a face. "What are you eating?"

"I'll ask the questions here, if you don't mind."

Adam held his hands out in mock acquiescence. "Please."

Never taking his eyes from Adam's face the man set the bowl on the floor and wiped his face with the back of his hand. He rocked back on the chair. Adam noticed the hair on his legs was as wild as it was on his head. Surprisingly, his sandals appeared to be new and of very good quality.

Adam's distrust turned to curiosity. Something told him, despite appearances, this man was anything but mad.

Both men sized each other up for some time before John the Baptist finally spoke. "I don't know if I envy or pity you."

"Why should you do either?" John rocked further back on the chair and Adam declined warning him about its wounded leg.

"Oh, I don't know," John said as he chewed off a fingernail and spit it onto the dirt floor. "To see every movement of God's hand on Earth. To have lived perfectly in Paradise with the mother of all mankind. Every mineral, rock, and element bowing to your will. The Almighty as an evening companion, discussing the day's events." John released a low, slow but impressive whistle.

Adam stared open-mouthed.

John's tone sobered. "But to have lost it all the way you did. My Lord, man. How have you survived yourself?"

Adam continued to stare. His mind could form no questions, nor response.

His guest was brusque, feral, and although brutally tactless, not without total sensitivity. He stood up and poured his host a mug of wine from a container sitting on the table and handed it to him. He poured one for himself, drank heavily from the cup, refilled it to the brim, and sat back down. He hummed a tune to himself and waited.

Finally, Adam composed himself enough to speak. "How did he tell you?"

"How he told me isn't important," John stretched and yawned. "My accusers say I'm crazy," he said lazily, never taking his eyes off his host. "When God first told me about you, I wondered if they were right."

"How long ago?" Adam choked out.

"About a month, I guess. I saw you walking on the road. That night I had a dream about you. You and God were walking in the Garden. There was a woman, a snake, and an exit. The next morning, he spoke to my mind and confirmed it. This morning, he said it was time to come to you. I knew I'd never have thought of it myself." He spread out his hands as if to say, "That's all I know . . ."

"Some people believe I'm an Elijah," he continued after a few minutes in order to break the uncomfortable silence. "You know, like him but not really him sort of thing?" he picked something out of his teeth. "I asked God if that's what he meant. You were here in the *spirit* of Adam."

John laughed and showed a partially chipped eye tooth. "The Lord said one word to me. 'Original.'" John let out another slow whistle. "Tell me that won't mess with a guy's head. Even one with a wick as hot as mine."

Even in his swirling fog Adam marveled at the man's faith. Not many people would have accepted such an idea, let alone acted on it, with simply a dream, an impression, and one word from the Lord. "That's why you're here?" he finally sputtered. "You had a dream and God casually mentioned you might drop by?"

"Wouldn't you come see for yourself?" John gave a short laugh. "What did I have to lose? Somebody new might call me crazy?" He spun his eyes around wildly in his head, stuck his tongue out, and threw his hands in the air to exaggerate his point, which Adam found quite unnecessary.

He scrutinized his guest once more. He found it noteworthy the Lord would be on speaking terms with such an unorthodox fellow. John was a prophet of sorts, Adam thought, although he certainly didn't look or act like a Pharisee or Sadducee.

"Who are you and why did God tell you about me?"

"I'm John," he said, "and I'm here to tell you not to worry." Adam lifted his eyebrows and John continued. "God's currently restoring all that was lost, re-opening the door to Paradise and," he said without humility, "I am *huge* in this story."

Adam's pulse started to race. "How?"

"Uh, read your Torah, Adam," he chided. "'Unto the world a savior is born.' He's on Earth now and I'm going to introduce him. I know everything about him. Ask me anything." He knew the impact his words would have, and he studied Adam's face to gauge his reaction.

When he was satisfied he had his host's complete attention, John continued. "The savior we've all been waiting on is here. The savior who, sorry," he looked at Adam and shrugged his shoulders, "is currently fixing what you messed up."

Adam couldn't contain himself. He jumped to his feet sending his wine sprawling. "Who is he? Is it you?" he sputtered. Through tears Adam scrutinized his companion and doubted the Lord would use such an unlikely tool.

"Sit down." John stood up and poured himself and Adam another cup of wine, mopping up the spill with his foot using a clean tunic of Adam's laying nearby, careful not to get red wine on his new shoes. He waited until his host had composed himself, which was no short amount of time.

When he had as much of Adam's attention as he could expect, he answered calmly, "The man is not me. He is, however, a close and dear friend and actually a relative of mine. He tells me everything," he bragged.

"Even so," he said more to himself than to Adam, "in every way he is far beyond me."

"A relative of yours?" Adam couldn't believe it. He jumped to his feet again, this time turning the chair over. "Take me to him." When John didn't move Adam roared, "Now!"

John thought for a moment and simply said, "No."

Adam stood still not knowing what to do, shaking with emotion. To be so close to God's solution! The one person who would return

Paradise to Earth. Restore God to his people. Finally, to set right all Adam had wronged.

Everything Adam wanted, prayed for, would himself die for, was known to the wild man in front of him. He was overwhelmed by emotion as he leapt toward John and yanked him out of his chair. Holding him by the tunic and breathing hard into his face he demanded, "Tell me where he is, and I'll find him myself."

"I can't," John answered calmly, "he's gone away, and no one is sure when he'll return."

"Where is he? I will go to him!"

John removed Adam's hand from his tunic, straightened it, and moved towards the door. "I'm leaving. You can't take any more excitement today. I'll be back tomorrow. Get more wine."

Adam stood without moving. John looked at him from the door. "Please tell me. I have to know," Adam choked out hoarsely.

John looked at his new friend with compassion. "I don't exactly know where he is, brother. All I can tell you is he's somewhere in the desert. He's by himself. He's been gone about a month. He's not to be disturbed. You'll have to wait until he returns to ask your questions," he sighed, "just like the rest of us."

Adam moved toward the door, helplessly following John's back. His guest was leaving. "At least tell me," he said desperate for information, "what exactly is he doing in the desert?"

John turned back around to look Adam in the face. "It's not what he's doing in the desert that's important. It's what God's doing *to* him that matters."

CHAPTER 25

"WHAT WAS JESUS LIKE?" GRACE ASKED, TREADING gently. He was after all, the "antidote" to the sin virus Adam had introduced. It was more than likely a sore subject.

Adam smiled at the memory and spontaneously broke into song, *"Simply irresistible . . ."* He felt her looking at him expectantly. He stopped singing, shrugged, and said, "Just like they say, he was perfect, Grace. Absolutely perfect."

"What's perfect look like?"

Adam leaned his head back against his headrest and closed his eyes. It was obvious thinking of Jesus brought him peace and not the discomfort she feared.

"Well, he didn't look or act like the traditional pictures or old movie portrayals."

"No?"

He mildly snorted. "Does the Jesus that comes to mind make you think of a guy who could catch a football or carry a couple of two by fours on one shoulder?"

She laughed. "Hardly."

"That's what I mean. The Jesus I knew was God *and* Man in the flesh. If he was around today he could run a mile in under five minutes, build a bridge, negotiate a helicopter rescue, and he'd probably drive a sports car and keep a truck in the garage. Jesus was fully alive, fully present, fully passionate, fully *masculine*. Yet in the old movies I've seen he always looks a wee bit foggy, like his head's in the clouds. Like he just woke up and isn't quite sure where he is. Never moves his head too fast."

"He wasn't like that?"

"Just the opposite. Jesus was human as well as God and he did both beautifully. He was a lot of fun, actually. There wasn't a day he didn't find something to laugh out loud about. His critics falsely called him a glutton and a wine bibber, but I can tell you he enjoyed a good meal. He also loved music, spirited conversation, a good play, and he really liked to dance. He made up songs spontaneously and his deep, rich baritone, when singing about something important to him, could bring a rock to tears. He used his hands to punctuate his expressions, you could hear his sneeze a block away, and he was by far the best friend I ever had."

"He was outgoing?"

"Um," Adam thought, "yes and no. Sort of a mixture. He liked to go off by himself and when he did his friends pretty much knew to leave him alone. He had a lot on his mind. But when he wanted company, he was totally engaged and engaging."

"What'd he talk about?"

Adam broke into song, *"People . . ."*

Grace reached up and pretended to ring her call bell. "I'm asking for a different seat," she quipped.

He smiled unconcerned. "He was passionate. Whatever he talked about came alive in front of your very eyes. He especially liked to talk about his mom, his family, and human nature." He shifted his weight in his seat and adjusted his seat back trying to get a little more comfortable. "But besides people, he mainly loved to talk about the Father. He'd tell us something God had told him that we could relate to and was always interested in whatever God was telling us as well. Even though God talked constantly to him and only periodically to us."

She smiled, interested in his perspective of Jesus the man and friend. "Anything else?" She found that she enjoyed giving Adam the opportunity to talk about something that obviously gave him great pleasure and she wanted him to continue.

"He was a great storyteller," he reminisced. "Animated as well as passionate. He had lots of charisma, and his stories were interesting but even though his messages could apply to anyone his words actually had a way of piercing the heart of each individual present. Every person listening walked away thinking he'd just been talking to them."

"I can see that," Grace said earnestly.

"Almost everybody who got to know him, not including many of the Pharisees, really liked him," Adam said. "He was self-confident, but not cocky. He was selective about who he let into his inner circle but once he made a friend he'd lend him the robe off his back. He never allowed anyone in his presence to trash someone else merely for sport whether he knew them or not. He gave us hope for a better tomorrow but was practical and aware of the temperature of the day."

Adam continued nostalgically, "He never ran from a fight but never picked one either. He's someone you'd want with you if you were ever in a fix. He was strong but not aggressive, easygoing but not a pushover. Women loved him. Men respected him. Kids flocked to him. He didn't exactly have a halo, but with all that, who needed one?"

"Wow," she said impressed. "Was he good-looking, too?"

"The women thought so. I'm not a hundred percent sure it wasn't his way with them and not necessarily his looks they found so appealing."

"Jesus had a way with women?" she asked, surprised.

Adam chuckled. "Jesus had a way with everybody."

"Why did women like him so much?"

"Mainly because he stood up for them when it wasn't convenient or popular. You'd have to understand the culture of the day to really appreciate it, Grace." He clucked his tongue in disapproval. "Women were disregarded and disrespected by the church, the government, and by most men. They had almost no rights and only the privileges their husbands allowed them."

"That's awful!" she said, appalled.

"It was the culture. A well-respected religious teacher who came before Jesus went on a campaign claiming women were not trustworthy. He was instrumental in changing religious law, making it easy for a man to divorce his wife for no other reason than he didn't like the color of her hair.

"As I am sure you're aware, women couldn't support themselves respectably at the time," he elaborated, "so they were often controlled by fear. They could be cast out of their homes, friendless and penniless, stripped away from their children and families simply because their husband didn't like their mother-in-law hanging around. It was brutal!"

"What did Jesus do?"

"Jesus came to change the status quo, Grace. It was one of the reasons he was so controversial, popular, and yet feared by those invested in tradition. So, in typical Jesus fashion, he advocated for the women repeatedly and publicly in ways no other man had done. It didn't matter what kind of woman, Jesus protected them all. Respectable women, outcasts, poor women, rich women, prostitutes. His mama raised him right, that's for sure. Because he was so well-respected his obvious and blatant regard for women elevated their position in much of society. At least in the women's circles he was a local hero even before he died.

"And If Jesus hadn't made his regard for women clear prior to his resurrection, he certainly made a major statement on the day of his return. He appeared first outside the tomb to the two Marys and Salome because he wanted to honor them by being the first to see him. By being the first and carrying the news of his return, it elevated their status among the disciples and others all the way throughout history."

"Wow! Did they change the laws?"

"Not totally, but a lot of religious leaders fought to make it harder for men to divorce their wives without cause after that. Jesus was a major influencer and his obvious regard for women helped many stop living in fear and get their self-respect back."

Grace was impressed. She didn't know Jesus was such an advocate for women. "What else do you remember?"

"Well, like I said, he's the best friend I've ever had. I miss him terribly even though I still talk to him 'online' so to speak."

"What makes him such a great friend?"

"He listens to me and talks to me about things that are important to both of us," he said simply.

"That'll usually do it," she said matter-of-factly.

"Talking with Jesus was a lot like talking with God when I was in the Garden, but our relationship and what we talked about was quite a bit different due to my change in circumstances."

"Did he treat you more like a student?"

"No. Not like that." Adam smiled and studied his hands. "It's difficult to explain. He was full of good advice, teaching, and healing and all but more than anything," he paused, "I guess I loved Jesus like the brother I never had, and he felt the same about me. He was God but still he treated me like an equal. He said he thought of me as an equal."

"If he was God how could that be?"

"He respected me. Even though I'd made some huge mistakes he said it was our commonalities that created our bond and the differences between us really didn't matter that much. He said neither of us had human fathers, that God was our father and that made us brothers in a unique way. He helped me almost remember what it felt like to be perfect and the exhilaration of feeling totally alive, operating on all cylinders, without the encumbrances of sin clouding my mind or self-confidence. He said we each carried secrets that others couldn't relate to, which made us both feel pretty lonely at times."

"What else did you have in common?" she asked kindly.

"Lots of things." He fumbled with his seat belt underneath his tray table, pulled it out, and decided to just leave it unbuckled. "We were both intent on ridding the world of sin because we know how good it feels to be free. We each understood things about our heavenly father that other people couldn't even imagine. That alone was like a glue between us."

"What kind of things?" she interrupted.

He looked down at his hands again and then said, "It's hard to describe, Grace, to someone who's never met God in person, never walked with him at night, never had him kiss your forehead, bring you presents, laugh at your jokes. But I guess I'd just have to summarize by saying that God was sort of a combination of majesty and over the top . . . love."

Grace faintly shook her head and agreed she couldn't imagine.

He continued, "We just wanted other people to see it too.

Comprehend it. Let go of their spiritual misconceptions, let God out of the box they'd put him in, the one the religious community had constructed, grab hold of the Beautiful Vision even if just a wee bit. We both wanted to take a machete to people's obstacles that kept them from seeing the truth. We knew if people could see God's heart, catch a glimpse of his nature and his dreams for the world, know him for who he is and not who people said he was then they'd love him like we did. Do," he corrected himself. "And people loving the Father was and is very important to us both."

"Why is that, do you think?" she interrupted again.

"Because he so deserves it," he said automatically. Grace saw that Adam didn't say it because he was supposed to say it, he said it because it's true.

He continued, "So it was highly frustrating to us both when the Pharisees and Sadducees misrepresented God's nature, his will for his family, and for the world. Remember, Jesus came to upset the status quo. He came to set things straight. Reveal the truth about God, dispel the BS the enemy had been planting for centuries.

"That's probably one of the reasons why he, Jesus the Rebel, was so insistent we learn to pray more effectively. Why he gave us the Lord's prayer and made us memorize and pray it daily." He quoted, "'Thy kingdom come, thy will be done on Earth as it is in heaven.' Jesus wanted to raise our expectations and impress upon us the power we have to change our neighborhoods, our families, our workplace, and our own lives. He wanted us, and still does, to find out for ourselves, and then demonstrate how to love God and one another, embody righteousness, wield God's power in doing his will, find our identities in Christ and our purposes, and not stop until our individual worlds are miniature heavens, wherever we are. Because if our own worlds look more like

God's kingdom, then given the domino effect," he held his hands out, "what's to keep it from spreading?"

Grace looked at Adam as he stared straight ahead, deep in thought, twirling his ring. It was obvious his spirituality, his religion, his beliefs, meant more to him than an outstanding obligation to God or to his descendants. More than even a way to soothe his conscience for the damage he'd introduced. Adam's passion stemmed from a deep well of love for God, his Son, his restored kingdom, but also from a desire to see the world and God reunited. Adam wanted the people of the world to see and experience God as he did—loving father, companion, confidante, protector, provider, cheerleader, foxhole buddy, and eternal BFF.

Adam drummed his fingers on his tray table absently as he further reminisced. "Jesus was grateful for my friendship, and I loved and clung to him knowing each day I had with him was limited and precious. I wanted to spend all my time with him and felt lucky he included me in his life." Even in the cabin dimness Grace could feel Adam's emotion. "I undoubtedly missed him more than anyone after he left. Maybe even more than his mom."

"Anything else?" she asked softly.

"I'm not bragging but we actually looked a lot alike. Looking at him was almost like looking in a mirror. We had the same dad, you know," he reminded her.

"Looked alike how?"

Adam batted his eyes exaggeratingly at Grace. "His eyes were stunning." She laughed out loud, and he said, "No really. He had the most beautiful brown eyes you ever saw. They weren't chocolate brown, they were more of a dark amber with flecks of blue and gold that reflected the light."

"He had a very slight chip on his front right tooth that gave him a look of mischief when he smiled, which was often because he had such a great sense of humor. He wasn't loud or the life of the party, but he could really make a group of guys laugh. His sense of humor was intelligent and subtle and lost on many people."

He recalled one of Jesus' early visits to his shop. Adam had owned a small store in the Galilee area and had hired a few men to build a counter to replace an old rickety table he'd been using. The men got into a disagreement over the best way to design it. The first man, Joseph, thought it should be shorter because most of Adam's customers were women and if it were too tall it would be harder for them to spread out and study their choices. His partner, Bartholomew, thought it should be taller because it would be easier on Adam's back not to have to lean over all day.

No one had seen Jesus enter the shop or saw him leaning against the wall listening to their conversation. After much discussion and contemplation, Adam and the two workers heard a voice ask, "Why not make it shorter but dig a hole for Adam to stand in?"

He said it with such earnestness, the three men nodded and stood silently for several minutes considering the possibility. They never realized he wasn't serious until finally they saw the grin.

Adam gave a whoop of laughter at the memory as he told Grace the story. She smiled when he was finished. She looked at Adam in the faint light of the plane. The look on his face reflected such love and fond memories. She thought wistfully, *I wish Jesus would come back and make me laugh.*

CHAPTER 26

THE MAN ACROSS THE AISLE WOKE UP AND PULLED OUT HIS computer. He adjusted his earphones and the screen lit up with the opening scenes of a recent Cowboy game. His wife woke up as well and nudged him. He pushed the pause button and stood to let her out to use the lavatory. He was a large man and accidentally bumped into Adam's arm. He apologized and seeing that both Adam and Grace were wide awake, engaged them in conversation. He said in hushed tones, "We're going on a cruise around the islands. Either one of you ever done that?"

They both shook their heads and Adam said, "No, but I'd like to. What cruise line?"

"Norwegian. My in-laws did it last year and said it was great. We'll see. My wife gets seasick, but she brought those patches along. We've never done a cruise before."

Adam said, "Good luck. I bet you'll have a good time."

The woman came out of the bathroom and Adam noticed pink fuzzy house slippers had replaced her shoes. She and her husband got re-settled. She pulled out the sleep mask handed out by the airline and covered her eyes, then leaned her seat back and adjusted her pillow while her husband resumed his game.

Grace said, "Something I've never understood," she asked cautiously, "is why do you think Jesus had to die? If he came to help people be born again and spread the Good News, wouldn't God's purposes have been better served by Jesus living a nice long life?"

Adam remembered the first time he'd insisted on an answer to that very same question. He remembered the devastation he'd felt when he first heard the news Jesus was preparing to die. It had been Peter who'd told him.

Peter, nor any of the disciples, were aware of Adam's true identity. John the Baptist insisted on changing Adam's name to Simon, as to not arouse any suspicion in the others. Adam and Jesus both had called him paranoid but it was one of John's more sedate requests, so Adam had begrudgingly agreed.

Peter knew Adam as Simon, that he was a friend of Cousin John, and one of the many followers Jesus had befriended along the way. If Simon was a friend of Jesus and John's it was good enough for Peter.

The two were sitting alone on a bench outside a local inn by the river having lunch. Peter, a big, strong, burly man with dark black shoulder-length hair and bushy beard, was gnawing on a piece of fish. Peter delivered the news surprisingly calmly. Adam, who had finished his lunch and was enjoying the sun and scenery, did not receive it in the same manner.

"Jesus said he's going to *die*?" he demanded, jumping off the bench.

Peter made Adam wait for an answer while he struggled with a catfish bone. He'd been relaying a conversation he'd had with Jesus. A conversation where he'd announced his time on Earth was finished, and he was going to die.

What Peter should have said, he thought later when he saw the panic in Adam's eyes, was Jesus *thought* he might die. Peter too had panicked but after consideration was certain his teacher had only been speaking metaphorically. Jesus was always talking about dying to the flesh.

"Don't worry," he reassured Adam, "Jesus isn't going to die. It's not possible." He was going to deliver them from Roman oppression and establish a new government. He'd told them so.

Peter patted his sword smugly. "Nobody's going to touch a hair on his head. Not on my watch." He turned his head and spit the bone to the ground forcefully then lifted the bottom of his tunic and wiped his mouth with it. Adam sat back down and eyed his friend skeptically.

Peter took another bite and said, with his mouth full, "This is how I know. After I told Jesus I didn't believe he would really die he said, 'Get behind me Satan!'" Peter swallowed and took another bite of fish. "I guess he told him! He realized the truth of my words and told Satan right there to quit taunting him. It was awesome." He washed the fish down with a drink from his stein.

Without explanation, Adam leapt from the bench and fled the scene, leaving Peter staring after him, a piece of bone stuck in his beard. Adam knew Jesus was not speaking metaphorically.

He found him waiting by the side of the road less than a mile from where he'd been having lunch with Peter.

"Tell me it's not what you meant," he panted. "Tell me you aren't the sacrifice."

Jesus looked at him more compassionately than anyone had ever looked at him in his life. "Tell me!" Adam shrieked and grabbed him by the shoulders, shaking him as tears streamed down both men's cheeks. Adam fell to the ground, convulsing in sobs, unable to think or breathe.

Jesus sat in the dirt beside his half-brother and held him until he could cry no more. "Let me do it," Adam hoarsely begged when he could finally speak. "If there is still a God in heaven who ever loved me, let me do it."

Jesus looked at him and shook his head slowly but sadly. "You know it has to be me."

"But it's not fair," Adam wailed. "It's my responsibility!" he insisted, knowing his words were a waste of time.

Jesus answered him. "You are the human son of God. I am the divine one. I am the only other person alive besides you who has ever been without sin. The only acceptable sacrifice Justice will accept." He looked at him compassionately but said candidly, "We both know you can't do it."

"No!" Adam yelled defiantly. He jumped up and ran, leaving Jesus sitting by the road mournfully watching his friend stumble away, leaving in the direction he came.

Adam ran until he could run no more. Eventually, out of breath and energy, he stopped in front of a large fig tree, threw himself onto the ground, buried his face in the grass, and sobbed until his sides ached with pain. Eventually he rolled over on his back and lifted his arms and voice to the sky.

"Abba!" he cried out to the heavenlies. "Have mercy, I beg you!"

he pleaded. He searched the skies and in his mind willed it to part once again to show him the face of his father. The sun shone bright, a few clouds rolled past, and Adam could hear the sounds of birds sweetly chirping from the branches above. Yet the heavens stayed closed.

Eventually he sat up, leaned against the tree, and shouted angrily, "I know you're still listening even if you won't show your face to me! So hear this!" He as much spat the words into the air. "I vow on this day to never speak your name again. I hereby renounce my oath to help restore your kingdom and undo whatever damage I've created. As far as I'm concerned it can all go to hell!" he screamed. He drew a deep breath and continued angrily, "I renounce my relationship with you, no longer call you Father, and commit to side with your enemies to destroy the rest of creation. From this day forward," he screamed frantically and then continued, "If you would dare to kill an innocent son when the guilty one is standing before you, prepared to face the consequences of my actions, then you are not the God or father I once knew. Consider me dead to you, to your cause, and to the world. From this day forth!" Adam threw himself back onto his stomach, broke into fresh sobs, and pounded his fists into the ground.

Lying face down, completely spent, he was surprised to feel a tender hand on his shoulder. He turned to see Jesus looking down at him compassionately. He simply said to Adam, "The Father has a response to your vow, Adam. 'I love you, you love me, nothing else matters between us. And nothing can change that.'"

Adam sighed as he turned his attention back to Grace. "Jesus' life shows us how to love and to be free. But his death and his resurrection," he said somberly, "are what give us the power to do it."

CHAPTER 27

THE BABY BEHIND THEM WOKE UP AND BEGAN TO CRY. THE mother rang her call button and Katie hurried past to the rescue. Grace noticed Adam's employee Nick stayed in the galley and waited for her instead of returning to his seat. Katie took a bottle from the mother and returned to heat it up.

The baby's cries turned from whimpers to impatient screams, temporarily halting any conversation. Adam took the opportunity to stretch his legs and use the washroom. Nick, a tall man with sandy brown hair and light freckles leaned against the lavatory door talking to Katie as she heated the bottle. "Too much coffee?" he asked and stepped aside to let Adam pass.

Grace looked out the window. Still dark outside, she looked at her watch. They were more than halfway to Honolulu, and she was still no closer to helping Adam solve his relationship issue with God. She now knew the dilemma wasn't ruining his life. Nor was it a head injury, chemical imbalance, or even a viable threat. She had no doubt at all that with or without her Adam and his God would certainly work the problem out and communication would be once again restored. Adam had even assured her his life had all but returned to a total paradise. However, the problem was currently significant enough for him to seek out the ear of a stranger.

Also, Grace had baited her seatmate into self-disclosure, she reminded herself. It had been unprofessional. Her motivation had been seeking evening entertainment and he'd certainly provided that and more, she thought, with no small amount of wonder. So, she owed him.

She glanced at the Cowboy game the man across the aisle was watching on his laptop and absently watched the coach yelling at a referee. Plus, she continued in her thoughts, she liked Adam. He had trusted her with his secret. For the first time in more than two decades Grace closed her eyes and silently prayed to a God she had no assurance would still be listening. "If you're there, help me help him. Please," she added humbly.

In a few minutes, Adam started to exit the restroom but paused to let Katie pass. She rushed by with the bottle of formula and delivered it to the mother who quickly placed it in the baby's mouth. To the relief of the other passengers it did the trick, soothed the child and restored relative silence once again to the cabin.

As a therapist Grace was trained to put herself in her patient's shoes and wonder how she would respond if she was in their situation. Katie returned to the galley and Grace looked towards the front of the cabin. She could see Adam leaning against the wall, obviously talking to her and his co-worker, but both were hidden from sight by the partition. It reminded Grace of someone in a confessional talking to their priest.

She saw a flickering of light from the corner of her eye and glanced again at the ball game. She saw a running back fumble the ball and a pileup ensued before the referee determined it had been recovered by the opposition, causing the other team's offense to take the field. She continued to watch as the camera followed the disgraced running back as he skulked off the field. She looked out the window again. She saw the vast emptiness of the nighttime sky and wondered, *Adam said God had forgiven him and all was well between them. Almost. Could the lingering problem possibly be that he believes God forgives but maybe doesn't forget?*

She glanced at the ball game again. Wouldn't Adam at least, at some level, still feel the devastation of surrendering the field to God's enemy? Every time he talked to God wouldn't every word be shadowed by all that wasn't being said? Undoubtedly both father and son had suffered mightily that day at the cross. If Adam thought he should've been the one to be crucified, not Jesus, and rightly so, could he ever truly let go of the deep pain of shame and regret? Down deep, would his father really want him to? Would Jesus? *Why would they?* she wondered silently. *Why shouldn't Adam be left to wallow in misery for what he'd done? Look at the people still suffering because of it,* she thought. *If Adam thought so too, wouldn't that explain the current barrier to his communication with God? What if God was silent with Adam because he was still mad at him, or worse yet, didn't love him anymore? Is that what Adam thought? Even subconsciously?*

She debated whether to gently broach the subject. She absently chewed at her hangnail and stopped, wondering if Katie might have a Band-Aid. She continued her internal debate. She could lightly question him about it but then quickly reconsidered. They were 30,000 feet in the air. What if things got messy? Deep wounds when exposed can be extremely painful and she was sure if this wound wasn't healed it would be no exception. If still active, the pain should be uncovered and dealt with slowly and carefully in a monitored setting. Certainly not miles in the air over drinks.

She debated the options and concluded it was not only unprofessional of her to attempt emotional surgery on Adam's subconscious on an airplane, but it could also be dangerous. She wondered how he would respond if she suggested they get together after their trip to continue their discussions in a more private and professional office environment.

She contemplated the plausibility of the plan. He lived in Fort Worth. She lived in Austin. Meeting again would be inconvenient. Still, it was just a three-and-a-half-hour drive down I-35. They could make it work. Or, she thought, she could just refer him to someone in Fort Worth. She had plenty of respected colleagues there. As she watched Adam approach, she thought to herself, *But what are the chances anyone would believe him? No matter how open-minded they claimed to be.* She shook her head and decided protectively, *No way. He needs me.*

Adam had asked Katie for two fresh glasses of water. He approached, handed both to Grace plus fresh napkins, sat down, buckled his seat belt, and said, "I was thinking in the bathroom God put you on this plane so you could help me. We don't have all night. You need to step it up."

She set the waters on the napkins on the tray between them. "I'm not your therapist. I'm your friend. Remember?"

He chuckled and said, "We both know you won't sleep tonight if you don't add one more win to your roster."

"Adam," she said gently but cautiously.

"Yes, Grace?" he responded expectantly.

"Do you think you'd like to stay in touch. You know," she faltered, "after tonight?"

He broke into a broad grin. He reached into his briefcase, pulled out his phone, opened up his contacts, clicked the add icon, and said, "Last name?"

She laughed happily and gave him her information. He entered it and showed her the screen. "Already in my favorites," he said and as she continued to grin he held up his phone, clicked the camera button, and took her picture.

"Hey!" she protested. "I wasn't ready!"

"I need a profile picture, I might forget you," he teased and showed her the photo. "You look fine." She complained she didn't have on any lipstick, he cropped it anyway and clicked the save icon. He put his phone away and said, "Okay, go."

She said, "So I really shouldn't help you outside of a professional setting. It's not ethical." She glanced at him sideways. "So maybe it's best if we wait and talk about this again in my office in Austin."

He reached over and took her by the hand and looked into her eyes. "Grace?"

"Yes," she said nervously, aware of the ruggedness and warmth of his hand.

"You're fired again. And if I come to Austin to see you, it certainly isn't going to be to sit in your office."

They held each other's glance for a moment and in the darkness of the cabin she couldn't tell if he was joking with her or not. She looked down, acutely aware of his nearness and the feel of his strong fingers wrapped around her small palm. She laughed nervously and pulled her hand away. In an attempt to change the subject, she asked, "What else do you remember about Jesus?"

Adam leaned his head back on his headrest, scratched his ear thoughtfully, and said, "Lots. When he talked about God there was nothing phony or preachy about him. If any of us had a problem, before giving us any advice, he'd stop, look up slightly, and ask the Father for help, like he was standing right there with us."

"Didn't that seem odd?"

"Not when he did it. It seemed perfectly natural and more than once I found myself looking around thinking maybe I'd see God walking across the yard just like the old days."

"Did you ever see him do a miracle?"

"Plenty of times. I personally never needed a physical healing, but he certainly gave me an emotional one. He was my original, and no offense, the greatest therapist I ever had."

"None taken. Jesus was your therapist?"

"Is. He doesn't have any qualms about being friend and therapist," he poked her arm teasingly. "He's called Counselor for a reason. I think a man owes it to himself to become all he's created to be. I'd gotten healthy enough to want that again. Jesus offered to help me, and I took him up on it."

Grace knew she couldn't even imagine the pain Adam had suffered. "How'd he do it?" she asked curiously.

"He helped me remember my value. My head was filled with so much crap about what God must think of me. I had to get born again. Jesus came along and dismantled those old lies and pain inside me like water pouring down on sugar."

"How?"

"It was a long time ago, Grace." Adam cocked his head trying to remember. "He'd pray, we'd talk, he'd hit a sore spot. He'd ask, 'What did you *decide* here?' Every time he'd ask me that, I'd see a bad decision, something untrue, like I was worthless, or God was terrible, or I should've never been created.

"All the pain and the lies were roadblocks standing between me and God. Jesus said it's important we exchange them for peace and truth, or it makes it hard for God's Spirit and resources to get through. Jesus would never let it go until I found the bad decision that was causing me trouble. Once I did, I felt an immediate release. It's what finally set me free."

"Garbage in, garbage out?"

"Right," he agreed. "But once we found the lie and named it, the truth popped up right behind it and took its place in my heart and mind. Then peace like a river."

Grace nodded, engrossed in his story of healing. "I've noticed some Christian therapists call those bad decisions 'arrows.'"

"Right. I've noticed that too. I call them glitches, faulty programming. But glitches, arrows, lies—whatever you want to call them—are the primary tools the enemy uses, sows, as weapons of spiritual destruction. Jesus would pinpoint the lies inside me by looking for the sore spots in my life and work them out of my psyche like a chiropractor does the knots in your shoulder."

"Bad code?" she asked, and he nodded.

"Bad code," he agreed. "Planted, nurtured, and guarded by Satan and his minions and caused me to malfunction."

"But Jesus got to the root?" she asked.

"On some things. Other things we simply prayed over and they were gone. That's why it's important to give your do-over to God. Only he knows where all the dead bodies are buried."

"So, no one-size-therapy-fits-all?" she asked.

He shook his head. "No cookie-cutter process, what works for one will work for all. It doesn't work that way. The only one who knows for sure what you need and how to deliver it is God."

"But Jesus helped you get born again? Get rid of your crap?"

"Yep. I don't know anyone who gets completely restored all at once. It's usually a process, I think. However, almost immediately he helped me dump the shame," he ran his fingers through his hair remembering. "The relief I felt was overwhelming. Shame over what Eve and I had done, what I'd done to God, to his world. Every murder, rape, every tear shed from all the never-ending pain and suffering that surrounded me. The constant torment of others almost drove me insane." He shook his head mournfully and admitted, "You can't believe how many times I tried to kill myself. But like that movie, *Groundhog Day*, I just kept waking up."

"I'm glad Jesus helped you," she said empathetically, and very truthfully.

"Thank you, me too. He convinced me that God creates all good and all evil for his own purposes, that he knows the end from the beginning, that Eve and I did not take him by total surprise, and what the enemy would use for evil, God can use for good.

"He said because God sees my heart, knows I'm sorry, what's left to judge? What's done is done. I needed to move on or else the enemy had already won."

"And you believed him."

"Well, I saw the truth in what he was saying but it was his 'Jesus power' that actually fixed me. That pain was tattooed on my soul. I couldn't have permanently erased it just because I saw the logic. The enemy had me trapped in a spiritual prison. It takes a stronger spiritual force than the enemy's to spring that kind of lock. Only God's big enough to heal your very soul."

He grinned at her boyishly. "After that I started to remember why I'm so lovable. And except for my recent small set back, which you have failed to fix, my life looks pretty good again."

She considered Adam's renewed self-acceptance and appreciation and she marveled at his recovery. It was almost unbelievable, especially considering how low he'd fallen, she told herself. As a therapist she knew she could never lay claim to helping any of her patients with such dev-astating wounds, achieve that level of healthiness and wholeness, and she was more than impressed with the healing powers of Jesus.

He continued, "After we dealt with my issues, he insisted I be bap-tized. After that, everything changed for me."

"Why did you need to be baptized?"

"It's all part of the do-over. When Jesus and John baptized me in the Jordan, they didn't have to tell me God loves me or about my place in the family and kingdom of God, they helped me remember it."

"Wow! Jesus and John baptized you in the Jordan River? Yowsa!"

He smiled proudly, "Yep. It was something to remember for sure. When Jesus first suggested it, I didn't know how to respond. I was too embarrassed to let anyone baptize me, especially them. But finally, with his and John's urging, I conceded. I thought, why not? What did I have to hide anymore? It felt good to watch all that crap go down knowing it lost its power to haunt me."

Grace was captivated by the story. Suddenly she was aware of a spiritual presence she recognized from her childhood. She looked up and around to see if there was a vent somewhere. The air around her suddenly turned dense, warm, sweet, and strangely comforting. It felt like being wrapped in a thick, warm blanket and hugged closely by someone actively loving her; someone she knew she could trust, re-lax, and lean into.

"The day we all met by the river all the disciples were there and some of my other friends. John prayed over me, but it was Jesus who lowered me into the water. When he did, I thought I was going to fi-nally die."

"Why's that?"

"When I was under the water, I had a vision I was standing in front of God seated on his throne. I was faced with the memories of the day

I ate from the Tree and how Satan and his demons had attacked me. I saw how weak, vulnerable, and alone I'd become after disconnecting from God. Suddenly the water surrounding me seemed to engulf me like a tomb. I felt a tremendous rush, like a part of my spirit was leaving my body, and in my mind I saw a door start to open. I thought, *So this is what it feels like to die.* The water had been so cold when I went in, but suddenly I felt strong, loving arms holding and comforting me as I faced the remnants of all the loneliness, pain, regret, and fears of a lifetime.

"Suddenly all the emotion passed and although I was still submerged, my lungs felt as if they were breathing in the water and it was as light and clean as fresh air. My heart was lifted and all that remained was a sense of happiness, well-being, belonging, and the feeling of light-hearted joy. Almost like I had been in a nightmare but finally awoke to an old comfortable and familiar reality, one where I truly belonged instead of the temporary hell where I'd been living. The sense of love and relief was overwhelming. I was born again, free and alive, remembering my beautiful self once more!

"When Jesus pulled me from the water and I opened my eyes, instead of the Son of God standing before me with me in his arms, it was the Father cradling and holding me as he had when I was a young man back in the Garden. He was smiling proudly at me, with a look on his face that reminded me of how he'd once promised me nothing could ever permanently separate us. Seeing him there like that I cried like a baby. I reached up and grabbed him around the neck hugging him so tight, overwhelmed with joy and relief to be held, loved, forgiven, and in his presence again.

"He tousled my hair and kissed me on the forehead and his eyes shone with love for me just like he'd done a hundred times before. Everyone else saw me hugging Jesus, but he and I both knew who'd really baptized, forgiven, and saved me that day."

Grace had tears in her eyes and reached into her purse to find a tissue. She dabbed her eyes, blew her nose, and said, "All's well that ends well, hmm?"

Adam laughed. "After that I started to remember how proud I was to be called God's son and started to act that way again. I remembered the look God had in his eyes for me, how proud he's always been of me, even when I gave him no reason to be proud. My father loves me and has always seen something great in me even when I couldn't. Jesus did that for me," he said. "He helped me remember how God looks at me.

"Afterwards the enemy tried to put shame on me once again. I struggled with it momentarily but took the problem immediately back to Jesus. He helped me see that I was keeping shame around as a reminder. I guess I thought I needed to hang onto it."

Grace nodded, understanding. "You thought the shame would keep you in line so you wouldn't make the same mistakes again, didn't you?"

"Yes, I felt I owed it to myself and to others to keep the shame as a reminder. I thought if I completely released it, I was denying that I'd ever made the mistakes in the first place."

He took a drink of water and said, "One night after that it was so hot I decided to sleep outside. I suddenly awoke because I heard a faint rustling inside my house. I jumped up and ran inside, armed with nothing but a piece of wood I'd found lying nearby. The house was empty and so thinking it was possibly only a dream, I returned to sleep.

"However, in the morning when I went inside, I noticed something was different. Beside my table lay the open box where I thought I kept the piece of pottery that Cain had destroyed, stained with his blood. The one piece of stained and broken pottery had been skillfully reassembled along with a new array of beautiful mosaic pieces, skillfully spun into the most exquisite urn I'd ever seen, accompanied by a note. In Jesus' handwriting the note simply said, 'Through receiving the Spirit we are all made members of the body of Christ. What God has joined together let no man tear asunder.'

"Jesus showed me God wants us to let go of the shame of our past mistakes. Shame and regret are the tools of the enemy, not God's. God's toolbox is filled with much better equipment."

Grace gasped and tears flooded her eyes. She looked at Adam and together they smiled in appreciation of the greatest gift Adam had ever received. Complete and total healing, forever cemented through a visual aid handcrafted by the Healer himself.

Adam said, "The forgiveness we give ourselves is the gift we give back to Jesus, acknowledging his gift to us at the cross. Hanging onto judgment and condemnation of self and others is a way of denying Christ's sacrifice, not honoring him for it.

Grace taking her cue from her seatmate started to lightly sing, "Let it go, let it go . . ."

Adam laughed and pulled out his phone and showed Grace a picture of the cutest puppy she'd ever seen. He looked just like a little lion. Adam announced he'd just gotten him and had named him Sebastion.

CHAPTER 28

G RACE ASKED, "COULD JESUS ACTUALLY TURN WATER INTO wine?" Adam nodded and she said, "That's something I could really use. If I was ever going to do miracles, I'd ask God to make that my first one."

Adam laughed. "I actually walked with him to the wedding where that first happened. You should've seen his friends go wild after that! We did everything possible to convince him to show us what else he could do."

"Did he?"

"No," he shook his head and chuckled.

"Why not?"

He admitted, slightly embarrassed, "He wasn't about to pull a rabbit out of a hat like some party trick."

She smiled. "What else happened while you were with him?"

"Lots of things. I'll jot down the best ones and find you in Austin. We'll have a 'best of' session." She nodded and smiled, and he silently thanked God again for her. Even if he didn't come up with any answers that night, the joy of having someone to talk to again brought him so much pleasure and relief.

He looked at his new friend whose pretty face still scrutinized his so closely for clues. Adam had convinced her that Jesus healed him from the terrible pain and shame of his fall, but she knew something was still standing in between him and his father and she wanted to help him find it. He said he was stuck. It bothered him.

Grace was convinced God wanted him to find the answer. *How hard can this be?* she asked herself impatiently. Finally, she asked, "What else can be bothering you, Adam. If you feel like you're back to your old self, what else is going on? Pray if you need to and then guess," she insisted.

She turned on the overhead light, leaned down, and reached into her purse to search for anything to wrap around her throbbing finger and found nothing but a tissue. With her head bent over he noticed again the hint of gold that weaved through her hair. He'd always liked Austin, he thought. He was already looking forward to the trip.

She wrapped the tissue around her finger, pressed it tightly, closed her purse, and pushed it under the seat again. "Well?" she looked at Adam expectantly.

Adam struggled to remember what he was supposed to be pondering. "Oh, yes. I'm supposed to be guessing."

She frowned at him. "Did anything else happen during Jesus' life you think we should talk about? Maybe after you were baptized? Some other glitch that snuck it's way in?" When he looked at her blankly she insisted, "Something's blocking your spiritual ears," she said wisely. "What is it?"

"Well, I was there when Jesus died," he suggested. "Even though I'm healed from the pain maybe the problem goes back to something that happened then. The whole event was certainly traumatizing."

That could certainly be it, Grace concluded quickly. Maybe Adam had only been partially healed. Deep wounds heal in layers, she knew. But again, should she broach it on a plane? What if he hadn't dealt with the worst of it? "Do you really want to talk about that now?" she asked gently.

"Why not? I dealt with the pain a long time ago."

She paused. "I don't know, Adam. Maybe we should wait until we land."

"You think I'll have a big breakdown and they'll have to call for a doctor?"

"I am a doctor," she reminded him drolly.

He was silent for a moment and said, "It's been a long time, Grace. I'm sure I've dealt with it."

"But are you sure it didn't damage your relationship with God? Even a little? I know you said you're over it, but guilt and shame are major stumbling blocks. Are you sure some isn't still hanging around?"

They sat silent for a few minutes, thinking, both sipping their water. Finally he said, "I have an idea. I'll tell you what happened, and we'll see where it goes. If something too painful pops up, we'll table it for later. Okay?"

"Perfect."

He asked, "Do you have enough tissues in your purse, just in case?"

She looked at him cautiously, saw he was messing with her, and shook her head disapprovingly. Adam suddenly sobered. "You'd need a whole carton of tissues if I told you everything. The crucifixion, and everything that led up to it, was so horrible for Jesus it caused the undoing of the rest of us. If he hadn't come back, those of us who loved him would've lost our minds. Peter probably would've killed himself."

"How'd you deal with it?" she said, shaking her head empathetically.

"Jesus helped us. He spent time alone with each one of us once he got back."

"Did he come to say goodbye?"

"More than that. Also to help us heal. I've never seen anything so brutal and unfair. The way it all went down," Adam shook his head. "It was surreal."

"I'm sure," she murmured.

Adam took another sip of water and wiped his mouth on the napkin. "Once the Romans arrested him it was like an evil force moved in and settled around Pilate's judgement hall and the surrounding area. It was like unexpected news had spread throughout the spiritual underworld and every demonic member dropped whatever they were doing to attend the event of the season.

"An almost tangible force of malevolence seemed to build and expand until it physically permeated the atmosphere. The whole event reminded me of the day Eve and I ate from the Tree of Knowledge. During both events I witnessed demons out of control with excitement like they'd been turned loose on a coveted, untouchable delicacy, trying to devour it while it was still alive before it could escape or die. It was like Satan's minions had been let loose out of hell for the day to attend a sporting event. They swirled in the atmosphere almost visibly emitting particles of odorous sulfur."

Grace felt hot. She took Adam's coat off her lap and set it to the side. She reached up to turn her air vent on.

"The actual event was worse than anything you could ever imagine. Seeing someone you love, admire, worship, really . . . hanging on a cross, alone, brutally punished and suffering beyond relief for something that wasn't even his fault. Knowing the whole time it should've been me up there. Knowing he was doing it out of love and obedience. So people could be free. So the devil couldn't have what God promised to us. So we could all have our do-over." He wiped his face with his hand as if to swipe the images off the slate of his mind.

"The only thing that saved any of us that day from completely losing our minds was that he didn't suffer for days. We'd all heard of crucifixions that lasted up to a week, and I don't think any of us could have recovered had it gone on any longer than it did."

Grace shook her head. "I don't know how anyone stood it, honestly."

Adam took a deep breath and sighed. "What choice did we have? The only disciple of the twelve who was there with us that day was John. He's Jesus' best friend and he stood at the foot of the cross as a show of support during the entire event. The others hid because they weren't sure if the Romans would still come after them. People got so worked up. It seemed things would never finally deescalate and settle back down."

"Did you hide?"

"No. But I wasn't in as much danger as the rest of them. But honestly, I almost wanted them to come after me." He sighed again. "When it was over I got drunk and stayed drunk for two days."

"What did everyone else do?"

"I don't really know. All I really remember was Martha sending Lazarus into the tavern to get me and take me home. I stayed there nursing my wounds until he came back on the third day and told me Jesus had come back and was asking to see me. I remember crying, throwing up, and taking a swing at him. I thought he was playing a cruel joke on me."

"But he wasn't?"

Adam shook his head. "Jesus was back. When I raced into the upper room and saw him standing there surrounded by everyone else, they all stared at me—smelly, dirty, hungover, with red blurry eyes. Jesus simply smiled that old familiar smile I'd seen a hundred times and said that of the two of us I was the only one who actually looked like I'd been in hell for the last three days."

Adam took the last swig of his water. "If Jesus hadn't come back there would be no church today to spread the news of who he is and what he did because not one of us would've survived the trauma of his death to tell the story.

"He had to come back to reassure us that not only is he the true Son of God, but he was all right. We had to see him whole and healthy, alive and the same as before, better even. Still sowing dreams in our hearts for a glorious future because our Savior lives and is still out there valiantly commanding the troops, preparing for the final battle where he'll return for good and kick any remaining crap out of the enemy."

Grace took another sip of her water. The therapist and human-itarian in her wondered who helped Jesus work through *his* trauma. Jesus lost his life, his friends, his family, his humanity. He had prayed for hours in the Garden of Gethsemane the night before, that God would take the cup from him if possible. He was stung by the betrayal of Judas. Denied by Peter. Forced to watch his mother and friends suf-fer helplessly at his feet as he died, naked, bleeding, humiliated, broken.

The Bible states Jesus cried out to his father on the cross, "Why have you abandoned me?" Why did God leave him? Could he not watch? Was it too painful? Did the sin Jesus carried on the cross cre-ate a barrier?

Undoubtedly Jesus suffered emotionally, not just physically, that day. Who helped him get closure once it was all over and done? Does

God even need closure? Did he find peace while on the cross? What did he feel when he descended into hell? When he returned and pushed the rock away? In the upper room seeing his friends again?

The Bible states Jesus endured the cross for the joy that was before him. What joy? Did he already get it? Is it being seated at the right hand of the Father? Wouldn't he have sat there anyway? Did he see a new future? Was it his wedding? Did he do it for his Bride?

Grace turned to the only person alive she thought might know. "You were there when Jesus died and afterwards? You were there for the whole thing?"

Adam nodded. "I was the man known as Simon of Cyrene. I carried the cross for Jesus up the hill to Calvary and was there to help Joseph of Arimathea and Nicodemus carry him down again. Yes, Grace, I was there for the whole thing."

CHAPTER 29

G RACE WAS SUDDENLY TIRED, AND ADAM'S STORY OF Christ's death had sobered them both. There was a myriad of emotions stirring within her heart and she started to wonder again if possibly Adam wasn't the only one God was pursuing that night. The warm feeling surrounding her when Adam spoke of Jesus was the same feeling she remembered experiencing as a child. When she still loved him. Thought he wanted to marry her. When they were dancing together on the balcony in her dreams. Grace studied her throbbing finger and asked herself, *Could it be Jesus has not forgotten me after all?* But if not, *why not*? Why would he still want her after all this time? She'd practically come out publicly and declared anyone an uneducated idiot who believed in him.

She further considered her options. Maybe as a child she hadn't been wrong. Maybe God did love her. Maybe still loves her, she allowed herself to consider. She tried to remember her spiritual journey as an adult. Or lack thereof, she admitted. She had rejected God. But what was her reason? Had she even given him a real chance? Had she simply rejected him because she didn't want to follow the crowd? Didn't want to fall into the category of conservative sheep? Too proud of her standing as an intellectual to lower herself onto an emotional crutch?

Grace considered her analysis. Was she spiritually lazy or was a bad experience with a youth group and the hypocrisy of her mother and her friends enough to permanently dissuade her from seeking answers to some very important questions? *Just because some Christians are wrong about some things, doesn't necessarily mean they are all wrong about everything,* she told herself logically. What about C.S. Lewis? Martin Luther? Mother Teresa? Great minds who wrestled with the existence of God and intellectually came to the conclusion to accept on faith what their human senses could not confirm. In the end, what argument persuaded them?

Grace mildly chided herself, *Why didn't I search for my own answers? Done the research. Listened objectively to both sides and weighed the arguments. Even gone to God and asked him for myself? As an adult, I didn't even try. But why not?*

She looked around her at the other passengers and rested her eyes on the aging grandparents across the aisle. Grace wasn't old but she wasn't getting any younger. She thought possibly she should start the process of considering where she wanted to live once she left planet Here and Now. And with whom and what kind of people did she want to share her eternity? Trillions and trillions of years? *That's a long time,* she told herself thoughtfully. Normally a long term and strategic planner, she thought it wise to reconsider her options.

If her parents and other Christian relatives and friends wanted to live with Jesus but she didn't, how would that work? Would she ever see them again? Could they leave heaven to come see her? Could she enter on a day pass? She considered the likelihood. She'd heard a woman speak on a TED Talk and the woman claimed heaven was in a different realm and inaccessible to people who didn't choose to be there permanently. So probably no to the day pass option.

So then would her Christian friends and family eventually forget her? Or remember her somewhat fondly as an old friend they once knew but no longer someone with whom they associated? They would all live together in the celestial Four Seasons and she'd be lucky if she even got a Days Inn? Her sister would love nothing more than a big "I told you so." Her family was going to be spending their eternal Christmases around Jesus' tree, not hers. Adam said God's house isn't a hotel for nice people just looking for a place to crash. So where would Grace go?

Her theory about God and the afterlife was "let's wait and see." Was that even smart? She scoffed and thought she certainly wasn't going to accept God simply because she was afraid of the potential alternatives. She had more pride than that and even though she didn't think she loved God anymore, she certainly wasn't going to stoop to simply using him as an eternal meal ticket. She had integrity.

However, something was certainly missing in her life. Adam said he was alive when God was with him, then dead after the Garden, now alive again because Jesus fixed him. He said his relationship with God makes him happy. He has passion. He operates on all cylinders. Obviously not taking an Uber to the first pot dispensary when they landed. Didn't she want to feel alive, Grace asked herself. Wasn't that her main problem? She felt so dull inside, like there was something missing that nothing seemed to satisfy.

Adam insisted God still loves her. *But why would he?* she wondered.

Did he even know her anymore? Grace had ridiculed people who believed in God, called them ignorant sheep. She grimaced at the memory. She'd probably said a lot worse. Would he forgive her? Would she have to go to church and repent? That would be so humiliating, she thought, especially if she had to do it publicly. The tissue had fallen off her finger and she studied her red throbbing hangnail.

She glanced at Adam whose eyes were closed. He knew Grace was deep in thought and he wanted to give her a moment to think. He took the opportunity to pray. In his heart he searched for the presence of his friend Jesus and said, "I know you're here for her as well as for me. Help me, help her."

Grace looked at Adam sitting with his eyes closed and did a quick reassessment. Logically, she told herself, his story *had* to be fabricated, or more likely the result of an unexplained illness.

She knew his story wasn't possible. Once she got off the plane and away from his spell, away from his smell and that grin, she would be embarrassed and ashamed for entertaining and participating in such a wild fantasy.

Grace certainly wouldn't discuss the night with her colleagues. If she even fudged a little, pretending Adam had been a patient and Grace had for one second considered the validity of his claims, she didn't know one associate who wouldn't suggest she get some rest and take a sabbatical from her practice.

Grace closed her eyes and leaned her head on the headrest. Cold again, she pulled his coat up and closer around her neck and smelled the delicious scent of its owner. She wanted to give him the benefit of the doubt. Nothing about him gave her cause for concern other than his fantastic story, which she admitted was the issue. However, the intellectual and emotional tools he utilized to deal with his issues were actually quite remarkable.

Madmen, she reminded herself, don't normally seek therapy and describe in rational detail their own culpability. They don't relay events in ways that result in their highly educated and respected mental health expert getting emotionally and spiritually challenged to the point of giving serious consideration to changing a lifetime of religious conviction either. She absently started to chew on her hangnail again, felt the pain, and sat on her hand. Still, there was not one shred of evidence, she told herself, to corroborate his story.

She heard Katie giggle and looked up to see her still talking with Adam's co-worker. Well, almost nothing. Grace thought of the unexplained account of Adam's older wife and how it tied into his story. Maybe she just needed to exercise a little faith, she told herself optimistically.

Deciding she sounded like her mother she chided herself sternly, *Do not exchange years of intellectual theory for one man's version of religious history regardless of how attractive the theory* or *the man based on faith alone!* She just couldn't betray her intellect and entertain a probable myth that existed with no basis of logic.

She considered Adam's assertion that spiritual events occur in the heavenlies of which people cannot possibly have knowledge. *Is there even sufficient evidence to believe in the ongoing spirit of a person?* she asked herself. *Does the spirit even exist?*

Yes, Grace finally decided after several contemplative moments. She believed all people possess a spirit; that intangible force within every human being that moves in and outside the mind, heart, and body. Something that spurs the Picassos, the Pavarottis, the Madame Curies to strive and create works and events outside the boundaries of mortal humans. Something divine, Grace admitted, that arouses and encourages the human soul to move towards greater love, hope, and achievement than what our minds and bodies tell us is possible.

She glanced again at Adam, still sitting with his eyes closed. He had answers for her. She knew he did. She could feel it. She glanced at her watch. It was late and she was tired, but she was not looking forward to the end of the flight or the adventure. She was reassured he might reach out to her once they got back to Texas. But then again, he might not. She'd exchanged business cards with a few fellow travelers before, but she'd never contacted or been contacted by even one after the plane landed. Still, no one had ever taken her picture.

She contemplated the ceiling as Adam fumbled in his briefcase. She finally admitted to herself that trying to solve a relationship issue with God, her own or someone else's, was beyond her reach. She herself needed help and therefore was in absolutely no position to help anyone else. Glancing at her seatmate she worried that once she admitted it to him they'd really have no reason to get together once back in Texas.

She said as lightheartedly as possible, "Well, I'm probably fired for good, aren't I? You're no closer to an answer than before the night started. It seems we drug all this up for nothing." She looked at him expectantly as she waited for a reply.

He studied her and then discerning her thoughts he said, "You're in my speed dial. Don't think you'll never see me again. You're the only person on Earth who knows who I am, and I've got other issues you know nothing about. You should be worried you'll have to get a restraining order," he quipped charmingly.

She laughed out loud and the man across the aisle looked at her and smiled. She felt strangely relieved and suddenly lighthearted. She said, "I'll risk it."

"I did realize though," he said more seriously, tearing open a bag of peanut M&M's he pulled from his briefcase, "there is a part of the story I haven't told you yet. In fact, it's sort of the best part."

Grace was surprised. "There's a best part?"

He offered her a red M&M and she took it and popped it into her mouth. He explained, "After the Fall, God promised us that eventually his seed and Satan's would no longer struggle within us. We all knew one day the swords in front of the Garden gates would come down and we'd be free to re-enter. God knew it, Eve and I knew it, and Satan knew it. Those swords came down the day that Jesus died."

She said, "Wow. I would've liked to have been a fly on the wall and seen the devil's face that day!"

He smiled and nodded, remembering the story Jesus had told him and the others after his resurrection.

Satan knew God planned to send a redeemer for his people and the plan was that savior would die for the people's sins, setting them free. Some people think that Jesus was a surprise to the devil, but he wasn't. The Bible prophesied a savior would come and the devil can read. So, although he knew he couldn't stop Jesus from coming, Satan thought he might be able to keep him from dying. Satan's only chance to hang onto his captives would be if Jesus, once he got here, refused to sacrifice himself.

Yet even a perfect God couldn't pay for the sins of Man as Spirit alone. He had to first become human, flesh and blood, for the payment to be accepted. The perfect Lamb would have to come as a man but not born through the seed of a man but be born under the law receiving no special favor from above. He would have to be given the opportunity to disobey God and refuse it. Then, still perfect and without blemish, freely offer the sacrifice of his own life for the sins of his fellow brethren. Knowing full well in advance many would never fully appreciate what it cost him or accept the gift.

There has only ever been one person qualified to make such a sacrifice, the magnificent and holy Son of God. Royal DNA came to Earth with no disqualifying virus running through his veins. Jesus answered the call of his heavenly father when asked to sacrifice himself to save once and forever all of God's family, past, present, and future.

Satan knew the reason Jesus was coming to Earth was to set the captives free. Forever release God's family from the shackles of sin, forever dethroning Satan from the minds, hearts, and flesh of his victims. He knew Christ was coming to depose him and that his crucifixion would forever demolish sin, captivity, death, and Satan's reign. Forever.

As Jesus equipped himself to leave his heavenly home, he reminded himself of why he was headed to Earth, the difficulties he would face, and who his adversary would be. The Father had prepared him fully and armed him with every necessary tool for his success. The Son of God was coming to disarm Satan; he was coming for war. And the inhabitants of both heaven and hell knew it and what was at stake. With every fiber of his being Lucifer vowed that although he couldn't stop the birth of Christ, Jesus would never finish his race.

Satan gathered and invested in every resource available. He got together with his advisors, and they strategized unceasingly. Once Jesus donned his humanity and vulnerability, Satan would use every friend, relative, mentor, and situation to tempt, confuse, and disarm him.

His attack would be two-fold. Initially he would try to get Christ to love his life so dearly he would be hesitant to give it up. Secondly, and decidedly more difficult, he would attempt to plant just enough doubt and confusion about the Father's true intentions and purpose for him that Jesus would ultimately second guess him and change his mind. Satan would make him believe he was more valuable to God's people alive than dead.

He would convince him, at least he hoped he could, that God's real plan was in the eleventh hour to provide an alternate sacrifice for man's sins, like in the story of Abraham and Isaac. God would send another lamb waiting in the wings as his replacement. Satan would plant in Jesus' mind the hope that God loved him too much to really ask him to drink from the cup of death. At the opportune moment Satan would whisper to Jesus that he could satisfy the courts of Justice by being *willing* to die. He wouldn't really have to do it. If Satan could manipulate those two factors and throw in enough pain, fear, and humiliation along the way, he might get Jesus to call the whole thing off.

However, throughout Christ's life Lucifer was thwarted at every turn. Jesus proved a stronger adversary than his enemy had feared. In the end Satan panicked. When the hour finally came and with the cross on the horizon, Satan called forth every minion in his kingdom and held an underworld summit. He would implement the emergency Plan B.

His message to his underlings was clear. Jesus could not make it through the cross. He had to be made to summon God's angels who would be waiting unseen in the heavenlies to free him. However, if Jesus would not break, which Satan couldn't believe but made himself consider, then Satan's warriors were to ensure that the King of Kings would be so insulted, abused, and tormented that the watching warrior angels waiting to free him would be so outraged at the abuse they would break rank, lose control, and rescue him regardless of his will to continue.

But God also held his summit. If Jesus even whispered the command, every warrior angel, thousands present and under the command of Michael the Archangel, would descend upon Calvary with swords drawn, ready to fight to the death. Their orders were to quickly, deftly, and mercilessly free their King and destroy his enemies and attackers. However, if no command was uttered, under no circumstances were they to unbind him until his mission was completely accomplished. Jesus was the only hope the world had to be free. There could be no mistakes.

Satan prepared his minions for battle. He barked orders, telling them to muster from their depraved imaginations every insult, every offense, every brutality, and hurl them at a vulnerable and defenseless Christ. This was their chance for payback, he baited them. For all the demons he had cast out, all the humiliation he'd caused them, this would be their one and only chance to get even and he encouraged them to use every tactic in their arsenal.

However, he didn't tell them the entire goal was to instigate the battle, one where his own troops would surely be defeated. He didn't divulge that he was perfectly willing, even desirous, to sacrifice every single warrior in his kingdom for the chance at getting Jesus to summon his angels and take him off that cross. The tortured whisper of "enough," not winning the battle, was Satan's goal.

Satan told his generals that any act of mercy, weakness, or leniency would be severely punished. Every demon was required to do whatever he had to do to keep Jesus from dying. In an act of desperation, Satan actually promised one third of his kingdom to the general whose warrior provoked the breaking of the final straw.

Yet at the end of the day the inhabitants of both heaven and hell stared open-mouthed as Christ's lifeless body was prepared for burial. The ordeal was nothing either side had expected. No one had really been prepared for the horror, chaos, and evil unleashed in both the spiritual and physical realms that continued until the Son of God took his last labored breath.

Thousands of God's warrior angels stood by helpless, frustrated, wracked in agony, yet perfectly aware they were forbidden to rescue their king from the injustice and agony he suffered. Nothing but death or an audible command from the Son or his father would finally call a halt to the agony and injustice of the day. Each one understood too much was at stake. They each had been created and chosen for such a time as this. If their Lord and King could withstand the pain and humiliation, who were they to force the hand of God?

Michael, the warrior leader, shook with pain and fury as he hovered hopefully yet helplessly, at times actually requiring physical restraint. He wanted nothing more than to rescue his Lord and massacre his enemies as part of the process. However, Michael is God's most trusted servant. He would never reach beyond his own authority and call his troops into an unsanctioned war.

Throughout the ordeal he had demanded silence, straining to hear any whisper, any groan of concession from above or below that might indicate his Lord was conceding. All eyes were on the leader of the host, waiting for his sword to rise indicating it was time to move. Yet until the torturous end, as total darkness covered the Earth, his weapon stayed in its sheath. Only when life left the Son's body did the entire host in one movement fall to their knees, beat their breasts, and release their pent-up fury and frustration through wailing and tears.

They beat the firmament with their fists and cursed their enemies' debauchery. Time passed in the supernatural realm as a sea of prostrate warriors covered the ground, spent, inconsolable and dazed.

Michael was the first to feel a sudden and forceful stirring from within. Suddenly the rage and indignation of the Almighty coursed through his body and he shook with the force of it. Momentarily confused, he feebly questioned, "Now, Lord? Isn't it too late? Your son is dead!"

Visions of the future of God's kingdom, complete with a victorious Jesus on the throne surrounded by a free and jubilant people, appeared before Michael. Pictures of generation upon generation of the sons and daughters of God creating new worlds and new creations living together peacefully and productively without threat or fear danced promisingly before his eyes.

Michael sprung to the air, boldly and confidently sounding the alarm each warrior recognized as the call to war. Michael pulled his sword and wielded it in the air. "He is the Alpha and the Omega. The Bright Morning Star. The Almighty, the Bread of Life, True Vine, Messiah, Holy One."

In time, others began to join in vociferously and with conviction. "Lamb of God, Lord of Lords, Master, Faithful, Light of the World." As the Spirit of God descended heavily upon the place where the loyalists stood, stomping their feet, proudly and enthusiastically thrusting their weapons high, thunderous voices soon rocked the heavens and the Earth. "Image of the Invisible God, Author and Finisher of our Faith, Lion of the Tribe of Judah, Son of Man, and King of the Jews." Finally, in an earth-rocking crescendo in unison they cried, "Our Savior and Lord, The Way, The Truth, and The Life! Jesus! The Everlasting Christ!"

Without warning the ground began to shake violently and long, thunderous claps filled the air. The angelic host was thrown off their feet and back onto their faces. Many involuntarily cried out in alarm. Would the world see the wrath of God delivered from his own hand? They covered their heads as the shaking and thunder continued unceasingly.

Suddenly the heavens parted and the familiar voice of God Almighty roared through the air, "What are you waiting for? Follow him! Bring me my son!"

The congregation leapt to their feet at once, relieved and ready to advance. However, looking expectantly from one to another, finally someone called out, "Follow him where?"

The descending Michael on mounted wings, with sword drawn, could barely be seen. His voice though, totally audible cut through the atmosphere, "To hell, Brothers, to hell!"

CHAPTER 30

I T WAS OBVIOUS JESUS HAD ARRIVED BEFORE THEM. IN AN offensive position Michael surveyed the scene before him. Immediately the other warriors landed, quickly drew their swords, and prepared for the battle of their lives. None of Satan's followers could be seen but the gates of hell had been ripped from their hinges. Michael and the others looked through the massive opening and saw a trail of light illuminating the cave-like walls of the tunnel leading to Satan's domain.

The fierce-looking angelic leader and his troops advanced and were soon surprised to see many of hell's centaurs laying silently on their bellies cowering in the soot, ash trails swirling about them. The ground shook where they lay, the aftershock of the footprints of their newest guest.

Heaven's warriors looked at each other incredulously. Each had been prepared for a search and rescue mission. They had expected to find their Lord in a weakened state. Possibly in shackles. Could someone else have gotten there before them? They shook their heads certain of the knowledge there were only two armies in the universe equipped with this kind of devastating power. They were one and the other was laying prostate at their feet, dazed and filled with undeniable certainty—Satan was in danger.

God's troops made their way into the hallway and headed for Satan's sanctuary. Moving at full speed, led by a trail of light, they were surprised to see the earthquake had not only ripped open hell's gates but had also destroyed walls, rooms, and even separated the ground, creating large, cavernous pits ending in nothing but a dark and lonely void. Imprisoned human souls were milling around, uncertain of whom or what was responsible for their sudden release.

Angelic warriors made their way aggressively yet cautiously through the rubble, such massive destruction they'd never seen. With such confusion and wandering of lost souls, they were unsure who were Satan's captives and who were willing followers. After careful scrutiny, they realized none were a threat and continued in search of their master. Most of hell's inhabitants followed not knowing what else to do.

Within a short time they heard the voice of their Lord. With shining armor and swords drawn they streamed into Satan's sanctuary and were surprised (and somewhat disappointed) to find the only enemy life-form remaining was the Prince of Darkness himself. Even Lucifer's inner circle of high priests and bravest soldiers had fled the scene armed with the same knowledge—their leader had grossly misrepresented himself as a worthy opponent to the one true king.

Michael and the others eventually saw Jesus standing in the middle of enemy headquarters. He appeared to be casually inspecting the elaborate but gaudy surroundings, much as a new owner surveys property he knows will eventually face a wrecking ball. To the relief of all save one, his body strong, his face triumphant, his demeanor said it all: "Behold, thy Victor."

Sitting alone, his rival stared straight ahead, feigning indifference at the overpowering presence of his enemy. It was obvious to all the one-time hopeful conqueror had quickly and unexpectedly become the conquered, his territory easily invaded and possessed.

His countenance refused to reveal the shock he still felt when Jesus had arrived unannounced at his door, not even weakened, but full of an unbridled force Satan and his warriors had never before seen. Later, they were to sadly agree, even during the war in heaven such unrelenting power had never been witnessed.

Upon receiving the news of his defeat, Satan had violently retreated to the sanctuary of his throne room, abusing then destroying everyone and everything that mistakenly came into sight. Seething with fury he had ordered the return of his generals and was already at work formulating the worst forms of torture and rebuke for their failings.

He had stood looking in the mirror, numb with the shock of such a devastating and unforeseen loss when he first felt it. He steadied himself against the wall. Quizzically he cocked his head to determine the cause of the sudden jarring. He heard the sounds of distant thunder in the background, faintly at first but then louder. His mind, briefly confused, wondered if someone had accidentally and erroneously set off the fireworks originally meant for celebration.

The rest happened so quickly Satan found difficulty in the recall of it. Still against the wall, trying to steady himself, he looked up in time to see Jesus enter the room. He took two long and purposeful strides, towered over his enemy, grabbed him by the neck, and threw him to the floor.

Satan cowered there refusing to look into the face of his conqueror, not only out of disrespect but because the light that came from Jesus' body was blinding. Momentarily, he managed to back up and crawl to his throne. He rose and lifted himself into a sitting position, picked up his keys from the armrest, and sat on them, as if daring Jesus to force them away from him.

He could see his former prisoners, recently freed, gaping at him in shock, astounded at the brazenness of Satan in the face of his obvious superior. He knew the keys to his prison cells were worthless but still they were a symbol of his power and a reminder he was once a worthy adversary.

"*Once* a worthy adversary?" he immediately scoffed. He sat up straight on his throne as hope filled his pathetic soul. *Nobody in the past has ever come to hell and been released,* he reminded himself. Wasn't this still his domain? Wasn't he *still* the Prince of Darkness? The Lord of Destruction? Hadn't God given him the kingdom? Taken for himself the land of the living and given him dominion over the dead? He looked at Jesus and his angelic warriors in command of his sanctuary and was filled with rage. Jesus had *died*. If he was in hell, he was Satan's rightful property!

Satan rallied. The unexpected presence of the Lord's warriors was not proof of victory but part of the bounty. They had been too weak to protect their king. God was disgusted with the lot of them and had sent them to hell together! He grabbed his keys defiantly and looked up menacingly, ready to call the bluff.

But Jesus was not bluffing. As soon as Satan raised his eyes the light and power of Christ shot through him and Satan was immediately catapulted off his throne. His body was thrown to the floor, his hand forcibly opened wide. The keys flew into the waiting and open hand of Jesus. Satan screamed as Jesus walked over, pressed his heel to Satan's protruding jugular, raised his arms to the sky, and let out a thunderous and victorious war cry that was heard throughout the universe, reaching the ears of the angelic spectators above.

Jesus was joined by the deafening sound of cheers, applause, and the clanking sounds of oversized warriors beating their swords on their chests. Amidst tears of gratitude and shouts of joy from the released prisoners he took Satan's keys and threw them into a gaping pit.

Satan's festivities for Jesus' arrival went to waste. The Son of God reigned over hell for three days, acting as host to hell's emancipated, serving them a different kind of food and drink—the living manna and waters that proceeded from his mouth as he preached the Good News of salvation and the promise of a new and brilliant tomorrow.

Heaven's warriors stood guard over Satan's recovering forces although everyone present knew no threat would be rallied. Finally, on the third day after the last of the prisoners were escorted from hell, Jesus re-entered the throne room and found Satan laying on the floor.

He cared not that Satan refused to acknowledge his presence. Jesus reached down and picked Lucifer up, drawing him to eye level. Satan closed his eyes petulantly but couldn't resist the will of Christ. He opened his eyes and stared defiantly into the blazing face of the Son. What he saw was the Father in heaven looking back at him.

Jesus spoke the words dictated from above. "Lucifer, in ignorance you waged war, not once, but twice against the Almighty.

Satan rolled his eyes and interrupted, "Spare me the sermon," he muttered.

Jesus continued, more for the benefit of those watching than for his captive. "In the Garden you dealt the world a mighty and crippling blow—one from which it will take us a long time to fully recover. But by attacking God and the world with unrelenting, unbridled, and supernatural strength, you have unwittingly made God's strongest point."

"Please, get on with it," he muttered again.

"You proved once and for all that no one, not even the Prince of Evil, can successfully wage war against God or his family and win. Unbeknownst to you, you provided the world with an unforgettable demonstration no one will ever forget. Not heaven, Earth, or the inhabitants of hell will ever forget what God himself is willing to endure and sacrifice for love of his family. God loves us, we love him, and *you* or anything you could ever throw at us, sure as this hell, certainly don't matter."

Jesus and the warriors recited in unison, and as they spoke a spark of fire picked up the sound and burned it into the walls of the enemy's domain as an everlasting reminder and remains there today. The sound was then picked up by an unseen breeze, carried through the walls, into the air, was captured by a Holy Wind, and finally carved into the universal journals of Providence. "For God so loves the world that He gave His only begotten Son, that whosoever believes in Him, will not perish, but enjoy everlasting life."

And with those parting words the Son of God dropped Satan to the floor, motioned to his warriors, and together exited the premises forever, leaving his one-time adversary defeated and alone to rule what was left of a crippled kingdom.

CHAPTER 31

THE LADY WITH THE TEASED HAIR IN THE BULKHEAD GOT up to use the restroom and the door hinges strained loudly as she entered the compartment. A young man, a few rows back in coach, got up and opened an overhead bin. He closed the door loudly, obviously not caring that most of the other passengers were still trying to sleep. Adam's friend had retaken his seat and Katie had gone to the back for additional supplies.

When Adam finished his story an enthralled Grace asked, "Wow! What happened when Jesus told you all the story?"

"Well, it took us awhile, but after we calmed down from the shock and awe of it, we were finally able to start processing all that had happened. It was so much, so overwhelming," he elaborated. "And we certainly needed his perspective. I mean, not just the horror of the events before the cross, but then his actual death, plus everything that happened with Judas, the Romans, God's part in it, our parts in it. There was just so much to process."

"I can't even imagine!"

"But besides helping us sort through it all, he was also there to help us grasp our future roles in representing him and telling the story. He wanted to make sure the word about him spread and the message was clear."

Adam continued, "You probably know this, but the resurrection is the greatest miracle of all time. Other people have done miracles, but no one has ever heard of, let alone seen, someone who's been publicly condemned, crucified, and then has risen from the grave. There was no doubt after that Jesus is who he says he is."

She nodded. "When he came back was he afraid to show himself?"

Adam looked at her, crinkled his eyebrows, and asked, "Of what? Upsetting somebody?"

She cocked her head slightly and conceded. "Do you think he came back because he needed closure?" The therapist in her was worried Jesus wasn't just there to minister to others. Maybe there was something he needed too.

"I don't know, Grace. If he did, I didn't know about it. If possible he demonstrated even more peace than before. It was like he did what he came to do, returned to the scene to make a point, check on his friends, and ensure we could do our jobs. He was more carefree and lighthearted than I'd ever seen him but also was there to make sure we each had our marching orders for the next chapter."

"Next chapter?"

"Sure. His job was done but ours were just getting started. Peter was chosen to plant the official church, but we were each commissioned to help spread the news. Jesus knew the enemy was permanently defeated but only temporarily crippled and would do whatever he could to abort the Christian movement. There would be plenty of future opposition and he wanted to make sure each of us was prepared to face it and make sure the story, his story, got out, took root, and spread."

"When was the last time you saw him?"

"The night before he left for good on the beach. We had dinner and he said goodbye to me then."

"What happened?"

Adam sighed remembering. "While he was back we all wandered from day to day in sort of a daze. Those who'd been hiding and not actually at the cross drilled those of us who were, asking repeatedly if we were sure we'd actually seen him die. I'm sure you read about Thomas saying he wouldn't believe it until he actually saw and put his fingers in the holes in Jesus's hands where his wounds had been."

"Yes, I do. Did that actually happen?"

"Oh yeah. You should've seen Thomas back down when Jesus offered to let him. He was all talk until he actually had the chance to do it. But anyway, Jesus did all kinds of miracles when he was back. It was almost like he'd never left. Eventually everyone had no choice but to accept it, settle down, and talk about what would happen next."

"What happened at dinner?"

"It was Jesus, Peter, John, and me and a few others. Things were somber at first because we knew he was leaving. But it turned out to be a night of healing and closure for us all."

"How so?"

"Well, you know about Peter and the drama that surrounded him before the events of the cross?"

She shook her head.

"Yes, you do. You've just forgotten. The night the Roman soldiers arrested Jesus they accused Peter of being one of his followers and he denied three times he even knew him. After he'd boasted to him in front of the rest of us he'd never deny him."

Grace was completely engrossed in the story. She had straightened her seat back, put her feet on the floor, and was leaning close to Adam to make sure she heard every word, eager for even the slightest detail. The night and events continued to feel unreal to her and she was sure in the light of day, and in the months, if not years, that followed she would question whether the encounter had occurred at all. She didn't know how she would ever completely process it. She was certain she wouldn't be able to tell anyone about it, colleague, family, priest, or friend. Still, somewhere inside she suspected she was in the presence of someone who'd been witness and participant in the greatest events of history. Regardless of how she planned to deal with it later, she wanted to capture every moment of the present.

Suddenly she reached into her bag and pulled out her phone. She hit the camera button, pointed her phone at Adam, and said "Smile," and clicked away.

"What was that for?" he asked surprised.

She reviewed the photos taken, nodded her head in satisfaction, and put the phone back in her purse. "Just making sure you actually show up in pictures. I'm sure I'll need it tomorrow when I wake up and start to replay all this in my head."

He laughed and said, "How about I just call you? Just to reassure you, you know, you weren't hallucinating."

She smiled happily. "We could compare notes and tell each other how our presentations went on zero hours of sleep. We may just ruin our reputations and need consolation."

He motioned towards his men in the row behind them and said, "I've got backup. I don't know what you're going to do."

"I'm going to wing it, that's what I'm going to do." Then said, "Tell me what really happened with Peter before they took Jesus."

Adam shook his head remembering. "Like I said, surreal."

"How so?"

"We were in the Garden of Gethsemane when the soldiers came. At first Peter was so brave, so confident. With literally no back up he whipped out his sword and cut off one of the soldier's ears, ready to take on the entire lot of them, all alone if necessary. He was prepared to die right then and there in battle. But once he realized Jesus wasn't going to fight and wouldn't let us fight and was going to let them take him, it took the wind out of his sails.

"Before the night was over he realized Jesus really was going to die. And not just die but be tortured and crucified on the cross. It was Calvary and all the gore, misery, and hell that would lead up to it that was the plan after all. Once the truth set in, he panicked. Peter the brave, in the end had a total freak-out moment."

Adam sighed again remembering the incident. "The denial was an automatic response out of fear, but he was devastated and so terribly ashamed. He regretted it immediately once the cock crowed three times, just as Jesus had predicted, but by then there was no way for him to take it back. He could hardly face Jesus when he returned, and it took no small amount of convincing on Jesus's part to get Peter back to the table with us."

"Oh, yes. I had forgotten about that."

"Well, anyway, we all went fishing that next to last day and then later that night we had dinner on the beach. We ate and things were overall okay, but subdued because we all knew Peter was still feeling guilty. Nobody really said much."

"All of a sudden, out of the blue, Jesus asked Peter if he loved him. Peter said he did. Jesus asked him again the same question and Peter again reassured him. But then Jesus asked him the third time and it was obvious to us all something was going on. Peter had denied Jesus three times and there was Jesus asking Peter three times if he loved him. We knew it wasn't like Jesus to rub salt in a wound so we couldn't figure out why he was confronting Peter, especially in front of us all. Peter's feelings were hurt because he thought Jesus was rebuking him, and publicly no less, for denying him. But that wasn't it."

"What was it?"

"Well, there's been a lot of debate about this. A lot of theologians over the years have made a big deal out of the word 'love' that was used in the interchange. Twice Jesus used the word 'Agape' love and the last time he used the word 'Phileo' love and by doing that some people have thought that Jesus was telling Peter he didn't love him enough. But that wasn't it."

"What was his point?"

"Jesus knew Peter had condemned himself and was wallowing in misery and shame even though he said he wasn't. Jesus wasn't about to leave him like that. Peter was destined to start the church. He needed a deeper healing for his own transgressions before he was ready to help others find forgiveness for theirs.

"By asking Peter three times if he loved him, Jesus was addressing the elephant in the room. He was saying 'You made a mistake. We're going to acknowledge it, get it out on the table, forgive it, and move on.'

"You see, Grace, even though Peter's destiny was to start the church, he was often intolerant of other people's sins and weaknesses. That's not a good quality for a person who's in charge of helping others find forgiveness and healing."

Grace nodded in agreement.

"But Peter's 'glitch' was he felt his denial of Jesus was unforgiveable and that disqualified him from being a decent follower of Christ let alone form the church. He thought the church should be led by some-one without sin and only Jesus could do that so no mortal man could or should call himself a spiritual leader. But that was a lie the enemy had planted and nurtured in Peter. Immediately after Peter's denial the enemy started working on him to destroy and cripple him because he wanted to take him out before he could become a real threat. If Jesus and the rest of us hadn't prayed him through it, it would've happened too," he assured her.

"But that night at the beach Jesus convinced Peter that every sin is forgivable and not just the importance, but the necessity of letting go of old mistakes. He told us all that sins don't disqualify anyone from anything Christ has called him or her to do. If anyone, including lead-ers, makes a mistake they should confess it, deal with it, and get on with their calling. They should lead by example and role model for-giveness and *continuing on*. Taking leaders out of their God-appointed positions because they make mistakes once they've owned up to them only sends the message to the people watching that sins are shameful, crippling, and disqualifying. Where's the Christ in that?" he insisted.

He continued, "So had Peter not forgiven himself and let it go, de-nying Christ would have prevented him from effectively achieving one of the most important roles in history. If the enemy could have perma-nently sown the guilt and shame seeds in Peter and allowed him to dis-qualify himself for the role, the Christian church would never be what it is today. And Grace, Jesus was not about to let that happen.

"He told Peter, 'Feed my sheep! Help people see Christianity is not about the absence of sin. It's not about being perfect. Christianity is about loving God, finding wholeness, and accepting ourselves and one another wherever we are in the process. We're family, Peter. He loves us. We love him. Nothing else matters. If our sin no longer separates us from God, why should it separate us from each other? Stop giving sin *so much power!*'"

Adam turned to Grace and said, "Leaders who tell good-hearted, committed Christians that God's goal is primarily good behavior and not relationship with him are not advancing the kingdom of heaven. All they're doing is keeping it stagnant and their parishioners' passion for Christ lukewarm."

"How so?" she asked.

"Because people do not fall in love with a God they don't think likes them. People won't risk forming an intimate relationship with God if they think he's bored, critical, or rolling his eyes when they talk to him."

Adam continued passionately, "You can try to please God by strict adherence to good behaviors, good works, and condemning yourself and others when there's a problem, or you can believe *in his heart* he's already let go of our issues and wants us to cut ourselves and each other some slack. Because you can't do both. The two concepts are diametrically opposed. It's just that simple."

She said, "I tell my patients all the time to be careful what they obsess over because eventually it's what they'll become. If you focus on people's mistakes, you'll become critical and judgmental, beating yourself up looking through the same lens. The only people I know who are free are those who take responsibility for their actions but who've also learned to forgive themselves and each other when they mess up."

"That's right, Grace. Now you're getting it. And that's why Peter was the perfect person to plant the church. Peter understood Jesus's message better than anyone. He had faith. He walked on water. He was zealous. But when Peter denied Christ so blatantly and publicly, not once but three times, it devastated him. He couldn't forgive his own sin."

Grace nodded. "I'm sure he was. Did he get over it then?"

"He did," Adam nodded. "Peter experienced forgiveness firsthand for something he was deeply ashamed of and his revelation of the beauty of it because of the burden it lifts was awesome to behold. Before the night was over Peter completely embraced that although many of us have good intentions even the best of human beings at times have flawed thinking and behavior. Nobody's perfect and that's okay."

Grace sighed and said, "It really is, isn't it?"

"Jesus told Peter and us all that night we can't let the frailties of this temporary human experience cripple us by making us feel less than who God creates us to be. You need to remember this, Grace," he looked her squarely in the eyes, "we are each perfect in our original design. The fact that we can't always see it is irrelevant. If God wanted us to be flawless, he would have given us the ability to do it. And then teach others how to do it. But we can't so obviously he doesn't."

Grace held up her hand indicating Adam should stop talking for a moment. "We can't get there from here," she stared in his direction. "No matter how hard we try we can't be perfect. God's not setting us up. It's not even possible." She paused, "But what about the narrow gates? Isn't that telling us to try to be perfect? Isn't that telling us to *work* at our salvation?"

Adam scratched his head. "It can get a little complicated but getting through the narrow gates is more about love and trusting God. But you have to work at it in order not to let fear immobilize you along the way. The focus of walking in unity with Christ isn't about the absence of sin, and it's not about white knuckling it trying to always do the right thing. It's about trust. Trusting that God loves you, and that anything he asks you to do or wants to give you is for your benefit. No matter what it looks like it might cost."

She thought for a second and said, "So getting through the narrow gates, for those so inclined, is more about 'doing it afraid' than doing it right. Trusting that God is paying attention, loves us, and has an amazing plan for our futures. And continuing to move forward with him no matter what. Is that it?"

Adam nodded, happy Grace was finally starting to see it. He said, "That's right. And for those Christians who say God is only pleased and proud of us once we've overcome our sins and earned our Sin No More merit badge, all I can say is they do not understand the foundation of Christianity. Peter never again could prove he wouldn't deny Jesus in the same way he did the night before the cross. He had no way of showing he'd overcome that particular sin. And yet Peter was called to start the church, not because he earned it, but because he accepted the role. Because in God's world good behavior is not the prerequisite to a dinner invitation or a job in the family business. The heart of Christianity isn't about what you overcome anyway. It's about coming over to God's side and finding out what that means."

Grace said, "That's pretty healthy."

"Once it was over Peter cried a bit and then let it go. It was awesome and so healing for us all. He and Jesus hugged, laughed a little, and we all knew it was time to move on. Then Jesus turned to me and said, 'And I don't need to remind you this goes for you too!'

"Afterwards he told us some stories, we sang some songs, drank some wine, and when we each left our hearts were light. The ordeal was over. Jesus had come back, he was okay, our mistakes were forgiven, and we could all look forward to the next chapter."

Grace studied Adam for a moment and suddenly said, "Then what is your dilemma, Adam? Why have you not found your peace with God?"

Adam had not expected the question. He stared at her, took a sip of his water, and placed the glass back on the napkin. He was silent for about five minutes. Finally he said, "When Jesus left I was healed, and

I was happy. But honestly, I've never been as fully alive as I was in the Garden."

"How do you mean?"

"Jesus healed me of my past. However, after he left I was faced with living life alone again without him. So, for a really long time I just kept busy. I helped Peter with his ministry. I was friends with John, Paul, and a guy named Tychicus. I traveled with them and together we did some amazing things all in the service of Christ. I was happy.

"I would say even since then I've been very content. I'm definitely living on Garden shores. My world looks a lot like it did originally. My internal heaven is reflected in my external circumstances. My heart and head are filled with love, confidence, faith, and peace. I would say I have a lot of personal power and am very free. But somewhere in the last few months I've decided I'm not so happy anymore and can't pretend I am. I don't seem to care about anything. I'm starting to wonder if any happiness I've had was really just busy-ness, me trying to fill a void."

Grace was alarmed. "What do you mean, you don't care? You love God. He loves you. You've talked about working so hard to help people return to the Garden! Find their heaven on Earth."

He stared down at his hands and twisted the ring on his right hand. "I have to be honest, Grace. I guess it's not enough after all. For some reason suddenly I think if every person were completely free and healed it still wouldn't be enough for me. I need more and I can't seem to get it."

"No!" she exclaimed, "That can't be true! How can you expect any more than you already have? Yes, there've been problems for you along the way, but I bet most Christians would give their eyeteeth to have the relationship with God you do. You're just in a dry spot. You know so much. Have seen so much. Have so many answers to the biggest of life's challenges. What could possibly be left?"

Adam shook his head slowly. "I'm not looking for ways to serve

God, I'm not looking for more Truth. It's not the blessings of his hand. It's not even seeing God do miracles I'm after."

"Then what do you want?" she asked, confused.

Tears sprung to his eyes. "I want *to be with him*!" he cried out. "My father. And Jesus!" he added. "We used to walk and talk every night. We fished. We told stories. We laughed. They wanted to spend time with me; they cared about me, kissed me on my forehead, shared their hearts with me. In conversation not everything was always about me."

"But you love working to help restore God's kingdom," she insisted.

"It's not enough," he said flatly. "I want God to talk to me."

"God talks to you all the time," she countered.

"*In person*, Grace. I want to talk with them both in person. On this Earth, face to face, *like before*."

Grace's face fell but she asked kindly, "Adam, what makes you think that's even possible?"

"God created me and put me in the Garden on Earth in the beginning. He didn't create any of us for a long-term relationship with him *in heaven*. He created mankind for fellowship with him, Grace, on *Earth*. Man was never supposed to die and live in heaven afterwards. I caused Man to die. Read Revelation. The New Jerusalem, where we live with God as his temples, is on the new Earth, Earth restored. The future for Man and God together is *here*. Like it was in the beginning? 'Tis now and ever shall be? World without end? Of course it's possible. God wants it as much as I do, probably more. I just can't figure out what's holding him back!"

Grace was speechless. Finally, the problem they'd been looking for. It was a dilemma Grace had never heard before in her life or career as a therapist. Somebody who didn't just want the blessings of

God, somebody who didn't want more Truth of God, someone who didn't equate loving God with serving him. Not even someone who wanted God to use them to perform miracles and raise people from the dead. Adam wanted to see God in person, tell him stories, hear him laugh out loud, hug and kiss him, and walk with him again in the cool of the evening.

She didn't even know such a thing was possible.

CHAPTER 32

THERE WAS A SLIGHT RUSTLING IN THE CABIN AS MORE people started to wake up. Adam got up to use the restroom again. The young newlyweds had physically separated—her head was on a pillow and she was leaning against the window. Her husband was awake, and Grace noticed in the gap between the seats he was watching a movie. Two actors popular in the 1980s popped up on screen, Danny Glover and Mel Gibson, and she wondered why he'd picked a movie made before he was born.

Adam returned to his seat and Grace waited for him to get settled. They hadn't solved his problem, but she felt great relief that at least they'd found it. Usually that was more than half the battle. Adam wanted to see God again face to face. She thought about Adam's hymn,

"As it was in the beginning, is now and ever shall be, world without end . . ."
Adam simply wanted his old life back.

Still, something didn't make sense.

"Adam," she said, "Jesus left more than two thousand years ago. You said you stopped hearing from God not all that long ago. You said you were fairly content until then. What changed?"

Adam thought for a few minutes, looked at his hands, and twirled his ring again. "In the Garden, years ago, God made me a promise. He said he'd give me whatever I asked him for and within a reasonable time frame as long as we were in agreement about what I was asking him to do."

"Okay . . ."

"Well, I guess about a year ago I asked him to come and visit me in person again like he used to. I told him it was important to me. He said he'd do it, but he hasn't." He shrugged. "I guess I'm mad about it."

Grace couldn't help but laugh. "Adam, that's a big ask."

He looked at her without comment.

"You seriously don't think God plans to come to Fort Worth and what, take you for dinner? Send you a text saying 'Meet me at Joe T's for Mexican food. Get a booth.'?"

Adam laughed a little but said, "Grace, God answers my prayers. If something is important to me and I ask him for it, he does it. Anything."

She shook her head and objected. "That's not possible. Maybe once, Adam, but not now. God doesn't come to Earth anymore and I have a hard time believing he'll do whatever you ask him to do. He doesn't do that for people."

"How do you know what God does or doesn't do?" he challenged. "He gave me what I asked him for in the Garden and unless there's a hiccup he gives me whatever I ask him for now. Within a reasonable time period. Which is why I don't understand this holdout."

She snorted. "Oh, please, Adam. Like if you ask him to win the lottery, I'm so sure he's going to do it."

"I don't need to win the lottery. But regardless, do you think I would ask God for something that stupid? He taught me how to pray and I know how to pray according to his will. Therefore, I get what I ask him for."

She stared at him blankly. "Well, I'd certainly ask to win the lottery."

He mildly rolled his eyes and shook his head. "Grace, Jesus redeems history. I've done the work. He said he'll do it. So why shouldn't things return to 'normal' for me? Like they were in the Garden? Why wouldn't I get a total do-over? God's all about redemption and restoration. Plus, it's not like he's against the idea of being with me in person. It was his idea in the first place."

"Well," she said confused, "smart people say Jesus won't return until a lot of other stuff happens first."

"What people and what stuff?" he challenged again. "Do you think God has a board of humans and they meet annually to discuss his options? What pride to assume people can predict God's behavior. And who says all God's plans apply to everyone the same? To intimate all plans are group plans? Where does the Bible say that?

"My relationship with God is personal. Why would our reunion not be? He came and visited with Abraham, questioned Sara when she laughed. He came to see Joshua in human form before the battle of Jericho. Moses saw his back. Jacob wrestled with God as a man. He was in the fire with Shadrach, Meshach, and Abednego as the fourth man. He appeared in human form with a staff in his hand to Gideon. He sent a personal chariot to take Elijah to heaven. So, I ask you, Grace, why do people claim to know everything God has planned for those who love him when the Bible says and shows so clearly that we don't?"

"Well," she sort of mumbled, "people who go to seminary, you know, people who study things, they all seem to agree it's sort of a group thing," and turned to look out the window suddenly feeling as narrow-minded as she accused her mother of being.

Adam said, "Well, I didn't go to seminary, but I can tell you one thing for sure. No one's ever going to put God in a box, and he certainly seems to favor revelation through hindsight not foresight. The Bible says even Jesus doesn't know the day of his return. Many of the Jews are still waiting for the Messiah because of the way their scholars interpret the prophesies. They say Jesus didn't meet the requirements. When John wrote the book of Revelation, God told him to leave out some of what he'd seen in his vision. That seems to indicate he's holding his cards pretty close to his chest."

"Judaism doesn't acknowledge Jesus as the Messiah because of the way they interpret the Bible?"

He nodded. "Yep. Not unless they're Messianic. Many people get it into their heads the way it's going to be and don't anticipate other possibilities. Yet Jesus tells people clearly to stay awake and don't fall asleep. He says he's coming like a thief in the night. To me that indicates he might come at an unexpected time but maybe in an unexpected way as well and we might do well to keep our eyes open and consider the possibilities. So, if God says he's sending me a chariot to meet him at the top of a mountain with Moses and Elijah or coming to see me in person and I get a text, you can bet I'll be waiting in a booth at Joe T's."

"Then teach me," she said suddenly. "I want Jesus to take me for dinner."

"Why? So you can ask him to help you win the lottery?"

A little hurt she said defensively, "No. I'd just like to meet him."

Adam was sorry he sounded so abrupt. "I'm not jerking your chain. I just want you to understand. If a person's motive is to get God to pull a rabbit out of a hat, they're going to be disappointed. Love works best when it goes both ways."

Grace contemplated his words and suspected Adam's shortness with her came from a sense of protectiveness towards God. He loved him, she was certain, and didn't want his friend taken advantage of, simply used by people who care more about what God can do for them than for his heart. She said contritely, "I know God's got a heart. You've reminded me of that tonight. He's not a genie in a bottle."

"But he can and will help," he assured her. "With anything. Everything. Some things faster than others."

"Such as?"

"Loneliness, fear, lack of belonging, having a purpose higher than yourself. You can find peace knowing you've entered into God's family eternally and your place after death is assured. You can know if you've invited him into your heart his Holy Spirit lives within you and will give comfort and guidance."

She admitted, "I don't feel anything living inside me. It honestly just feels sort of stagnant. If I'm honest, a little dead. Can he help with that?"

He looked at her compassionately, a little surprised by her confession. "He's living waters, Grace, and you've never experienced such a flood as when he comes pouring in. Especially once you get rid of the dam. I have friends who say they don't know how people find any joy in life at all without knowing God. He's the passion and the purpose of the day once you get to really know him. And a *lot* of fun."

Grace looked at him in disbelief. Never in her life had she heard anyone describe God as fun. "So, you think he can fix depression?" Adam looked at her sideways. "Asking for a friend," she said.

"As you know, Dr. Grace, depression often stems from stress, fear, lack of hope. When people can't see any change coming and their current situation seems intolerable."

Grace sighed and nodded in agreement. "Or afraid that any change might be worse than what they've already got."

"Yes, God can help fix depression," he assured her. "But solutions for depression, fear, anxiety, worry, alcoholism, sexual issues, control issues, weight, money problems, legal issues, anger, powerlessness, literally anything Grace, don't usually happen immediately and just because you follow Jesus. Even for those of us committed to finding the narrow gates back into Eden on Earth. You can't always expect a microwave fix to slow cooker problems. Usually big issues are cumulative effects of long-term thoughts, emotions, behaviors, and events."

"But if you do what he says, God will help fix your problems?"

He nodded. "Yep, but two things are required. Prayer and faith. We've got to ask God for what we need and then trust he's on it. Nothing moves the hand of God but prayer. Faith is the substance of things hoped for not yet seen. That means if God sends you something invisible from the spiritual world it's our faith in him that acts as the spray paint that turns the gift from invisible to visible. God can technically deliver something to us but without faith it can be very difficult, if not impossible, to collect. It's like a pitcher and a batter. Both have to do their jobs to knock one out of the park."

"So, nothing happens without faith?"

"Not much. To the victor go the spoils and no one ever walked on water without first stepping out of the boat when Jesus makes the call."

"So God will give you whatever you pray and have faith for?" she asked skeptically.

"No. He'll give you whatever you pray and have faith for that he says he will. That's the key and the only way to avoid disappointment and frustration with God. I knew a guy who was in love with his high school sweetheart and prayed that her husband would die so he could marry her. He claimed his faith in it every day for years. It never happened. It was because God never told him he'd do it and never made such a promise. So the guy prayed to absolutely no avail. He eventually dumped God over it and lost his faith."

"Because he didn't get his genie?"

He nodded. "He didn't get his genie. But if you ask God, and God promises you he'll do something and you have faith for it, follow him, keep talking to him about it, don't jerk it out of his hands, and don't give up, then in time it will be yours. I can't say guaranteed, but it has happened 99% of the time for me. I say 99% because I'm still waiting for that dinner at Joe T's."

"But how does a person hear from God, Adam? If you're just a beginner? How do you know what he's telling you to do?"

"Well, it's hard to hear someone you doubt is talking. But once you get off the fence, the first thing is to start paying attention to your spirit. That's where God lives and most communication occurs there."

"Pay attention to what?"

"What's going on in here," he pointed to his chest. "God's Spirit lives inside our hearts and moves around within us. Makes adjustments as necessary. Changes our perspective, as well as moves externally in our life circumstances. It helps if we pay attention. Look at different things that pop up. Possibly a thought or emotion that suddenly changes or intensifies. Something that's not easy to ignore. Maybe you find you're headed to the right and a new idea surfaces and gently re-routes you to the left."

"Audible voices?" she asked skeptically.

"No. Not audible voices. Anything audible or insistent is highly, highly suspicious. I'm not saying impossible, but God's voice is gentle, subtle, and as soothing as a gentle wind. When in doubt if it's him speaking to you ask him to confirm it. Then if he does, have faith and move gently and cautiously forward and see where his Spirit leads you. And always, always, pray for protection from anything and anyone the enemy would use to confuse, mislead, or derail you. Don't worry, Grace. God's not going to let you get hurt if you stay tucked up underneath him and don't go running ahead."

"I said I was asking for a friend not necessarily for me," she countered. But then after another moment she questioned, "How could he confirm it?"

"Move again in a different way. Maybe say the same thing through a call from a friend or maybe through an unlikely coincidence. If you ask him, he'll find a way. Just pay attention. Also, I like to use the open door/closed door method of following God. When I pray for something I ask him to open a door for me, a new logical and viable opportunity for me to explore. If I see one, I gingerly walk through it. If another one opens, I continue, keeping him with me the entire way. If the door is closed, I might tug slightly but if it stays closed I ask him to show me another way. God is faithful Grace. He knows he's hard to hear sometimes. He doesn't want us to be misled but he does want us to learn to walk, run, and then fly with him."

"How close to God can a person get?"

"Well, he uses the terms Bride and Bridegroom for a reason." He indicated the couple sitting in the row ahead of them. "He'll never be the one to say, 'Close enough.' How close is up to us. But Grace," he said and waited for her to look at him, "it's going to be difficult to do if you think he's scowling at you. Or that your behavior, past, present, and future is the end all. Getting close to God includes the ability to relax in his presence. It may be difficult at first but once you get used to it, you'll discover how easy it becomes. Just try it," he offered. "You'll see."

"Would I have to read the Bible?"

He said, "Well, it could certainly help. Jesus is the Word. God uses the Bible to talk to most people, at least sometimes. And it's an excellent plumb line. Nothing else he will ever tell you will contradict what's in his Word. So it's a safe and reliable source."

"So he's not going to tell you something if it's not in the Bible?"

"I didn't say that. John said that if all the things Jesus did and said were written down, all the libraries of the world couldn't hold them all. So obviously there could be things he'll tell you that are not necessarily in the Bible."

"Did he ever tell you to do something not in the Bible?" she asked.

"Yes. He told me to recycle my plastic. He told me I need new tires. He told me I should hire the two guys behind you. He told me not to watch *The Exorcist*. He told me I needed more fiber in my diet. He led me to the ranch I bought. He woke me up in the night and led me to the barn. I had a horse in trouble. He's told me thousands and thousands of things. We live together, Grace. It's a *relationship*."

He continued, "But within the relationship the Holy Spirit will never contradict the Bible. He's never going to say, 'Why don't you steal that car? We need a new one,' when obviously the Bible teaches that stealing is wrong. But walking closely with him has required that I not limit him to only one form of communication."

"Like what other methods can he use?"

"Anything. Music. Any form, not just Christian. Books, not just self-help. Nature. Movies. Other people. Even therapists," he smiled. "The Holy Spirit can use anything if your phone's turned on. Remember, God once used a donkey to speak through. The key is you have to relax, pay attention, give it time, and find a good Christian friend, with a proven track record, who will help you not go down some weird rabbit trail. Once you find one, don't worry too much about being wrong.

Because even when you are wrong, *and you will miss it from time to time,* but you stay connected to God, he'll get you back on track.

"But the most important part," he added, "and I should've mentioned this before, is to ask God to help you fall in love with him. To not just love him but to fall *in love* with him. There's a difference. Some people call it asking him to put a hook in your heart. To woo you. Partnering with God, learning your true identity in him, finding your heaven on Earth, is all so much easier when you're in love with him and know he's in love with you too. And it certainly helps later when you have to deal with the messy parts."

She looked at him sideways. "Like I said earlier, I don't want to get to the Superbowl, Adam. I'm not like you. But I think maybe I would like to go to heaven after I die. Maybe even talk to God now and then while I'm still here. I get lonely by myself all the time. And I certainly would like him to take us both to dinner when you come to Austin. However, I think I'll deal with the messy parts on my own."

CHAPTER 33

S HE KNEW THE PLANE WOULD BE LANDING BEFORE TOO MUCH
longer and so asked, "Anything else important?"

He nodded. "Yep. No matter what, don't give up on him.
The enemy will do whatever he can to derail you. But try reading the
Bible. If you get stuck or unsure about something, phone a friend. Best
if he's from Fort Worth. We know things."

She smiled at the offer. "But what about all the parts of the Bible
that don't make sense? That I don't agree with. Like the parts about ho-
mosexuality, women submitting to their husbands, not wearing pearls
to church? That's a big one for my mom. She'll wear a two-carat diamond stud in each ear, but she won't wear her pearls to church because
the Bible says not to."

"Well, I don't know about that," he laughed lightly. "The Bible is a living book, Grace. Do you remember the picture of the woman that if you looked at her one way she was an old woman but if you turned your eyes slightly she looked young?" She nodded. "That's the Bible. If you read it with your head it might seem legalistic, boring, and lifeless to you. But read it with your heart, looking at it from God's perspective, asking him to show it to you through his eyes, and you might see things a little differently."

She was quiet then said, "But what about all the rules? Do they still apply? If you break the wrong ones accidentally or on purpose does God ever get mad? I know we can't be perfect but if we don't even try would he think we're blowing him off?"

Adam furrowed his brow and she continued doggedly, "How do you know what's not important to him? Would he care if my mom wore her pearls to church? She won't even let my dad take the trash out on Sundays. Could there be something a person still thinks is a sin, but God doesn't? Or the other way around? Something he might even send a person to hell for?"

Adam was surprised by the question and told her so. "Grace, it doesn't work that way. Sin isn't some mystical, intangible concept. It's abuse. It's damage. It's unhealthy. Sin is destructive. Unchecked it would destroy all that's good in the world. God's not a control freak who gets his kicks asking people to jump through irrelevant hoops. He isn't old-fashioned, prudish, uptight, sitting around in a robe listening to harp music all day while his world and family live and struggle in the current century. God knows the meanings of lol, gaslighting, and bougie and can use them in a sentence, I promise you. Remember when I said earlier I think you should revisit your beliefs about God? Update them a bit? Cut him some slack?" He started to sing, *"What a friend we have in Jesus . . ."*

"No, don't sing." She touched his arm and gently shook her head.

"Anyway, you're probably right," she continued but was still obviously troubled. "It's just that I grew up thinking God was old, angry, punitive, and unreasonable. And every Sunday I still feel this constant judgment, spoken and unspoken, coming from my mom and sister about how my mistakes are going to catch up with me someday."

Adam continued, "Don't think you're alone. Lots of people have to deal with family members who use the Bible as a means of trying to control them. But shame and condemnation are tools in Satan's toolbox—"

Grace interrupted him and blurted out, "Do you think I could go to hell because I slept with an old boyfriend in a one-night stand a month before I got married?"

Suddenly speechless, Adam stared at his seatmate in the dim cabin light. He noticed her face was tight and when he didn't answer right away she started to chew on the problematic hangnail again. "Grace," he said finally, "who told you that?"

"My mother. My sister. They said I'm going to hell and tried to show me in the Bible where it says so. My mother even told her friends to pray for me! The whole church found out about me sleeping with that guy. My sister called me a slut in a youth group meeting. I was so humiliated!" she hurled violently.

Grace suddenly and unexpectedly experienced an emotional upheaval. "I absolutely hate God because of this!" she cried out. "I've been a good person my whole life! I've spent countless hours listening and helping others! Gone out of my way to do everything I can to better humanity and if God's going to send me to hell for that then I'd rather live there than under the rule of a dictator! My mother said good works don't mean *squat* to God. He only cares about following all his goddamn rules!" She started to cry.

Adam was quiet for several moments. He noticed the man across the aisle who was watching the Cowboy game had stopped and was instead looking at Grace. Adam reached up and turned off the overhead light and moved slightly to obstruct his view. He took his water glass off his napkin and handed the napkin to Grace who dabbed her eyes. They sat in silence for several minutes. The co-pilot came out to use the restroom and Katie took his place in the cockpit. Finally Adam said, "Grace," and waited until she was looking at him to continue. "It's not true. That's no place in the Bible and if it was, which it isn't," he said soberly, "then hell would be a hell of a lot bigger because how many people out there haven't done something in their lives they wish they hadn't?"

Embarrassed by her emotion she said earnestly, "That's the problem. I don't regret it."

He laughed out loud and shook his head surprised by her honesty.

She looked both angry but concerned. "So?" she challenged, "I'm not sorry. I think to call it a sin, even a mistake, is ridiculous! If I hadn't slept with him, I would've pined for that idiot my whole life. It was so awful I cried for the hours I'd spent mourning that he'd dumped me before I got the chance to sleep with him when I was in high school. I even told my fiancé and after he got over being mad about it he said, 'Thank God you got that out of your system before you married me!' And he was right! So there's no way I'm going to honestly say 'I'm sorry and repent," she said sarcastically, "or ask for forgiveness." She turned and looked him squarely in the face. "That would be so hypocritical and stupid. I'm not doing it."

Adam shook his head again and answered truthfully, "I think you might be missing the point. You've slipped back into thinking God's legalistic and punitive. I'm not exactly sure about the specifics of hell, but I can tell you for sure what it's not. It's not a place God sends teenage girls who sleep with their boyfriends or for people who are just trying to figure out how to make their way in life. Like I said earlier, he's the person of Love, Grace. Think about that."

"Then why has every conversation I've ever heard about God, until tonight, start and end with a person's behavior and how God feels about it?"

"I don't know. Maybe you're just hanging around the wrong people. Not every Christian thinks God's focus is their behavior."

"Then what is? What does God *want* from us?" Adam thought she sounded confused and a little desperate. She then added, "I just don't want him to think I'm a loser. A total waste of time. Sorry he ever made me because I'm such a disappointment."

Adam's heart hurt for Grace. Obviously there was a lot of religious abuse in her past. He touched her hand gently and said, "Just for you to let him love you, Grace," he said simply. "And hopefully to love him back. And to love others. God is love. So doesn't it make sense this whole thing is also about love? About life? And exploring all that means. Together? Living life to the fullest with the One who made you. Loving, appreciating, and protecting the relationships he's given you with friends and family? Experiencing passion? Having something to get excited about? Using the gifts he's placed inside you for yourself and the betterment of society. To name a few. But behavior is definitely not at the top of the list."

She was contemplative before asking, "Then does behavior even matter?"

"Of course it matters. Morality, truthfulness, honor, righteousness. Communing with God on lofty topics and operating at full capacity is hard to do if you're in and out of jail or rolling around drunk in the gutter. The healthier the person, the healthier the life. But it's the person and the life that's God's end game. Not if we lose it in traffic or take a swing at the neighborhood bully. That's like saying I went to school to become an engineer, never learned to build a bridge, but got an A on my report card in conduct. How anticlimactic."

She nodded, understanding his point. "I've been hung up on the sin. I thought it was all he cares about."

Adam shook his head and said, "Grace, I guarantee, build an intimate relationship with Jesus and you won't need to worry about any sins. Nothing unhealthy can last for long in close proximity to that kind of love. Focus on him and watch it all melt away like butter in the hot sun. He'll handle it all. You can trust him. He's sweet." She looked at him and he smiled at her reassuringly.

She said to herself as if to reinforce the concept, *He's sweet.* She nodded her head, thinking about her relationship with Jesus as a child. "Suddenly I feel like I'm back in grade school. I feel like I got criticized for coloring outside the lines, so I quit when maybe I was a mini-Picasso." She added remorsefully, "What a waste."

He shook his head. "You're still a Picasso. You just need a new canvas to start over with and some fresh paint. Not those old dried-up things you're still using from your childhood."

"And you think that's what God wants for me too?"

Adam nodded. "Isn't that what you'd want if you had kids? To love you, join you, and create something great together?"

"Of course." She released a heavy sigh and looked down at the floor. Finally, she said practically but somewhat miserably, "But I'm afraid it's too late for me. I'm so clogged up I haven't thought straight about God for years. If ever." She shook her head dejectedly, "I don't think I can see my way through this, Adam. I've lived without God for so long I don't even know how I'd begin to live with him."

She added, "I honestly don't know how I'd get over thinking he's still judging me. It's too engrained in me. I can't just flip a switch and say he doesn't see my crap anymore or care about it. I have no idea what else I'd talk to him about other than praying for what I need. Then I'd just replace him as judge and jury with the genie in the bottle. Then grow cold when he wouldn't grant me my three wishes.

"Plus," she continued, "I have dinner with my family every Sunday night. Right and wrong and how I live my life are always on the menu. I need something real, something from the Bible to show them, and me, that God's on my side. Something I can hang onto, trust, and fight back with."

He drummed his fingers on the table and said, "Everything in the Bible shows that God's on your side. But speaking of finding a new and fresh perspective, have you ever thought about making dinner once a month, not once a week?" he offered.

She nodded. "I'm a therapist. I understand good boundaries. But the relationship is complicated. I'm working on it."

He said, "I understand. But I wouldn't try to argue with your mother if she's got her mind already made up about what constitutes a good Christian. I'm pretty sure it would be pointless. I think most people have decided by the time they're forty pretty much what they believe. And most people don't really see a need to add or take away much from that. The tools we have make sense to us or we wouldn't keep them around. And many times, there's nothing wrong with that. But it is a primary reason most of us don't talk religion or politics at dinner. So, I would ask God to help you redirect, Counselor."

"That's too healthy." She pressed him, "Don't you know at least one verse in the Bible, Adam? Something I can quote to prove to my mother I understand what's important, but I don't want to discuss religion with her? And that I'm sick of having to constantly defend myself?" She trusted Adam and wanted his advice. "I can't avoid the topic with my family forever. No matter how much I redirect. And I need something to say to myself to remind me that God loves me and we're okay. Especially on the days I act like an idiot and know he's watching me."

He nodded. "I get it." He then quoted, "'For God so loves the world that he gave his only begotten Son that whosoever believes in Him shall not perish but have everlasting *life*. John 3:16.' If you decide to follow Christ, then tell your mother. But tell her firmly that you and God will work out the details and she needs to trust the God within you. It's all that ever needs to be said."

Grace was delighted. "Okay! Thank you! I'll try it."

He added, "Your mother is a Christian. She knows John 3:16 is the final say on the issue. Plus, as a Christian she probably understands you are God's to mold if you choose, not hers any longer. But if she keeps talking, drop the rope. It takes two people to play tug of war and it's the stronger one, not the weaker, who can end an argument going nowhere with four simple words. 'I'm dropping the rope.'"

Grace slightly nodded and said, "I'm dropping the rope. I like that."

He grinned. "I have a neighbor who told me that's what she says out loud but in her mind she translates it into Texan speak, 'Well, bless your heart,' which in her circle of friends can mean a lot of things."

Grace smiled but turned her head to look out the window and could see the early morning sun start to break through the clouds. Her eyes teared up once more and she thought of her mother, her sister, and all the wasted years of anger and shame she'd buried but hung onto, all because she thought God was going to let her rot in hell for something her family still harshly judged her for to the very day. And until now, she didn't have any effective tools to help lift her out of her hell and onto some high ground.

She pulled open her purse and threw the used napkin inside. She pulled out a compact and a tube of lipstick. She reached up and turned on the overhead light. She looked in the mirror, licked her finger, and rubbed off the smudged mascara under each eye. She put on a fresh coat of pale pink lipstick. She flicked the light off again, put her makeup away, and pushed her purse back under the seat in front of her. She turned to her seatmate and said simply, "Thank you, Adam. I think tonight you might have just saved my life."

CHAPTER 34

ANNA CAME TO THE FRONT OF THE PLANE AND STOPPED AT their row. "Did you two solve the problems of the world while it was sleeping? You certainly didn't get much rest. I hope you don't have big plans for the day. You need to go to your hotel and crash." After a second thought she asked sweetly, "Are you two married or just dating? I hope I find someone I'll want to talk to all night long."

Adam shook his head with mock sadness and said, "I was born married and went to work the next day."

Grace ignored him and said to Anna, "We just met."

Anna blushed and apologized. "I'm so sorry. I just assumed . . ." her voice trailed off.

Changing the subject Grace asked quickly, "Do you happen to have a Band-Aid? I have a hangnail that's giving me fits."

Anna said she had one in her purse and scurried to the front. Soon she returned with a bandage and a tube of antibiotic cream. "Show it to me," she commanded officially, and Grace held out her finger. Anna squeezed a small amount on the nail and gently dabbed it on the wound before sticking the tube into her apron pocket, unwrapping the bandage and carefully wrapping it around Grace's finger. "There you go! Right as rain!"

She smiled again and Grace thanked her as she walked away. Thinking she was the sweetest young woman she'd ever met, she reminded Grace of her little niece. She said to Adam, "She's missed her calling. She'd make a great nurse."

Adam agreed and said, "We're about to land pretty soon. How we doing? Did you get your questions answered? Got your glitch worked out? Maybe thinking about re-thinking the whole God thing?"

She shrugged non-committedly but grinned and answered, "Maybe."

He said, "Then give me your takeaway after wine, coffee, tea, water, three trips to the bathroom, one stained pair of pants, one or two rants, a few tears, and a chewed off finger."

She looked at him drolly and retorted, "Life's not a bitch and then you die. At least it doesn't have to be according to Adam, the cowboy who I still think was in a cigarette ad but won't admit it."

He ignored the bait and asked, "What else?"

She pondered for a moment. "Well, I'm not going to hell. That's a big one," and they both gently laughed. She added, "How embarrassing. But funny how something can get stuck in your subconscious and you not even know it's there or how painful it is. Or maybe how awful it really is that my family thinks I deserve to go to hell." Her face darkened again. "Well, they're certainly going to hear about it, that's for sure."

"Well, I might be careful. The Bible says not to throw your pearls before swine." He added quickly, "Not that I'm comparing your family to farm animals and your mom obviously has an issue with her pearls." He took a small sip of water and said, "But who knows? I might meet them some day."

She felt overwhelmed with happiness but refusing to show it said simply, "Well, I'm definitely going to arm myself with a few Bible verses. However, if I start quoting scripture my mom isn't going to have to worry about whether there's a rapture's or not. She'll probably die of a heart attack."

They both laughed and she quipped, "I'll risk it though." Then on second thought she said, "But the only thing I'm still a little confused about is how our lives can look like heaven just because we give them to God. I just see so many people in my practice who say they've done that to absolutely no avail. What's missing, Adam?'"

He shrugged. "I don't know, Grace. Every Christian has complete power within themselves to have their lives transformed into heaven on Earth."

"But why would so many Christians' lives indicate otherwise?"

He replied, "I don't know. No matter the situation we face, no matter how daunting, no matter how much it looks like someone else has the keys to our happiness, we all have all the power we need to change what's going on in our lives."

"How?" she insisted.

He said simply, "By looking to heaven and saying, 'Take this.' And then doing whatever God tells us to do. And not jerking it out of his hands if he's slow. That's it."

She shook her head. "I'm not sure I can believe it's that simple, Adam. Let's just take the situation with my mom. No matter what I do or say she's never going to change. She's always going to be critical; she's always going to judge me. I have dinner with her every week. I'm miserable every time I have to go. I can tell her I'm dropping the rope, but I know she'll just keep harping at me. Or making her not so subtle innuendoes about my choices. It's her and my sister's primary form of entertainment—to goad me. How's that going to be any different as long as she's alive?"

He looked at her and suggested, "I'm not God, but can I pretend for a moment?"

She smiled. "Go for it."

He lowered his voice an octave and, doing his best Charlton Heston imitation, said, "Grace, tell your mother if she continues to criticize you, you will start limiting your visits."

Grace studied her wounded finger and answered practically, "Yeah. God, I don't think I'm hearing you very well because you have no idea what a problem that would cause."

"Then tell me," he drawled deeply, sounding more like the Wizard of Oz behind the curtain.

"Well, I love my little niece. But the only time I get to see her is at those family dinners. If I limit my time I won't get to see her anymore. My sister will side with my mom, and she may never let me see her again."

Still using his God voice but much kinder and softer, Adam asked, "Will you trust me to work out the details?"

Grace looked at him and stared. "I don't honestly think I could."

Adam said in a normal tone, "And there you have it, Grace. Like I said, some people don't have the stomach for it. That's why the gate is narrow. No criticism there, by the way. It's totally understandable. But some prayers take more time for God to answer than others. Like you said, parking spaces are easy. God's not a genie in a bottle but he is a miracle worker."

She sighed. "I get it. The power for heaven in my life is completely within me because I can give God anything and he promises to take it and eventually fix it. It's just up to me if I can let him do his job."

He shrugged and said, "You can give that to him too. He can even help you find the strength to find the strength."

She interjected, "You make it sound so easy. Like he's the great panacea."

He smiled. "Centuries of experience, Grace. I consider myself God's oldest cheat sheet. I have wisdom born out of great suffering. And great restoration. I know what's possible. I see the pot of gold at the end of my rainbow, and I know it's not a fairy tale because I'm enjoying it. I'd like to help others find theirs. That's all. Nothing in it for me God hasn't already given me. I just want to spread the love."

She frowned at him. "That's not true and you know it. At some level we're all your family too. You want to see God and Man both happy. With life, the way it's all going to turn out, and with each other. This is still your world, and you want to see the enemy kicked out of it. You want us to move onto to where you and Eve left off. You want the plan. You need closure, Adam, in addition to your dinner date with God."

He said thoughtfully, "You might be right."

They looked at each other in the early morning light, now streaming in through the window. Adam reached for her hand, lifted it to his lips, and kissed it. "Thank you, Grace. You certainly live up to your name."

Through the heavenly throne room window Jesus and the Father watched from above and when the couple finished speaking, each gave a happy sigh. The Father put his arm around the Son and asked, "So, do you think they'll see each other again?"

Jesus answered, "I don't know. She's pretty bougie."

God laughed. "I hear you. She might just wake up in the morning and think he was gaslighting her."

They both laughed softly, and Jesus asked, "Remember how it all plays out?"

His father smiled. "I'm just going to enjoy the process. You?"

Jesus said, "Well, I am thinking about a trip to Fort Worth. Care to join me?"

God said, "Lol. We'll see."

CHAPTER 35

GRACE CLOSED THE WINDOW SLIGHTLY TO SHADE THEM from the bright light streaming into the cabin. Morning was upon them and their adventure almost over. Katie walked up and said, "We'll be serving breakfast soon, but I've got some coffee going. Are either of you ready for a fresh cup?"

Adam said he'd take some and Grace asked if she had any cranberry juice. Katie said, "Cranapple," and agreed to bring Grace the can. Soon she returned with Adam's coffee, some cream and sugar, fresh napkins, and a stir stick. Grace had pulled out her tray table, left it only half-open, and waited for Katie to bring her juice.

The man across the aisle had finished watching the Cowboy game and was playing Solitaire on his computer. Katie also brought him a cup of coffee and sat it on the table between him and his sleeping wife.

Soon she returned with the can of juice for Grace, a glass half filled with ice, and another napkin that Grace placed on her tray table. Katie said, "Some people add prosecco to it. It's really good. Do you want to try it?"

Grace shook her head but thanked her. She poured half the can of juice into the glass and took a sip. "It's pretty good," she told Katie. Adam tore open a sugar packet and emptied it into his coffee, tore the lid off the creamer and poured it into his cup. He stirred both and said, "Well, I feel better. Do you? It seems we both got a bit unclogged this trip."

She nodded. "I definitely do. I didn't realize how mad I was at God, the church, and my family. God found me when I was little, I just couldn't hang onto him. I trusted people I thought knew more about him and what he wanted for me more than I trusted myself. But it wasn't my fault. I was too young to know."

"But now you can be born again and start all over. With better paint, little Miss Picasso."

She took a sip of her juice and slightly nodded. In the bright morning light she saw Adam's face more clearly than since she'd met him. *Such a kind and handsome face,* she thought happily. She rested her hand on his arm, looked at him squarely, and said, "Thank you again, Adam."

He dipped his head slightly and said, "And back to you."

She removed her hand from his arm, smiled, and asked, "Still mad because God won't come see you?"

"Yet," he said, tapping the coffee off his stir stick and setting it on the napkin. "He'll do it. He said he would. I'm going to just be patient."

She nodded and they both sipped their drinks and contemplated the mysteries of God.

"Do you think you'll hear from him soon?"

"Oh yeah," he answered assuredly. "I already feel him. It was just the mad blocking him."

She poured a little more juice into her glass. "You're lucky you hear him so easily."

"I forget that sometimes."

She said teasingly, "You could pray for the rapture. You'd see him that way."

He smiled. "I could but I don't want to. I want to be here when it all comes down. I want to be part of the transition team."

"Aren't you afraid of the mess?"

He thought about it. "Nothing worse than I've probably seen before. But I believe he's setting up places on Earth something like spiritual sanctuary cities, embassies. You know, protected from what's going on outside."

"I hope it's in my neighborhood," she said honestly. She waited for a few minutes and then cleared her throat. "Well, unless you've got something else you'd like to talk about I have something I'd still like to discuss."

"Sure. What's on your mind."

She hesitated, took a long drink of her juice, looked out the window again, and then turned back to Adam. "I've given God such a bum rap."

"You think?"

She was pretty sure his comment was a little tongue-in-cheek but ignored it. "I do. I've let my biases get in the way. I owe him an apology. And I need to rethink the entire subject." She paused as light tears covered her eyes. "I've got a hole in my soul, Adam, and I can't find anything to fill it. Not my work, not a man, not better family relationships. There's nothing on Earth that's going to do it. Something's missing. Or maybe someone. The only time I remember feeling the way I want to on the inside was as a kid when I loved Jesus and thought he loved me too. So, for better or for worse, even if I'm being stupid and/

or duped, I think I'm going to give God another try. Especially since you say your own life is working so well, minus your little hiccup, and you seem so keen on it."

He smiled kindly and said, "That's right, Grace. I'm keen on it." He leaned over to see if he could see Katie in the galley and wondered when breakfast was coming. He waited momentarily before asking, "And you don't think it would make you delusional? You know, talking to people who aren't really there?" he lightly teased.

"I re-pent of saying that." She exaggerated saying the word and he smiled into his coffee. "Actually," she continued seriously, "I was thinking maybe you could give me some advice."

"Like what? I've told you everything I know."

"I doubt that. But that's not what I mean," she explained. "I accepted Jesus when I was a kid. I sort of backed out, but do you think it still 'took?'"

"It doesn't matter what I think. It's what you think. Do you think it 'took?'"

Grace examined her bandaged finger and resisted chewing on it. "Maybe I should tell him again. It's been a while. And I know I never asked the Holy Spirit to live inside me."

"Okay. Do you want to tell him now?"

Grace asked quickly, "Here?"

"Any reason not to? I have a direct line."

She giggled slightly and said, "Good point. You call him." He sat down his coffee cup and held out his hand to take hers and she looked at it tentatively. She slowly placed her hand in his and said, "You don't think this is too weird?"

"No. I would be honored, Grace, to talk to God with you. Do you want to start, or do you want me to?"

"You do it. You get us started and then I'll jump in."

He noticed her hand was cold and he was careful to avoid the troublesome finger. An unexpected wave of joy crossed over him and he mentally made note of the moment as one he knew he would never forget. He looked into her eyes, smiled, and squeezed her small hand gently. He then looked past her, out the window, and said, "Hello, God. It's Adam and as you know I've got Grace with me."

"Wait," she interrupted quickly. "Aren't you going to bow your head or close your eyes?"

"You can if you want. But I don't close my eyes when I talk to God. I think better with my eyes opened."

"Oh, okay. Sorry. I didn't know you could do that."

He continued, "Anyway, as you know we're on this plane and I'm sure you've heard us talking and she has something she'd like to discuss with you. But before she does, I just want to say thank you for putting her on this plane with me tonight. Grace is smart, honest, and such a good person." He was quiet for a moment and Grace felt he was saying something to God that was private.

After a moment he resumed his prayer aloud. "It was so great of you to send her to me, and I can't thank you enough. She's helped me tremendously and I'm grateful she took such a risk. So, regardless of what happens between the two of you, I'm asking you to mightily bless her for her willingness to listen to a stranger and share her heart and talents when she wasn't sure about the patient or the outcome. It just goes to show what a kind and generous person she truly is."

He paused and squeezed her hand gently indicating it was her turn. She was silent for a moment before asking Adam, "Hold on. Exactly who am I talking to?"

He hesitated. "Well, you have choices. You can either talk to God the Father or Jesus. You could also talk to the Holy Spirit, but we haven't really gotten that far yet. I'd pick one of the others to get started."

"Okay. I know Jesus from before."

"Then I'd start there."

She cleared her throat, bowed her head, and closed her eyes. "Jesus, it's Grace. First of all, I want to say I'm sorry I dumped you. I don't really have a good excuse and I hope you'll forgive me. I was just mad and confused but it doesn't look like I had all the facts." She opened her eyes and said to Adam, "Do you think that's all I need to say about that?"

He nodded. "Yep."

She closed her eyes and bowed her head again. "So, when I was young I asked you to forgive me for my sins and I asked you into my heart. But I've made a lot of mistakes since then, a lot worse mistakes in the last twenty years than I made in the first fifteen, which we can talk about later if you want. Anyway, I just want to say thank you for not holding them against me and for dying on the cross and all."

She took a deep breath. "Adam says you would like me to be a part of your family. I know I thought when I was young we were going to get married and now I think that was probably just silly so I'm not holding you to it. But I would like to be a part of your family and, honestly, I think I'd like to be friends." She paused and added a little more quietly, "Maybe even put a hook in my heart so I fall in love with you again. I loved you so much when I was little. There had to be something to that."

Her voice returned to normal. "I don't really know what all this means but I'm open to finding out. I also don't want to just come to you when I need something. So maybe you could tell me something about yourself and what you want out of all this. It would be nice to have a two-way conversation, and everything not just be about me all the time. I know you don't need a therapist, but I am a good listener." She paused as if considering the possibility and then concluded, "I'm just saying."

"But I need you to teach me," she coached him, "and we need to start from scratch. I've got so much garbage where you're concerned I don't know how you're going to separate all the fact from fiction, but Adam seems to think you can do anything so . . ." Her voice trailed off before she continued, "But at least I do know this, thanks to Adam. It's not about going to church. It's not about religion and it's certainly not about acting all holy just to make my critics happy. You know me and that I could never pull that crap off anyway so why start out by faking it? If we're going to do this thing it's going to be about you and me. That's it. Nobody else. I honestly don't give a rat's ass what people think anyway. I'm going to talk to you where no one but you and me know what we're talking about, and we'll just see where it goes from there. Adam says you're sweet, so actually," she added, and Adam knew she was trying to give God some encouragement, "I'm already starting to look forward to the journey."

He thought she was finished but then she added, "Also, I'd like for the Holy Spirit to live within me and act as a guide to help me walk with you and have a good relationship if that's what you want too. But I'll tell you now, so you don't get your hopes up, I'm not coming in through any narrow door. I'm not like Adam. I don't have what it takes to give up everything in order to enter into any Paradise. I'm okay in Austin. So no Christian Superbowl for me." She paused for emphasis to make sure he had heard her and understood. "I know that about myself and I think I need to be upfront before we get started. I just want to go to heaven when I die, and I want you to fill the hole in my soul while I'm alive. That's it." It was obvious to Adam that Grace was setting the ground rules because she didn't want there to be any false expectations.

She was quiet and then added, almost as if conceding a little, "But I would like to give you my proxy so you can change my world a little, but you'll have to show me first how that works. You might start with how I've been feeling on the inside about my prospects. Again, I'm sorry for all the damage I've caused. Especially to my sister," she paused and lowered her voice again, "you know what I mean."

She paused and then momentarily added, "So that's it, really. Maybe you could work with Adam to give me some useful pointers. And, by the way, speaking of Adam, thanks for helping him figure out his dilemma and if possible please come see him. In person. It's important to him." She paused and then continued, "Honestly, I don't even know how it would be possible, but I guess if you did it once you can do it again. But if there's anything else I can help him with just let me know."

"By the way, he also says he doesn't want to be raptured and I don't even know if that's your plan but if it is will you please make sure not to forget my mother? She doesn't want to be part of any transition team and she's really counting on getting out of the worst of it here, you know, before it all hits the fan. And honestly, she loves you but she's probably not going to change any of her thinking or deal with her old issues unless you do a miracle. I've already tried. She likes her life just like it is and that's probably okay, according to Adam. But I guess that's up to you and to her and I should just set a boundary and leave her alone about it.

"And lastly, would you please help me be the best therapist I can be? Maybe you could teach me some of your healing techniques. I have a lot of patients who could really use some advanced treatment options." She paused and not knowing how to end it, she simply said, "So keep up the good work and I guess I'll talk to you later. Maybe when I get to the hotel."

She opened her eyes and saw that Adam was looking at her tenderly. "Was that okay?"

"Perfect."

She squeezed his fingers and let go of his hand. She picked up her juice glass, swirled it, and looking into the contents said, "I know this night didn't start out about me, but I feel a lot better."

Both of them, suddenly tired, laid their heads back on their head-rests. The hum of the engines would have been enough to put them to sleep if the sounds of Katie starting to move through the aisles announcing breakfast hadn't kept them awake. In a few minutes, with her eyes closed, Grace asked aloud, "What are you thinking?"

Adam was silent. Then he said, "I was making up a song."

She smiled and said, "Of course you were. Tell me what you've got so far."

She heard him gently start to sing, making up his own lyrics but singing it to the tune of an old Van Morrison song she recognized.

When the sun sets this side of moonlight
When the timing seems just about right
Brother, could we meet up
In the heart of this old Cowtown.

She smiled and said, "That's pretty good. Make one up for me."

In a surprisingly short amount of time, he began to sing to a tune she recognized but couldn't remember from where.

It took us one whole night
But in the morning light
I stopped searchin'
You forgave your churchin'
316 was one heck of a flight.

She reached her hand out, laid it softly on his arm, and decided to let it rest there. The young woman in the seat in front of her woke up and said something to her new husband. Grace could see he put his movie on pause and the screen went still as the couple talked quietly. Soon Katie approached and presented their breakfast options. Grace lightly gasped as she glanced in between the seats and saw the image of Mel Gibson looking exactly the same as Jesus had once looked in her dreams, smiling expectantly at her.

Goodbye, for now . . .

NOTE FROM THE AUTHOR

The idea for this book started about twenty-five years ago on a flight from Dallas to Washington. I had been upgraded to first class and was seated next to a hostage negotiator who had just completed an overseas mission.

We were having a drink and engaged in casual, fellow passenger chitchat, when unexpectedly the president of the airlines, seated behind us, tapped him on the shoulder and said, "Excuse me, but I just want to thank you for what you just did." He and the man seated next to him both stood and beamed with admiration and approval. My seatmate introduced me as "my new friend, Rita," and we all shook hands.

Of course, once seated, I asked, "What was *that* about?"

He smiled and said humbly, "Have you been watching the news lately about the hostage negotiations?" I nodded. The story was everywhere. He said, "Yeah, that was me. I got all those people out and not one soul was killed."

Impressed, I said, "Wow! Can you talk about it?"

He answered, "Well, I haven't discussed it with anyone yet. You'd be the first." His face went dark, and he added, "And I'm having a problem with the way it all went down . . ."

Never one to shy away from a person with a problem, especially on a long flight, over drinks, with a few hours to kill, I listened to the long and harrowing tale and in the end understood why he was troubled.

Once he'd finished, I asked, "Have you talked to God about it?"

He answered truthfully, "I tried but he doesn't talk to me anymore. Probably because I gave up on him a long time ago." He went on to explain, "I just can't buy the party line about God, religion, Christianity. It just doesn't make sense to me."

Always ready to help God out with his familial relationships I quickly asked, "Would you like a different perspective?"

For the next few hours we talked about God, Christianity, and I answered at least a dozen questions the best I could. As the plane was landing, he pulled out a pen and handed me his cocktail napkin and said, "Write down what I need to do. I think I'll give God another try."

I got to the hotel room and as I fell asleep I told God about other recent encounters I'd had on planes that were similar. Suddenly I had the idea to write the key points of the story down and make copies so when I met people who needed relationship help with him, I wouldn't have to rush to record the bullet points as the plane was landing, I could just hand them a copy.

The next morning, I got the idea to turn my document into a novel with Adam as my main character, talking to a fellow passenger who had lost her faith in God. Why not? The research was easy. In my business and career, I've flown well over a million miles and during that time logged dozens of hours listening to non-believers and non-practicing Christians explain their reasons for excluding God as a viable alternative to self-reliance. Explanations that ranged from thinking God to be either fictitious, a collective consciousness, too distant, too unpredictable, too scary, or too holy to seek an actual relationship with. Yet almost all started the conversation with "I've got a problem that I can't resolve myself. There's no solution in sight and the problem could potentially dismantle me."

That's when I offer God as a solution. That's when I tell people about the practical benefits of partnering with Jesus.

My book is intended to tell the story, not with heaven after death as the ultimate finish line but with man reclaiming heaven on Earth, in full partnership with the Father, Son, and the Holy Spirit. Success is in our spiritual DNA. Happiness and unity with God, living and creating together, operating on all cylinders, meeting our God-given potential is the Father's ultimate desire for every one of his children. He loves us and if we love him, then nothing else matters. Much.

Flight 316 is a fictional love story where God creates Man, God loses Man, God gets Man back. The Bible is the oldest and the greatest love story ever told. I just wanted to try to recapture parts of it and tell them in ways that hopefully make some sense to those of my fellow travelers who need God and don't know where to find him and who may have had difficulty with how they've interpreted the message along the way.